I0823157

I Hope You Find What You're Looking For

I Hope You Find What You're Looking For

A Novel

BSRAT MEZGHEBE

Liveright Publishing Corporation
A Division of W. W. Norton & Company
Independent Publishers Since 1923

Printed in the United States of America
First Edition

For information about special discounts for bulk purchases, please contact W. W. Norton Special Sales at specialsales@wwnorton.com or 800-233-4830

Manufacturing by Lake Book Manufacturing
Book design by Chris Welch
Production manager: Lauren Abbate

ISBN 978-1-324-09249-0

Liveright Publishing Corporation, 500 Fifth Avenue, New York, NY 10110
www.wwnorton.com

W. W. Norton & Company Ltd., 15 Carlisle Street, London W1D 3BS

1 2 3 4 5 6 7 8 9 0

I Hope You Find What You're Looking For

Prologue

THERE WAS SO MUCH ZEWDI WANTED TO TELL LYDIA, SO MUCH she had to make sure the girl understood. She wanted her to know that men and children were a woman's only protection. Women were at the mercy of those who sired them, those who married them, and those they birthed. If they were like Zewdi, unmarried and childless, they were nobody at all.

A thirteen-year-old in Eritrea would have known that was true. But time in America slowed in all the wrong places. From their building lobby, Zewdi would watch Lydia walk home from the bus stop, reading as she crossed the parking lot. Elsa, Lydia's mother and Zewdi's cousin, wouldn't mind if the girl walked into light poles doing all that reading. But Zewdi knew that a young woman had to know more. She had long taken charge of Lydia's education, spending more time with her than her own mother could. Elsa never said thank you, but when did she say anything at all?

When Elsa arrived in Alexandria twelve years ago—with a child and without a husband—Zewdi was the one who took her in. Elsa offered a terse and inadequate explanation that Lydia's father had died in the war. Zewdi didn't bother to ask if they had been married—the war for independence had changed many things.

But here Elsa was, along with Zewdi. They were doing their very best, in their own ways, to make a life that justified the choices they made. Lydia would have to do better.

May 1991

I

LYDIA HAD NEVER MET BEREKHET BEFORE OR EVEN SEEN A PICTURE of him. But when a skinny teenager appeared in the Dulles Airport terminal, she was somehow certain that he was who they were waiting for.

From as early as she could remember, it seemed like Eritrea was emptying out, and all the Eritreans in her apartment building opened their homes to relatives and friends fleeing the war. Now there was someone new, and Berekhet's arrival meant that Lydia would be displaced to Elsa's room. In what world did a teenager have to sleep in the same bed as her mother?

In the weeks before, Lydia had been forced to empty out her closet and dresser and store her belongings under her mother's bed. Elsa set out matching sheets and towels and hung nautical-striped curtains purchased at full price. On Lydia's mirrored vanity tray, she positioned registration brochures from Northern Virginia Community College and a framed picture of Dr. Alazar, Berekhet's father and Elsa's uncle, taken when he was a medical student in Italy.

As Dr. Alazar's only son, Berekhet, was expected to surpass his father's career. Dr. Alazar even called Elsa, which he had never done before, to tell her that Berekhet was leaving Ethiopia, where they lived, to join her in the States.

"Of course, Dottore," Elsa replied. She never called him "uncle" and didn't expect him to ask if she had the space, money, or energy to take his son in.

Lydia expected to be asked. She was no longer a kid, having just turned thirteen. Her classmates received appropriate gifts for reaching the milestone—trips to New York, their own televisions, double ear piercings. A few lucky ones even got their own phone lines. What did Lydia get, besides a customary cake and some new clothes? An announcement that a stranger was taking over her bedroom.

"That's the problem with you American kids," Elsa had said to her. "You want a reward for living to see another year. The bar is pretty low, no?"

In the international arrivals hall, Elsa assumed her position next to a bank of chairs that Lydia claimed a seat in. She stood ramrod straight with her hands behind her back, like the freedom fighter she once was. Elsa could lecture, when she wanted to, but mostly she was tightlipped about the things Lydia actually wanted to know: the details of her childhood with Dr. Alazar, her years fighting in the war with Lydia's father, and pretty much everything that had happened back home.

Lydia looked up from the book she was reading. She caught her mother, as she often did, watching her with an inscrutable expression, as if Elsa either wanted to decipher some mystery or tell Lydia something. On the other hand, Mama Zewdi, who had joined them to welcome Berekhet, always examined Lydia with transparent intentions, reviewing her clothes, posture, and hair, and logging, as carefully as Lydia did, any fluctuations to her weight. She made Lydia change her outfit twice before they left for the airport, finally approving a V-neck blouse and denim skirt, which Lydia feared made her look frumpy. As they waited, Mama Zewdi, who was sitting next to Lydia, turned her attention to the people milling about the hall, angling her head to see if she could spot anyone she knew.

Lydia held her mother's gaze as she positioned her bookmark and closed the book. With her other hand, she nudged Elsa's arm. "Tell me again the last time you saw him?"

Elsa readjusted her arms. "I think he was two years old."

"Can he speak English?"

"How would I know?"

"Do you remember anything about him?"

"Not really." Elsa shrugged. "I didn't see him much."

"Why not?"

"We didn't live with each other. Dr. Alazar put us up in a separate house."

"But you weren't always around?" Lydia shifted in her seat so that her feet were nearly touching her mother's. "Like the way that Mama Zewdi spends so much time with me?"

"Lidu, I was slightly older than you are now when he was born. I was busy with school and then . . ." Elsa waved her hand in conclusion, as if the gesture summarized everything that happened after.

"And then you left to join the war."

"Yep."

"You were eighteen when you left, right?"

"Yes, Lidu. You know this," Elsa said, her voice growing weary.

"And you didn't tell Dr. Alazar you were leaving, right?"

"No, I didn't. But things were different back then."

"I think that's him!" Lydia pointed at a young man dragging a suitcase with broken wheels. Berekhet was dressed like a waiter, with a white collared shirt and black dress pants that stopped inches too soon. Like most Eritrean men, his bony shoulders were narrow, making his slight belly appear bigger than it really was.

Elsa waved. "Berekhet!" she called out. He didn't smile as he made his way toward them, but he looked closely at Lydia as he leaned forward to accept Elsa's embrace. Lydia averted her eyes.

Mama Zewdi snatched the limp carnations Elsa had just thrust into Lydia's hands, replacing them with the bouquet of yellow lilies she had gushed about purchasing on the drive there.

"Go kiss your brother," she said to Lydia in Tigrinya, pushing her forward.

Lydia hesitated before approaching Berekhet, thinking that he wasn't the ugliest person she had seen but that he had a face that made her want to figure out what was wrong with it. Maybe the proportions were off. His eyes bulged well beyond the grasp of their lids, the tip of his nose wider than the bridge suggested, his chin propelled forward by a greedy underbite. When he smiled at her, the first smile he offered since being greeted, he looked even stranger, all his features seeming to want to touch each other.

Lydia pressed her cheeks to his, unwilling to lift her arms and return his hug. Mama Zewdi snatched the lilies back and pressed them to Berekhet's chest, ululating so loudly that the family next to them flinched.

"I am Zewdi Naizghi Weldegebriel," she declared. "Weldegebriel is the brother of Deres, who is the father of Ghebrealfa, your father's father. So, my grandfather is the brother of your great-grandfather."

She punctuated each statement with a kiss. Berekhet looked at Lydia as if he wanted her to rescue him, but it was Elsa who finally intervened, taking Mama Zewdi's hand out of his and leading him toward the exit to the parking lot, saying that he must be very tired.

"Of course, of course," Mama Zewdi agreed. "Come along, Lydia," she said, reaching out her hand to hold Lydia's. "The poor thing must be exhausted."

Lydia was grateful that Mama Zewdi had invited herself to come along. Her mother didn't like to talk while she drove, only commenting on drivers who sped or followed too closely. But Mama Zewdi always had something to say. As Elsa maneuvered out of the lot, she twisted around in the passenger seat to ask Berekhet about the health of his father and the rest of the family back home.

"I never met your father, but I hear he is a serious, hardworking man," Mama Zewdi said. "Right, Elsiye?"

"Your father showed what can be done with opportunity,"

Elsa said, eyeing the eighteen-wheeler in the next lane. "Just stay focused and you'll do fine."

Berekhet responded in Tigrinya, with as few words as possible, his chin pointed toward the window. Elsa's van was full of items for her food cart, so they put his luggage in the backseat, forcing him and Lydia to squeeze close together. Lydia tried to make sure their limbs didn't touch. She placed her book on her lap, noticing that her thighs were bigger than his.

"I hope you don't feel homesick already, Berekhet," Mama Zewdi said. "There are so many Habesha in our building, let me tell you. You aren't going to feel lonely at all."

Berekhet nodded as she went on. Lydia had a feeling he wasn't really listening. She snuck more glances at him, trying to detect any resemblance to his father, whom she saw only in photos. Besides being fair, they didn't look much alike.

"We have so much to be grateful for," Mama Zewdi continued. "You're here, and independence is close. Everyone says the war is going to end any day now. Isn't that right, Elsu?"

"That's what everyone is saying," Elsa said.

"Are you hot, Berekhet? It's only the first of May. Just wait until the summer starts. This part of America is a swamp. It's not dry like back home. Stand in the shade here and you'll still sweat . . . Elsa can tell you. She's stuck grilling meat in that box all day, poor thing. But you know, air conditioning isn't good either. It gives you headaches, be careful. Lydia, why aren't you talking to Berekhet? Ask him if he's happy to be here."

"I don't know how to say that in Tigrinya."

"Yes, you do," Elsa said.

"She understands Tigrinya," Zewdi explained. "But she gets shy with speaking."

"I am happy to be here," Berekhet said in English, sparing her. "Very happy."

2

ELSA WOKE UP IN A PANIC, HER HEART A JACKHAMMER IN HER chest. It was important that she remain calm and determine what the conditions were. She inhaled deeply and steadied her breath. She was comfortable and warm and tried to remember when she got such a nice blanket. It was quiet; not even the crack of a branch or scurry of a lizard could be heard. Why was it so quiet?

"Hey," she whispered to her comrade next to her, pressing against her back. "Wake up," she said more urgently.

Something was wrong. They were all alone, which meant their unit must have already started on their trek. Elsa shook her harder. "Get up! We have to catch up with the others!"

The curled shape sat up and grabbed Elsa by her arms, pinning them down.

"Mom!" she said. "What are you doing?"

Elsa dropped her shoulders as her eyes adjusted to the darkness. She understood now. She was at her home in Southern Towers. Her daughter was lying beside her. She had to get up and go to work.

"I'm sorry," she said to Lydia, patting her arm. "I just got confused. Go back to sleep."

Lydia hesitated before lying back down and turning to face the wall. Elsa rubbed her daughter's back, trying to comfort them both.

Elsa's commute first took her five miles past her place of business. On a normal morning, by five thirty a.m., she steered her white Chevrolet Astro onto 395, taking her over the Potomac, where she could nearly make out her spot on the National Mall, before the highway went belowground, tunneling under the U.S. Capitol and emptying her out on New York Avenue. Driving farther east, away from the Mall, she usually reached the garage by six a.m., well before any of the other hot dog cart owners. But this morning, she was running late, and all the Eritrean vendors were already there. They were gathered around Aster, a usually subdued mother of three who was gesturing and smiling more than Elsa had ever seen her do.

"Elsa's here!" one of them called out. "Tell her what happened."

"When I woke up this morning," Aster said, turning to face Elsa, "I had this really strong feeling that I should call home."

"But it wasn't a bad feeling," said Tsega, a hyperactive vendor from a village outside of Keren, Elsa's hometown. "Like when I knew my little sister got hit by a truck in Khartoum. Six thousand, five hundred miles away, and I could feel exactly when it happened."

"Yeah, it wasn't that I knew that something terrible had happened," Aster said. "It was just this feeling, you know?"

Elsa did know. She also knew that time was money and that they had to prep their carts and get on the road. The non-Eritrean vendors in the poorly-lit garage eyed them curiously while loading up.

"I called Asmara, and my mother picked up. As soon as she heard my voice, she started screaming, 'He's back, he's back.' Then it sounded like the phone dropped. I could hear people shouting in the background, and my father got on the phone and said, 'Aster,' and I said, 'Yes, Father,' and he said, 'Aster, my daughter, is that you?' I said, 'Father, it's me.' He said, 'Do you believe in God?' I said, 'Of course I believe in God.' He said, 'Do you swear on your life and on your children's lives?' I said, 'I swear.' He said, 'Do you swear on your mother's life and on mine?' I said, 'Father, on everything I hold dear, on my martyred husband's soul, I believe in God.'"

Tsega gasped, her eyes welling with tears. Estifanos, the only man among them, hugged himself. All of them were listening with rapt attention, as if this were their first time hearing the story.

"He said to me, 'Your brother is alive. I saw him with my own eyes. He is alive!'"

They all gave shouts of joy, and Aster teetered unsteadily. Elsa gripped her elbow and sat her down on a folding chair, eyeing the clock above them as Aster continued to explain her good news.

Aster's brother, Samuel, hadn't been heard from since he left to join the rebels ten years prior. Over the past few weeks, her mother swore she had caught glimpses of him in their neighborhood, but her father dismissed the sightings as the delusions of a desperate mother—until he locked eyes with his son himself. It wasn't safe to trust anything or anyone in this war, so her father said nothing. Late that night, he heard a tapping on his gate. He peered through the gap between the frame and door and saw his Sami, his last born whose scruffy beard couldn't hide how hollowed-out his cheeks had become. Her father crossed himself and rushed back inside to his wife, whispering that she better not make a sound when she saw what he was about to show her. Then he let their son in. Samuel told his parents that the war was almost over. He had been stationed on the outskirts of the capital and didn't even want to think about how he'd be punished if his superiors knew where he was. But he just couldn't help it. He wanted to tell his parents himself that Eritrea would be free.

"Didn't I tell you guys independence was close?" Estifanos said.

"We all knew that," said Mehret, who was the most recent to have joined their ranks. "When Massawa fell last year, it was just a matter of time."

Mehret gestured at their mission control in the corner, an

oversized utility cart they commandeered for their wargames. Eritrea, the shape of a key tilted 135 degrees, was always visible to their eyes and invisible to the rest of the world. They mapped the country over the cart's surface, designating condiment bottles as mountains to be defended and snaking utensils through them as Ethiopian convoys to be attacked. When the rebels liberated Massawa, Eritrea's most important port, only the capital, Asmara, represented by a bottle of Windex, remained under enemy control.

"By May's end, our tanks will get every last Ethiopian out of Eritrea," Estifanos predicted. He was the savviest entrepreneur among them, working a spot until he built a steady clientele and then selling the unofficial rights to the next vendor-in-waiting. "I should have put some money on it."

"It's not too late," Mehret called out from the sink, where she was rinsing her tongs. "I bet you fifty packs of franks we'll capture Asmara by next Monday, the thirteenth."

Estifanos rubbed his chin. "No, that's too soon. I think it'll be the next week . . . the twenty-fifth . . . no . . . Friday the twenty-fourth. Our commander knows better than all of us though," he said to Elsa. "When do you think it'll happen?"

They all turned to face her with hopeful expressions, Aster angling her face upward from her seat, the tears still glistening in her eyes. Elsa clenched the rag in her hands and stepped back. There weren't any other former Eritrean People's Liberation Front rebels in the D.C. area, which had the largest Eritrean community in the States. Elsa assumed there had to be a few others in the rest of the country, but she was sure that she was the only female one. She was a rare breed, and everyone deferred to her in a way that felt unearned. The rest of her comrades weren't leaving the war unless their mission was achieved or they died trying. But here Elsa was, having accomplished neither of those things.

Elsa looked back up at the clock on the wall. The garage was already empty of everyone else; only the Pakistani owner who leased out the stalls remained, shouting on the phone in his office.

"I think we need to get ready for work," she said.

"You heard the general," Mehret said.

"All right, let's go." Estifanos walked Aster to her cart. "But we're not working these jobs long, right?"

"No!" they all answered.

"This time next year, we'll be back home, right?"

"Yes!"

"And are we taking these hot dogs with us?"

"Hell no!" Aster said with a giggle, the first time Elsa had ever heard her curse.

At seven a.m., Elsa hitched her cart to the porter's truck and reversed her commute, heading west on New York Avenue. The thoroughfare offered little in terms of scenery—an industrial stretch of warehouses and depots that hid narrow row homes and abandoned buildings from sight. After a left turn on North Capitol and right on Louisiana, just after Union Station, the city became the nation's capital, the greenery well-manicured, streets smooth, and facades well maintained. D.C. was a strange town, all its contradictions, the most powerless and powerful, compressed into seventy square miles. Even after ten years of working on the Mall, Elsa was still awed by that final turn on Constitution Avenue, the transition into that great and grand lawn that was open to everyone, but still a place she would have never spent time in if it didn't earn her a living.

Once the porter dropped her off at the southwest corner of Twelfth and Madison, in between the National Museums of American History and Natural History, she set up shop, an activity she could do in her sleep. First, she turned on the propane tank for the burners. Then, she placed the buns in the shelves, unwrapped tubs of relish, chili, and caramelized onions (her specialty alongside the expected sauerkraut), and lined up the squeeze bottles of ketchup and mustard. Outside of the cart, she unfurled the umbrella and extended the front counter, arranging the boxes of candy and clipping the individual bags of chips to their stands. At the cart's base, she nestled soda, water, and juice in two ice-filled coolers.

When Elsa first started, all she could afford was a small cart that came up to her hips. After braving her first winter of standing outside, Zewdi loaned her $10,000 to buy a stainless-steel cart that could house her. There wasn't enough space inside for her to extend both arms, but it kept her warm. She alternated between sitting on a stool with a slim panel for lumbar support and standing on a thick mat Zewdi swore would absorb any damage to her knees. While she wouldn't trade her covered cart for being exposed as she once was, she missed being able to see the area around her, her view now limited to the Plexiglas front panel she could open and close. The whole world seemed to be going by, tourists from every continent, students on school trips, ducks that wandered up from the Tidal Basin, and the fitness junkies who jogged around them. But in her cart, she saw nothing of that, only the faces that appeared to order and the strip of the gravelly walkway and hopeful pigeons that pecked at crumbs.

Business was steady that day, a good omen for the upcoming peak season, which would start once schools closed. After the lunch rush, Elsa realized that with all the commotion that morning, she forgot to restock her napkins. She grabbed her cash and walked down to Aster's cart, which was in view of hers, just a bit farther down Madison Street, to see if she had extra.

Aster was standing outside of her cart, in the middle of an exchange with a tourist family of five, all sporting fanny packs and fresh haircuts that hadn't quite settled.

"You really won't take our money?" the mother asked, clutching a twenty-dollar bill.

"Not today," Aster said with both hands over her heart. "It's a special day. My country has been at war but will be independent soon."

The family expressed the range of emotions Americans displayed when you talked about war. The mother looked uncomfortable. The father wanted to know more. The children grew bored.

"We're from Eritrea. We've been fighting for thirty years for our freedom."

"Thirty years?" the mother asked, stepping back and holding her youngest's hand. "And we've never heard of it?"

"Yes, we're fighting against Ethiopia. She can tell you more," Aster said, pointing at Elsa. "She was a freedom fighter."

The Americans looked at Elsa with a mixture of alarm and disbelief.

"Ethiopia, you say?" asked the father. "That's in Africa, right? Didn't they have a famine or something?"

"Yes, but it was man-made, government neglect," Aster said. "Tell them, Elsa."

The children started to pull their parents away, eager to eat their hot dogs. Elsa wasn't keen to give them a lecture on their vacation.

"It's a long story," she said. "You all go and enjoy your day."

"What's your problem?" Aster hissed at Elsa as the family walked away. "They need to know our story."

"They don't care, Aster. And they'll forget it by the time they get to the Lincoln Memorial."

"No, this is diplomacy. This is how you educate them."

"You really haven't charged anybody today?" Elsa asked, shielding her face from the sun with her hand.

"Not one."

"What are you going to do when independence comes? Give your cart away?"

"Girl, who cares about this thing?" Aster slapped the counter. "I've already given up much more. You must be anxious to hear from your comrades," she said, her expression softening. "I'm sure you can find a way to contact them when the war ends."

Elsa pulled down on her T-shirt, smoothing out a wrinkle only she could see. Not all the news after the war ended was going to be good.

"I should really get back to my cart. I just came to ask you for napkins. Do you have extra?"

Aster looked as if she wanted to say something else but just nodded and reached into her cart. After handing the stack to Elsa, she looked westward toward the Washington Monument. Elsa followed her gaze, suppressing the urge to walk as far away as she could from their carts. She wanted to move her body. She wanted to see what everyone else had come to see, walk alongside the Reflecting Pool and around Mr. Lincoln, across the Memorial Bridge into Virginia and past Southern Towers altogether. How long would that take her, she wondered.

3

"SWEET VIRGIN MARY," MAMA MINIA SAID TO THE RAW T-BONE Zewdi presented to her. "That's a beautiful cut of meat."

Of course it was. Fatty and perfectly marbled the way she liked it. Zewdi had the butcher at Giant cut it right in front of her—this wasn't a plastic-wrapped slab set out for the masses.

With a nod of approval from her guest, Zewdi turned back to the hot pan on her stove and proceeded to sear the meat in butter on both sides, adding only salt and a single rosemary sprig. As the fat popped and sizzled, she prepared a tomato-and-red-onion salad and plated it alongside the finished steak.

"Ecco," she said, setting it down on the table.

Mama Minia took a deep breath before her first bite. "Mother Mary."

She took a second bite and clapped her hands. "Do you know how long it's been since I've had red meat? I don't know who's crueler—my daughter or my doctor."

"Oh, hush. How can you say that?" Zewdi moved the piles of fresh injera she had baked that morning to the dining table in her living room. No customers had stopped by yet, and she was hopeful it would be quiet just a little longer so she could enjoy her time with her guest. She took the other seat at the breakfast table and sipped her cooling tea.

"You know they just want you to live as long as you can."

"Don't defend them. They should want me to enjoy whatever life I have left."

Mama Minia was in her early seventies, around the same age Zewdi's mother would have been if she was still alive. A year had passed since Mama Minia came from Asmara to visit her daughter, a sweet and health-conscious hospital lab tech who lived a floor below Zewdi with her Ethiopian husband. Mama Minia never referred to her son-in-law by name, only as "him."

Mama Minia was one of the few elders who came from back home to visit their adult children forging new lives in the States. Their arrivals were always dramatic: tearful reunions at Dulles; introductions to American-born grandchildren seen only in pictures but just as mute, their tongues resistant to Tigrinya; the proud distribution of homemade spice blends and custom clothes; and conversations late into the night about the happy memories and those they had lost.

The U.S. government might have been generous with visas, but American employers were stingy with PTO. After a few days off, a week if they were lucky, the children went back to work, and their visiting parents sat alone in unfamiliar homes with the televisions left on to mask the silence.

Zewdi sold injera from her apartment and had an open-door policy for anyone who needed coffee and conversation—an elder daycare, she liked to think of it. Lord knows they needed the company. They were bored out of their minds. They couldn't comprehend why you needed a car to get everywhere. The food had no flavor. Their children were spoiling their children. The doctors were making them sicker. In Eritrea, they had been consumed with the thought of their loved ones thousands of miles away, but now that they were reunited, all they could think of was going back home.

Zewdi doted on them all, but Mama Minia was her favorite. With only one English expression under her belt ("ten cue"), she made Alexandria, Virginia, her own. Sometimes Zewdi would spot her waiting for the bus on Seminary Road or traipsing along Beauregard by herself, her head covered and small frame clad in a colorful, ankle-grazing chiffon dress. Every Friday, she treated herself to a single scoop of butter-pecan ice cream at Baskin-Robbins, presenting the index card on which her daughter wrote her order. She understood the limits of her power and, conversely, the infinite power of God's will. Two children who died young, another two who joined the guerrillas, and a husband who suffered greatly from a stroke and eventually succumbed to it. There was a choice to be made. Mama Minia chose to count her blessings, to will herself to not just accept what had happened but to also find pleasure and enjoyment in the life that was left. Zewdi wished her own mother had been able to do the same, instead of her constant preoccupation with what could have been.

"You sure I can't serve you anything else?" Zewdi motioned to the fridge. "I have some potatoes I can fry up quickly."

Mama Minia shook her head while wiping faint grease from her mouth. She was leaving the States that evening to visit her eldest daughter in Stockholm before she returned to Asmara and had requested steak as her last American meal.

"Please, I'm about to go to the land of potatoes. I don't even want to look at those things." She pushed her plate forward and leaned back in satisfaction. "This was all I needed."

The kitchen table abutted the window, and the early-afternoon sun bathed Mama Minia in golden light. Her face was almost sultry, with pouty lips and upturned eyes that defied her age. Her rich, dark skin was also only barely lined, her full head of gray hair the only attribute giving her age away.

"I don't even know if I'm allowed to eat potatoes anymore," she said with her eyes closed. "Every appointment they ban something new."

Zewdi made a sympathetic sound but could tell that Mama Minia was worried about something other than her new diet. She reached out and covered her hands with her own.

"You'll see them again. God willing."

Mama Minia nodded, her eyes still clenched shut. "If I don't, I'll be proud of their sacrifice."

Zewdi gripped her hands tighter. For the first time, she didn't envy a woman who had children of her own.

"Come on," she said softly. "I'll make you some tea. It'll help you digest all that cholesterol."

Mama Minia opened her eyes, widening them mischievously. "I think I need something stronger."

Zewdi sighed and stood up to pull out a half-full bottle of Johnnie Walker from underneath the kitchen sink and two small tumblers she would have used for the tea.

"Your daughter is going to kill me."

"Don't worry about her. Just pour."

Zewdi laughed and filled their glasses to the brim.

"What am I going to do without you?" she asked.

Mama Minia took a healthy swig and motioned that Zewdi do the same.

"If you ever want to see me again, you'll have to come to Asmara. I'm never setting foot in America again. I don't want to die here."

"Don't talk like that!" Zewdi said, even though she loved that there was someone more dramatic than she was.

"I'm serious. I don't care what they diagnose me with next. I'd rather die in my country than be hooked up to all those machines. In fact, I'm just going to go straight back to Dekemhare so I can drop dead right where my husband was buried. Drink."

Zewdi obliged and took a paltry sip.

"Listen, the war is going to be over any day now. When are *you* coming back home, my dear?"

"I will. Soon." Zewdi did want to see where her mother was buried. She was an only child and not tracking the whereabouts of siblings and their children the way that others were.

Mama Minia patted her hand as if she could hear what Zewdi was thinking.

"Your life is here now. I understand. Everyone says they're coming back to Eritrea for good, they're going to pack up their homes and take their kids, but it's not going to happen. You all have become American . . . and these children . . . forget it."

She was right. Zewdi couldn't imagine Lydia resettling in Asmara. One bucket shower and she'd beg for a seat on the next flight back.

"We're not going anywhere, at least not anytime soon. Lydia's starting the eighth grade in the fall. Berekhet just got here. I never know what Elsa's thinking, but I'm sure her plan is to stay."

"Well, if you want to see me again, come to Dekemhare."

"Wait." Zewdi realized that she had missed something obvious. "I've been looking for the family of a fighter named Efrem Negash. He's from there too. I think he died in '78 during the retreat."

"What's his grandfather's name?"

"That I don't know."

"Who is he? What else do you know about him?"

Zewdi looked over her shoulder, as if someone else could be eavesdropping.

"He's Lydia's father. He was martyred before she was born. Elsa won't tell me anything else about him, and from what I can tell, I don't think she knows his family or has ever tried to find them. I've been looking—discreetly, of course—but I haven't had any luck. Maybe you can ask around."

The moment Lydia came into her life, Zewdi harassed Elsa about tracking down her father's family. Children need to know where they come from, yet Elsa seemed resistant. First, she said she was waiting for Lydia to start school, then she claimed it would be best to wait until she finished the sixth grade. After Lydia's elementary school graduation, Zewdi privately reminded her of her pledge. But Elsa said she thought it best to wait until she was admitted into college so that it wouldn't affect her grades and performance on the SATs. Nonsense. She was stalling as clearly as a sinner avoiding confession.

Mama Minia gulped the rest of her whiskey and set her glass down. "I'll ask around. But let's talk about you. What's next for Ms. Zewdi?"

Zewdi took another slow sip, pondering the question. She had some ideas about expanding her injera business, maybe supplying restaurants, catering beyond the few requests she accepted each year, and some other entrepreneurial ideas that weren't fully baked yet—and that she didn't talk about for fear of attracting the evil eye. Either way, she had the feeling that her work wasn't what Mama Minia was referring to.

"There's something I want to talk to you about before I leave." Mama Minia lowered her voice. "It's about a man."

"What man?"

Mama Minia raised her eyebrows and looked at her meaningfully.

It couldn't be. Zewdi was almost fifty years old, and now someone finally wanted to set her up? That window of her life had come and gone.

"You don't need to say anything," Mama Minia said. "Just listen to me and finish your whiskey."

4

IF LYDIA DIDN'T LEAVE THE HOUSE IN EXACTLY FOUR MINUTES, SHE was going to miss her bus and be late for school. The problem was that she was in desperate need of her book, *Roll of Thunder, Hear My Cry.* She always had one book that she read to and from school and another book on her nightstand that she read before going to sleep. Before Berekhet's arrival two weeks ago, all her books were in reach, which allowed her system to run smoothly. But now that he had taken over her room, things had gotten more complicated. And she realized that the book in question was still on her bookshelf.

Unfortunately, Elsa had given her strict orders to not wake Berekhet up or go into her room without his permission. Lydia had already wasted a few precious minutes knocking on the door and blasting the radio in the kitchen in the hopes that he would come out. But her cousin either slept like the dead or was pretending to be asleep, because he never emerged. So Lydia was on her knees in her mother's closet, pawing through her belongings for the right book to read on her ride.

As she searched, she knocked over the lid of a large cookie tin that she had never noticed and sifted through its contents. Underneath the "PAR AVION" envelopes and yellowed handkerchiefs lay a single photo. Lydia turned it over and recognized her father, Efrem. He was bright-eyed and grinning widely, poised at the base of a mountain with his arms gripping the two young women on either side of him. Lydia at first confused her mother for the other woman. They both had light complexions, heart-shaped faces, and their noses crinkled in the same way when they smiled. Even though they were nearly identical, the other woman was prettier in a way that had more to do with her presence than physical features. She was caught in mid-laughter, tucked comfortably under Efrem's shoulder, and looking straight into the lens. Elsa appeared to be suppressing a smile and was looking away.

Lydia was out of time. She darted out of the closet, grabbed her book bag from the living room, and bolted out of her apartment, clutching the photo as she rode the elevator down eleven floors. Maneuvering through the lobby, she sprinted outside and across the parking lot, hearing the faint whine of the bus grow louder. She forced herself to stop and look both ways at the blind spot at the end of their building's driveway before turning left and picking up speed toward the 7A Metrobus that had just pulled up to the stop. Out of breath, and with her thighs starting to chafe under her pleated skirt, she plopped down on the first empty seat.

Lydia returned to the photo with laser focus, as if its four-by-six dimensions could reveal much more than the scene it captured. She never expected war to look so photogenic. She always imagined darkness and gloom or scenes like the illustrations in her schoolbooks of white guys in pea coats charging toward each other. Her parents and the other woman looked like they were in an Eddie Bauer ad with their rugged confidence and bare legs. The only giveaway that they weren't just camping was the three rifles peeping over their shoulders.

For normal families with boxes of albums and two living parents, finding that photo wouldn't have been a big deal. But Elsa had always claimed that the photo of Lydia's dad in their living room was the only one she had. Lydia couldn't understand why Elsa would have kept this picture from her. She was always at the mercy of whatever her mother claimed to be true, and there was never a paper trail or enough credible witnesses to corroborate her assertions.

Her birth date, for example, was supposedly April 30, 1978, but how could she be sure of it? She was born in rebel territory, and while she had been issued a birth certificate by the guerillas, Elsa maintained that she didn't bring it with her to the States. There was a baptism certificate from a church in Khartoum, but its paper quality and typeface didn't inspire much confidence in the institution that issued it. The document didn't include a photo, and her name was written in a script she couldn't read. She hadn't learned that "Efrem" was her legal middle name until second grade, a fact she discovered while working on a school project. That assignment, to tell the story of her name, forced an explanation from her mother: Elsa had given her a middle name because she thought it necessary for their American documentation, but in Eritrean culture, there was no such thing as middle or last names. On official forms, they listed their first names and the names of their father and paternal grandfather. Children were taught to recite the names of their father, his father, and each preceding father for as long the genealogy was known. Mama Zewdi could list sixteen names and swore that her father could go as far back as David ("Yes, *that* David"). Elsa knew twelve names in her ancestry but recited them reluctantly since she didn't know Lydia's father's line, the one that mattered. At the very least, Lydia would have appreciated a meaningful story about the choice of "Lydia," something akin to the eager retellings she sat through in class. But Elsa couldn't even give her that. All she said was that she liked it.

Elsa's furtiveness made Lydia question everything. Who's to say that she was actually thirteen years old? She was much smarter than she let on (people already thought that she was very smart) and she was also one of the tallest people in her class. How did she know that Berekhet was actually her cousin? Most of the Eritreans presented to her as family were eventually revealed to not have any shared ancestry. There was some mysterious formula of shared hardship, village proximity, and tonnage of coffee consumed together that resulted in the dubious status change from friend to family.

Lydia returned to her own home after school, instead of going straight to Mama Zewdi's apartment as she normally did. She felt an obligation to check up on Berekhet. She walked into the kitchen and found him stationed at the table, wearing an oversized Bart Simpson T-shirt that Elsa must have gifted him.

"Greetings, cousin!" Berekhet said. He was holding up a box of Raisin Bran. "If I eat this, will I become big like you?" He inspected the side of the box before starting to read the ingredients out loud.

Lydia tilted her head, as if that would help her determine if she had heard him right.

All of their packaged foods were fanned out across the table: Ritz crackers, Oreos, cake mixes, Lunchables, Fruit Roll-Ups, and the illicit Pop-Tarts Lydia bought without Elsa's permission and hid in an empty granola box.

"Why is all of our food out?"

"I want to bulk up." Berekhet flexed his arms. "Everyone knows that American food makes you big. Isn't that what happened to you?" he said, gesturing at her. "You looked so different at Faniel's wedding, even your color changed."

When Lydia was eight, she had been the flower girl at a family wedding in Charlotte. A picture had been sent to relatives back home and apparently was the last they had seen of her. In the picture, her positioning in the light made her appear as fair as her mother, and her hair, flat-ironed for the first time, finally reached past her shoulders. In the five years since, yes, she had gotten bigger—both tall and fat, the two ways Eritreans meant the word—all while her hair hadn't grown an inch. How kind it was of Berekhet to point this out.

"Not sure." Lydia wasn't sure if she was more irritated by what he said or the fact that he was eating all her snacks.

In Elsa's room, Lydia changed into a T-shirt and sweatpants and put the photo back where she found it, making sure that nothing in the closet looked out of place. She reluctantly returned to the living room and found Berekhet with a bowl of cereal in hand, walking around the apartment as if it were a gallery. Lydia wondered if he noticed the things she did: the stained windowsills, uneven beads of chalky paint that covered the ceiling like a rash, and torn upholstery on the plaid burgundy sofa. He stopped in front of the television and turned it on with the remote.

"I thought there were supposed to be hundreds of channels in America," he said.

"That's if you have cable, which we don't. Mom doesn't want me to be distracted from my schoolwork." Lydia wanted to ask how many TV channels he had in Addis Ababa, but she held her tongue.

Berekhet circled back to the dining area and stood in front of a framed poster of a beautiful, smiling boy with silky hair and three faint lines carved like parentheses in each cheek. His teeth were as white as the lettering of the caption, which read "Eritrea." He was also Lydia's first crush, even though she'd never admit it.

"We liberated this poster, I see." Berekhet pointed at the caption.

"What do you mean?"

"The poster used to say Ethiopia, but the kid is Eritrean. Good to see we corrected it." Berekhet grew up in Addis Ababa, the Ethiopian capital, so he must have only seen the Ethiopian version of the poster. But to Lydia, the boy had always been Eritrean; it said so on every poster in every house she had been in. Mama Zewdi even swore that on her way to Sudan, she saw that exact same boy herding camels. Once, however, Lydia had seen the Ethiopian version in a mini-market. She pointed it out to her mother, which she immediately regretted as Elsa geared herself to challenge the shop owner. Elsa rarely ventured to the Ethiopian-owned stores in the nearby plaza, and when she did, she spoke in English, pretending not to understand Amharic, even though she was fluent in the Ethiopian language. Later, her mother explained that the photo had first appeared in the *National Geographic*, with the attribution to Ethiopia since Eritrea had been annexed by Ethiopia by that time. With the popularity of the photo, the Ethiopian Ministry of Tourism started using it in its campaigns.

"What's the difference between Eritreans and Ethiopians?" Berekhet asked.

"What do you mean?" Lydia said. "We're not fighting for independence to prove that we're different. We're fighting because it's our right to."

Berekhet turned away from the poster and considered Lydia more carefully. "And why is it our right to fight for independence?"

"Are you asking me because you don't know or because you want to see if I do?"

Berekhet smiled. "I want to see if you do. Come on," he said with a wave of his hand. "Tell me why we're at war. Explain it to me as you would to your classmates."

"My classmates don't care."

"Pretend they do."

"Well, Ethiopia took over Eritrea without the people saying that was what they wanted."

"When did that happen?"

"In 1961. The UN had decided that Ethiopia and Eritrea should be in a federation, but then Ethiopia just took us over. They arrested and killed people, took away our rights—like our freedom to speak our own languages. They shut down our businesses and moved them to Ethiopia."

"Who did this?"

"First, it happened under Emperor Haile Selassie. Then things got worse under the Derg, who are communists."

"Well, yes, *technically* they were Marxist-Leninists. So how long have we been fighting for?"

"Since 1961. It's been thirty years." Even though Lydia knew the answer, it was hard for her to imagine anything, much less the war, lasting that long.

"The first shot was fired in 1961, but we've been fighting for much longer. The nonviolent resistance started at the end of World War II in 1941, when our fate was to be decided. Everyone had a say except us—the Italians, the British, the Americans, and the Ethiopians all had their interests. We protested, we pleaded in the press and at the United Nations, but greater powers prevailed." Berekhet walked over to the sofa and sat down. "You know more than I would expect from an American kid though. How did you learn all this?"

Lydia couldn't remember a time when she didn't know the reasons for the war. It was all anyone ever talked about—her mother, Mama Zewdi, the Eritreans in her building. She had never actually articulated it before and now felt as if she'd accomplished something, and maybe proved herself to Berekhet, even though she didn't like the feeling of caring what he thought.

"Well, I'm impressed," he said. "And I think your father would be too."

Berekhet pointed to the grainy headshot that hung over the television. The picture was taken by the rebel authorities when her father first enlisted. Elsa told Lydia, in one of the rare stories she shared, that she had begged the administrator to give her an extra copy.

Berekhet hopped up from the sofa and examined Efrem's picture more closely.

"You do look like him. He's skinny, though, so I wonder

where you got your weight from. I think it's time for more cereal. Want some?"

Lydia felt all the goodwill she was just starting to develop for Berekhet disappear. She wanted to tell him to keep his hands off her cereal and find somewhere else to sleep.

"You know what?" she said pointedly. "I'm going to Mama Zewdi's."

"Oh, wait for me," Berekhet called out from the kitchen. "Let me just finish this cereal quickly."

"Don't worry, I'll be back down in a bit."

Lydia rushed out of the apartment and up two flights of stairs, letting herself into Mama Zewdi's unit without knocking. She threw herself onto the plush sofa and huffed, grateful that no one else was there.

"Lydia, is that you?" Mama Zewdi called out from the kitchen.

"Yep."

"Let me call you later," Lydia heard her say into the phone. "My daughter just got home from school."

Mama Zewdi emerged with a steaming batch of injera that she set on the dining table.

"Where's Berekhet?" she asked as she patted Lydia's cheek.

"I don't know, I guess he's in the house."

Mama Zewdi's gentle touch became firm as she turned Lydia's face to hers. "I know you didn't leave him down there by himself. He's a guest, Lydia . . . and he's your brother."

"He's not my brother, and he's definitely not behaving like a guest. Eritreans are so annoying. You meet them once, and they act like they've known you forever."

"Well, these Americans can know you for years, smile in your face all day, but ask them for help once, and they act like they've never seen you before. Does that sound better to you? Now, get up and get to work."

Lydia groaned as she heaved herself off the couch. She was

the sole and sometimes paid employee in Mama Zewdi's injera business. Lydia's only responsibility was to package batches of ten injera in clear bags, affix "Made by Zewdi" stickers on them, and sort the bags into orders for those who called ahead and those who just stopped by.

Mama Zewdi readjusted her scarf that had fallen to her shoulders, briefly exposing her long, glossy waves, and headed back to the kitchen. Lydia hoped the lecture was over.

"And another thing," she called out. "You should be happy that Berekhet is here. It'll be good for you and your mother to have a man in the house."

That's what Eritreans always did, reveal their own concerns by attributing them to others. Lydia knew that Mama Zewdi would have been happier as a married woman. It was harder to tell with Elsa.

"I can treat you like you are an American if you want," Mama Zewdi continued from the kitchen. "I can lock my door so that you can't come in whenever you please and eat my food. Would you like that?"

Lydia listened absentmindedly as Mama Zewdi carried on. A large burgundy tapestry of the Virgin Mary with cherubs in the bottom corners presided over the dining table. When business was busy, the stacks of injera got so high that it looked as if the angelic babies were nestled directly on top of them. Today was a slow day, and the cherubs were resting in the clouds instead.

"No, I don't think you would. I didn't give birth to you, but you're still my daughter. You were just a baby when you and Elsa came, the cutest, chubbiest thing I had ever seen. I couldn't let go of you. . . . I just knew you were mine. Elsa begged me to stop holding you so much so that you could learn to walk. I planned your first birthday party, it was right here in this apartment. Your mother, God bless her, put you in that daycare right here next to our building, even though I begged her to let me watch you and save her money. I would just stand outside and watch you play, and one time I saw you eat those disgusting bright orange crackers right off the floor. That's when I told Elsa enough! It was time for you to come home."

Lydia didn't want to admit that Mama Zewdi was partially right. Berekhet's arrival was what she had always wanted, someone else around to keep her company. It was probably why she felt so attached to Mama Zewdi, who would talk to her, tell her stories the way her mother wouldn't, not just accounts of events but how those events made people feel. Unfortunately, Mama Zewdi hadn't crossed paths with Elsa back home, so she couldn't tell her anything about her past and the mystery photo. The stories Elsa told Lydia, which weren't many, always ended right where Lydia wanted them to keep going, as if there were an entire emotional realm that didn't exist for her mother.

Lydia finished packing the injera and threw herself back down on the sofa. Mama Zewdi had moved on to recount the details of Lydia's first birthday party and the custom Minnie Mouse cake she ordered to match the dress she'd picked out for her. The proof was right there on the wall, a large framed picture of Mama Zewdi smiling down at Lydia, both their hands gripping the knife and poised to cut the cake. Elsa looked like a shy teenager, an invited guest standing behind the stars of the party, her eyes catching the lens unexpectedly, as if she had tried and failed to avoid the camera. There were others in the photo, residents of the building that would become the only family that Lydia knew. But then, they were all strangers, and Lydia wondered what her mother felt like surrounded by all those new faces.

Lydia turned her attention to the framed photos in the shelves of the television stand, each taken when Mama Zewdi was traveling with the Saudi royals she used to work for. She was alone in every picture and always touching something, as if to prove that she was actually in that place. Lydia knew everything about her adventures, the food, the clothes, the conversations; there were boxes of photo albums she could narrate on command. There was Mama Zewdi in front of the Il Duomo in Florence, both hands resting on the pink and green marble panels. At the Tidal Basin in D.C., she caressed a cherry blossom: "That was in 1977," Lydia could hear her say, "before these Habesha even knew what a cherry blossom was." Overlooking Lake Cuomo, she held the stem of a Champagne flute: "Ginger ale . . . I was still working after all, but what do you think they were drinking? Not soda, I can tell you that."

Lydia sank deeper into the cushions, burrowing her right thumb and index finger through the thick roots at the nape of her neck. What could she say about the one photo she had of her parents? Not one thing.

5

ZEWDI HAD TRIED TO SEEM CASUAL WHEN MAMA MINIA RECITED the biography of Dr. Asgedom Beyene, the man her unexpected matchmaker wanted to set her up with. He was the son of her neighbors in Asmara (which meant she knew the caliber of his family); a doctor (fantastic); not a medical doctor (that's fine, he still had his PhD); divorced (good that he had some cohabitational experience); a father of two children (perfect, since Zewdi was too old to give him any); Catholic and quite observant (could this be any better?); he lived in California (not ideal).

Zewdi agreed to pass along her number, and every time the phone rang, she felt a flutter in her chest. It was the stuff of sappy movies and love songs, absurd for a woman her age. After two weeks with no word from the good doctor, Zewdi wrote him off, wondering if she had imagined the whole scenario.

But two weeks later, Asgedom did call—at an inopportune time, of course.

It was the Thursday before Memorial Day. The end of the week was always busy, but demand was even higher for the holiday weekend. Zewdi had sold more injera than expected and was rushing to bake batches for the two customers waiting in her living room. When the phone rang, as it had been all afternoon, she was manning four griddles on the counter.

"Genet! I know I said five o'clock, but I need a bit more time," she said, cradling the phone between her shoulder and ear. "Tell that husband of yours to wait!"

The voice on the other end cleared itself. "Good evening. May I please speak to Ms. Zewdi?"

The flutter in her chest returned, and her hands froze mid-pour.

"Oh, yes, yes! This is Zewdi. I am Zewdi. So sorry," she said with a girlish laugh. "I thought you were someone else. Can I please ask who is calling?"

She tilted the pan, trying to evenly distribute the batter, but it was too late. The injera had somehow taken the shape of Russia. It was unsellable.

"This is Asgedom Beyene. I was given your number by Mama Minia."

Miriam, one of Zewdi's earliest customers and a resident on the seventh floor, appeared at her side.

"First you make me wait and then you don't even offer anything to drink?" she said with her hand on her hip. Zewdi pressed the phone closer to her ear with her shoulder and jabbed a finger toward the jug of water on the counter.

"Oh, yes, of course. Hi, Asgedom. So good that you called. How are you?"

"I'm well, thanks be to God."

"You don't have anything that's cold?" Miriam asked with her head in the fridge.

Zewdi snapped her fingers at Miriam's back until she turned to look at her. *Ice . . . ice*, Zewdi mouthed, pointing at the freezer.

Miriam sighed. "No, I can't use ice. It'll give me a headache."

"Wonderful," Zewdi said to Asgedom. "I heard that you—"

"Fatima!" Miriam yelled to the living room. "Do you want water? It's not cold!"

"Please! I'm on the phone!" Zewdi yelled back, not bothering to cover the mouthpiece.

Asgedom cleared his throat again.

"Is this a bad time?"

Zewdi still didn't know what kind of doctor Asgedom was, but she imagined that he was sitting in his office, tapping his fingers on a solid desk made of dark, polished wood. She felt that he could somehow sense that she was standing in her confined kitchen with buckets of injera batter at her feet and a plastic shopping bag tied around her head, covering a homemade hair mask of avocado and egg yolks.

"No, not at all. Please, go on," she said, breathing deeply as Miriam finally left the kitchen.

"Well, I just wanted to introduce myself and then schedule a time when we can properly chat."

Zewdi dabbed at the sweat beading above her lip. A professional like him knew the right way to do things.

"Great thinking. You're two hours behind, right?"

"Three hours. Pacific Coast Time is three hours behind Eastern Standard Time."

"Of course, of course. That's what I meant. I used to travel to California quite a bit actually. How about this Saturday at six? That would be three your time."

Zewdi plated the misshapen injera and sat at the table, peeking over at Miriam and Fatima, who were whispering and looking back at her.

"I try to keep Saturday open for my children. My son is more independent, he skipped a grade and is starting college in the fall, but I take my daughter to her lacrosse games and violin lessons. She's sixteen. Would Sunday work instead?"

"Sure, that works perfectly," Zewdi chirped, without stopping to think if it actually did.

That Sunday, at five forty-five p.m., Zewdi spritzed herself with perfume, girded her wrists with gold bangles, and sat in the living room, waiting by the phone. At exactly six p.m., it rang. Zewdi let it ring three times before answering with a breathless "Good evening." Who in the world answered the phone that way?

"Good evening, Zewdi. This is Asgedom. Is this still a convenient time for you?" he asked in a measured tone.

At the sound of his voice, Zewdi was suddenly on her feet, pacing. She walked with the handset to the dining table, untangling the extra-long cord along the way.

"Yes, I am available to speak. Thanks so much for calling back. How was your week?"

"Oh, it was very productive," he said. "I didn't have any obligations after work, as I often do . . . lectures, fundraisers, activities for my daughter, you know, those types of things . . . so I was able to get home at a reasonable time and garden, which I so love to do, and I also started a bit of repair work on our fence. I have hired someone to do the bulk of it but I'm helping, which is good because I stay active and also I can make sure he's managing his time well, which is important."

Zewdi eased into a dining chair as Asgedom droned on. He certainly was sharing more detail than she needed, but he had a pleasant manner of speaking.

"How was your week?" he asked.

"It was productive for me as well. That's how I like things. Idle hands, you know? Tell me about your daughter. You mentioned that she plays the violin?" Zewdi decided that it would be wise to not bring up whatever lacrosse was.

"Yes, we're very proud of her. She's quite the natural, and we're not sure where she got it from. Neither I nor her mother are very musical."

Zewdi tensed at the mention of his ex-wife. It seemed a bit early to bring her up. Asgedom then began to tell her about himself, in the way that correspondents on *60 Minutes* described a person before they began to interview him. He shared that he no longer ate red meat, walked five miles three days a week, and called his parents in Asmara on the first Sunday of every month. He discovered after his divorce that he rather enjoyed his own cooking ("Eritrean cuisine is often too oily"). Zewdi didn't appreciate the generalization, as it could have been at the hands of his ex-wife or his mother (God bless the latter). But she let him continue, until, finally, he explained his profession. After completing his early education in Asmara, he received his undergraduate degree at Addis Ababa University and a scholarship to get his PhD in pharmaceutical sciences at the University of Illinois in Chicago. He had planned on returning to Addis to help manage the national laboratories, but when the war intensified in the late '70s, he moved to Los Angeles, where he recently became the dean of the University of Southern California's School of Pharmacy.

Zewdi wanted to ask if he had supported the independence movement at all, possibly helped stock the underground labs the rebels had built in Nakfa. But at 6:20 p.m.—Zewdi was keeping track of the clock above the television—he cleared his throat.

"Why don't we stop here?" he said. "May I call you again next Sunday? I'm looking forward to hearing more about you."

Zewdi curled the cord around her fingers, her eyes traveling to the treetops visible from her balcony, stretching nearly unbroken until the shimmering glint of the Potomac. She let her fingers relax, freeing them from their bondage.

"Sure, I'd like it if you called me again," she said.

How could she not agree? And there was some consolation: he did expect her to eventually speak.

For that entire week, Zewdi thought carefully about how to present her biography to her suitor. It wasn't like she had much practice. There had been only one other man, and that was fourteen years ago; but Zewdi certainly wouldn't tell Asgedom that story, nor would she narrate the events of her life in chronological order. She wanted to model a more relaxed conversational style.

She would brag about Lydia for a bit. The girl might not play the violin, but she read like a fiend and her grades were always perfect. Then she would explain her work. She wouldn't call herself an entrepreneur, as she did with Americans. Injera production or any kind of food service wasn't held in high esteem among their people; but running her own business was certainly something she was proud of. Her time in Saudi would get brief coverage, so that she could instead talk more about her nursing experience, which wasn't very long and limited to Eritrea, but at least could provide them with some common ground.

But the following Sunday, at the sound of Asgedom's steady, authoritative voice, Zewdi's perfect plan went out the window.

"Well, I was born in Keren," she heard herself warble. What was happening to her? She sped through the nursing bit, while mentally calculating when best to bring up Lydia, before he interrupted her.

"May I ask why you didn't continue your nursing career in the States?"

Zewdi had to recount the years she lost working for the Saudi princess, plus the licensing requirements in America, which she would have been able to meet if she hadn't also had to make a living. He expressed his understanding and didn't sound judgmental, citing relatives who hadn't been able to continue their careers for similar reasons. But this line of discussion sent her down a fretful path, forcing her to remember how disheartened she felt by the awareness that she had become an entirely different woman with different prospects. She was still resentful at the gnawing conviction that if she had been married, her husband might have been able to support her while she studied for her exams.

Zewdi heard an intake of breath and the beginnings of a throat clear, Asgedom's cue that he was about to wrap up their conversation. The clock was at 6:19, but she had to get the conversation back on track. She sped through her booming business and ended up describing herself as an entrepreneur, saying the word in English.

"That's wonderful," he said. "Not everyone has the constitution to run their own business. I don't think I could. I applaud you."

"Well, thank you," Zewdi said, smiling for the first time while talking to him. "You're right, it's not for everyone. But I'm good at what I do."

"I would like to continue getting to know you. I'll be coming to D.C. for a work trip next month. Could we meet in person when I'm in town?"

"Of course. That sounds good. I look forward to meeting."

After the faint click of the call's end came the sound of Zewdi's belated exhale.

6

ON THE MORNING OF FRIDAY, MAY 24, ELSA DIDN'T WAKE UP because she never went to sleep. For much of the night, she lay on her side, watching Lydia sleep as if she were a baby again, as if they were sheltered in the guerrilla maternity ward, or nestled together on their cot in Khartoum, the time between Zager, Sudan, and Alexandria collapsing into a single memory.

Elsa kept her back to the alarm clock. Through the window next to the bed, the faintest hints of blue challenged the inkiness of the night sky. Born from years of observation, she could tell from the precise proportion of light to dark when it was 4:30. She turned over to confirm her accuracy and eased out of the bed, repositioning the blanket over Lydia. She shuffled to the living room and, after struggling with the sliding glass door to the balcony, curled up in the sole lawn chair. From eleven floors up, over the parking lot and 395 and lush treetops, she watched the night turn into day.

"You're gonna do good today, boss lady. Real good."

Ricky made this proclamation confidently, eyeing the crowds teeming on the Mall like a herder assessing his flock.

"This might be one for the books, Els. You should treat yourself . . . get a new bag or something. I can tell you what's in style. I know what the ladies like." He dabbed his brow with a white hand towel that was always tossed over his shoulder.

Elsa laughed and stepped out of her cart with her stool for Ricky to sit on. Ricky was a D.C. native and self-appointed steward of the National Mall. After a freak accident in which he fell down a manhole while splicing cables for PEPCO, he lived off workman's compensation and spent most of his days, weather and pain levels permitting, making his rounds among the food-cart owners, Smithsonian security guards, and National Park Service police. His brothers were both high-ranking officers in the Air Force and Marine Corps, but he preferred being "a man of the people," as he liked to put it.

Elsa dug out a bottle of Lipton Iced Tea from one of the coolers and handed it to Ricky, hopeful that his good cheer would be contagious. The only times she had known him to be anything less than agreeable were when he got on the topic of Marvin Gaye, who grew up a block over from him near the Anacostia waterfront and had somehow transformed himself into a national heartthrob, when no girl would even look twice at him back in their day. It didn't help that Ricky resembled Marvin Gaye—or rather that Gaye resembled him—and considered himself to be the real ladies' man, even though Elsa thought him much too sweet for that.

"I hope you're only buying things for one special lady," she said.

"All women deserve to be spoiled, Els. I'm just doing my part." He rested his cane against the cart and placed his hand in the center of his chest. "I'd get you something, too, but you're going to clean up today. Shoot, I should ask you to treat me to something!"

"What you need is *one* good woman, and I can't buy you that. A good woman has no price, Ricky."

"Ain't that the truth."

Elsa did expect to do well today. Business on Memorial Day weekend was always brisk, and this Friday was shaping up no differently.

A car started honking furiously. Elsa turned toward Madison Street as the offending vehicle, a speeding taxi, pulled over at the crosswalk.

"I bet that's one of your people," Ricky said.

"Just because a lot of us are cabdrivers doesn't mean—"

Elsa stopped when she realized that the driver wasn't just one of her people but Mengist, a fellow Southern Towers resident who lived three floors down with his wife and four children. According to Zewdi, they were distantly related to him, but Elsa hadn't known his family, who were from a village north of Keren.

"Elsa!" Mengist shouted, waving frantically.

"What was that again?" Ricky asked with a grin.

Elsa hurried toward Mengist. "What happened? Is it Lydia? Is everything okay?"

"It's over, Elsa. It's over!" He hurled himself out of his taxi and gripped her arms.

"What are you talking about?"

"The war! What do you think? Our tanks are in Asmara!"

Elsa was unable to fully process what he was saying, her arms going slack in his grip.

"Are . . . are you sure?" she heard herself stutter. "How do we know the Derg won't retake it . . . maybe it's just a temporary break in their hold."

"This is not temporary, Elsa. Believe me. It's over."

Mengist squeezed her shoulders and grinned before hurrying back to his car, yelling that he had to tell more people. Elsa watched him drive off, honking his horn like a madman, before pulling over at Aster's cart.

Elsa looked up at the bright sky, feeling as if she had just been dropped down into unfamiliar territory. Ricky walked up alongside her and touched her arm gently.

"What happened?"

"It's over," she whispered.

"What is?"

Elsa just shook her head, lost in her shock, and set off toward

Aster, hearing Ricky say, "Oh, this is about your people! Your war is over!"

"Watch the cart!" Elsa called out over her shoulder. She started jogging down Madison, feeling weighed down by her age and overly supportive sneakers. Sixteen years ago, she could trek for hours with rubber sandals and her rifle slung across her back. But now she heard her breath shamefully quicken on the flat terrain and started to laugh as Aster struggled to run toward her as well.

"Stay there!" she called out. Elsa had the advantage of being slim, but Aster was pear-shaped with wide hips and thick thighs.

Aster slowed down. "God, please tell me it's true, it has to be true!"

They ran into each other's arms at the clearing across the street from the Museum of Natural History, both bursting into tears as soon as they made contact. Elsa's sobs sounded foreign, as if they were coming from someone else.

"Is it true? Elsa, tell me it's true!" Aster wailed into Elsa's neck, before falling to the ground and shrieking her dead husband's name. Several tourists were looking their way, and a sinewy jogger with graying temples stopped before them.

"I'm a doctor," he said with kind eyes. "Does she need medical attention?"

"No, no. Thank you," Elsa said, trying to calm Aster down.

"Berhane! My God, Berhane, you should be here to see this!" Aster clutched her midsection and rocked back and forth on her knees.

"Are you sure?" he asked. "She seems to be in a great deal of pain."

"No, she's actually happy. She's in shock, but she's happy."

The jogger gave a skeptical look but continued on his run as Aster kept screaming out. Elsa joined her on the ground, cradling

Aster's head to her chest and thinking of the man she had heard so much about.

Berhane was an EPLF covert operative who carried out assassinations of high-ranking Ethiopian officials who had terrorized Asmara's residents. In June 1975, Ethiopian security police stormed into a birthday party, rounded up the seven guests, young women aged thirteen to twenty-two enjoying their Fanta and cream-filled pastries, and gang-raped them at an army camp before shooting them dead and tossing their bodies in the street in front of the home they had gathered in. Aster held her three girls close when she heard the news, unaware that her mild-mannered Berhane, who ran a garage in Gejeret and served as a deacon in their church, had murdered the squad commander in revenge. A few days later, a stranger appeared at her front door, telling her that Berhane had been arrested and that she and their children needed to leave the city the next day. Aster didn't believe him, demanding to go to the prison and see Berhane herself. The stranger said that Berhane expected her to say that and if he was ever in danger to recite this to his wife: "Whether you turn to the right or to the left, your ears will hear a voice behind you, saying, 'This is the way; walk in it.'" Isaiah 30:21 was their most cherished verse, and they would sometimes stay up late, long after they put their daughters to bed, reading the entire chapter to each other. The stranger told Aster to pack light and wait for a man with a folded newspaper under his right arm in front of Bar Hamasien right before curfew. Most important, she couldn't tell anyone, and he meant not one single person, that she was leaving, unless she wanted to endanger their lives too. The next day, they embarked on a weeklong journey to Sudan by foot, camel, and bus. In Khartoum, she later found out from another undercover operative seeking refuge that Berhane had been electrocuted, strung up by his feet, and whipped, in the hopes that he would reveal his collaborators. He refused, and was shot in the head and thrown off of a mountain.

As Aster's sobs slowed to a gentle whimper, Elsa helped her up to her feet. She blinked up at the sky again and started to feel her own senses begin to return.

"I have to go," Elsa said. "Lydia . . ."

Aster also appeared as if she had regained consciousness and looked back at her cart. "Yeah, me too."

Elsa made her way back to Ricky, who was faithfully standing guard.

"I sold some water for you." He handed over a dollar bill.

"Thank you, Ricky. That's the last thing we'll sell today. I need to go home."

"Home!" Ricky gestured at all the activity around them. "Come on, Els. Just put in a few hours."

Elsa shook her head and started draining the ice from the coolers.

"I'll make money another day. Come on and help me pack up."

Elsa pulled into the parking lot of St. Francis nearly an hour before school let out. She couldn't remember the last time she had done drop-off or pick-up. Zewdi took care of all that until Lydia began taking the bus in the sixth grade. Lydia eventually appeared, shuffling out by herself with a book in hand. She hunched forward slightly, and even though she had perfect vision, squinted off in the distance as if she were nearsighted, just as her father had. Elsa watched her from the car for a bit longer before Lydia noticed her and stopped in front of the statue of the school's namesake.

Elsa got out and waved Lydia over, smiling widely to counter her daughter's furrowed brow.

"What are you doing here?" Lydia asked with unconcealed suspicion.

Elsa resisted the urge to kiss her as she had when Lydia was younger, which would have only put her at a further disadvantage since Lydia was two inches taller, having scaled five-foot-six at the start of the year.

"I have good news," Elsa said as she held open the passenger door.

"Berekhet's moving out?"

"No, and not funny. Watch your hand."

Elsa walked around to the driver's side and eased herself in, turning to face Lydia's skeptical expression.

"The war is over, Lidu. We liberated Asmara."

Lydia looked at once surprised and concerned, as if the war's end somehow had a catch. Elsa brought her in closer, the gear digging into her side, and Lydia muttered a hoarse sound of happiness before bursting into tears and pressing her face into Elsa's shoulder. Lydia had never been a crier, her dry-eyed stoicism unnerving Elsa since she was a baby. Elsa would sometimes pinch her infant thigh, desperate for a reaction, fearful that her silence indicated some great harm perpetrated by a mother who didn't know what she was doing. But these waterworks were far more terrifying.

"What's wrong, my dear? We should be happy." Elsa hesitated. "Your father would want you to be happy."

"I am happy," Lydia said, hiccupping through her tears. She seemed just as taken aback by her own response and steadied her breath until she finally composed herself.

"It's kind of hard to imagine it being over because it's been going on for so long . . . and it's so far away. But I think I'm so . . . what I'm wondering is . . . do you think he knows . . . like, can Dad see that it's over?"

Elsa reached for napkins in the glove compartment to dry Lydia's face, and to stall for time. In Elsa's imagination, Efrem was not watching over them from a billowy cloud. She saw him as he was, a memory of a man who deserved more than what he got, not least to witness this very day. And she saw death as darkness that didn't transition into an enviable view of the light. While there was much Elsa couldn't do as a mother, she could and often did lie. The secret was to make sure that it was always accompanied with much more truth.

"I think he knows that the day he sacrificed for is finally here. He would want you to be proud." Elsa nudged Lydia's chin. "More than anything, you should be proud."

Lydia nodded and turned her attention to the front of the school, where her classmates were still horsing around. Elsa put her key in the ignition to start the car when Lydia said, "I found a picture in your closet of you and him in the war."

Elsa let her arm go slack, trying to determine how best to respond.

"Why were you keeping it from me?" Lydia turned to face her. Her voice quivered. Elsa prayed that she wouldn't cry again; she wouldn't be able to handle it.

"I . . . I don't . . ." Elsa struggled to find her words, to find some truth. The car chimed, reminding its owner that the key was still in the ignition.

"Is there something you don't want to talk about . . . something you don't want me to know?" Lydia's voice and gaze were steady.

"No, Liduye. I don't know why . . . it's just really hard for me to think about that time of my life and your father's death."

The chime seemed to be getting louder. Elsa cursed and yanked the keys out, accidentally dropping them at her feet.

"Now that the war is over, shouldn't it be easier to track down my father's family? Wouldn't they want to know about me?"

"Of course they would. But I've tried, trust me, I've tried." Elsa took Lydia's hand and felt it slacken. "I've tried to explain to you how things were, that as fighters we didn't know much about each other, we didn't talk about our personal lives. I wish I could just look them up, but it's not that easy."

"What about the other woman in the photo. Could she help?"

Elsa slowly released Lydia's hand and clasped hers together. "No, she can't."

"Why not? Who is she? I actually thought she was you at first. Is she family?"

"She was in our unit . . . and no, we're not related. She can't help because I don't know how to reach her either."

Lydia slumped back in the seat. She seemed tired, more tired than a girl her age should be. Elsa reached down for the keys and drove them in silence back home.

Later that night, when the darkness returned and the world was still, Elsa sat at the dining table cradling the sides of the telephone. There was one person, above all, whose voice she wanted to hear, but instead she called someone she could reach.

"Hello, Dottore. It's Elsa."

"Elsa," Dr. Alazar stated as if he was expecting her.

Elsa imagined him in his home office, which she was only ever summoned to for "pertinent matters," as he referred to the issuance of her report cards. The space had seemed cavernous to her as a child, with shelves that reached from the floor to the ceiling, crammed with books and reports in Italian, English, and Amharic. A massive, framed map of the world hung on the far wall, with countries shaded in natural tones and the oceans and seas a perfect, dreamy blue. Dr. Alazar didn't have much patience for children, but he appreciated intellectual curiosity at any age and took note of Elsa's fascination. In her earlier visits, he would let her gape at the map and choose a country, before steering her to a mighty book on a lectern in the corner that he called an atlas. After flipping to a specific page, he would reveal the world of that country, the name of each city and body of water, tables of impressive data, and pictures of sites of significance. Elsa once stood on the tips of her toes, trying to put her whole head through Peru. In a solemn tone, like a priest reading the scripture, he would recite the information listed, translating the Italian into Amharic, not Tigrinya as she would have preferred. The islands were Elsa's favorite, those seemingly insignificant specks claiming space in the equality of the atlas.

Dr. Alazar's office was thick with vegetation; any surface unclaimed by books was occupied by greenery of different shapes and sizes. Elsa offered to come more regularly and water them, thinking it a clever way to pursue her geographical adventures. But Dr. Alazar practically recoiled and said no. Just like that the spell had been broken, and he never invited her to explore the world again.

"I suppose you're calling because you heard the news," Dr. Alazar said. "Are you happy now?"

7

The Father of Boys

HADDISH, THE SON OF DERES AND FATHER OF ELSA, PREDICTED that his firstborn would be a son. When his prophecy proved true, he broadcast the news himself, as if everyone didn't already know everything that happened in Keren. His second child, born the next year, was also a boy, as was his third. Petros, Yakob, and Yohannes, named after Jesus's most trusted disciples, and the fattest babies anyone had seen.

"Look at these boys!" he bragged to his friends. "Good luck with your daughters. Will they help till your land?"

The next three names were already chosen: Michael, Gabriel, and Rafael, the archangels who served before the glory of the Lord.

"Start saving your dowries now," he advised. "Your daughters will be lucky to marry them."

But the next time he left his home to wait in his fields while his wife was in labor, he didn't know that the baby brought forth by her heaves and screams was a girl. He also didn't know that the midwife wrapped the baby in cotton cloth, set her down, and told his wife to push again. His second daughter met the world. In the final act of God's absolute and mysterious sovereignty, Haddish's wife bled out on the cot her babies were conceived in and died. Word spread even faster, as only bad news can, that the father of boys, now a widower, was no longer.

Hiwet and Hewan. The twin girls held their father's gaze, and their hair was as straight and thick as a horse's tail. Haddish swallowed his grief, telling everyone that his daughters were more beautiful than theirs, that their sons were not worthy.

As was custom, he quickly remarried a shy teenager named Manna who could mother his orphaned children. Ten years passed without his bride's body indicating any sign of new life. It was the eye of others, Manna thought, and also the terror of the bed that had claimed her predecessor. But then Elsabet was born. There was no legend about her arrival, no speculation about who she might become. The time of great pronouncements had passed, and there was only talk that she was quiet and underweight.

Months later, as Manna was boiling milk with a sleeping Elsa strapped to her back, she felt a pulsing in her thigh. She massaged the discomfort, thinking nothing of it, but then the sensation turned into a stabbing. Elsa let out a bloodcurdling scream, as if she could feel the pain herself. Manna took the pot off the charcoal and hurried to the fields, finding Haddish on his back, lying still on the turned dirt. One hand was on his thigh, and the other on his chest.

It was a pulmonary embolism that killed him. Embolia polmonare, Haddish's younger brother, Dr. Alazar, announced with a flourish twelve years later when Manna finally visited Addis and recounted that fateful day.

Dr. Alazar had accomplished many firsts. Not only was he the family's first doctor and the first Eritrean to ever receive a medical degree, but he was also the first Ethiopian subject to be trained in obstetrics and gynecology, having completed his studies in Turin the same year that Elsa was born. Upon his return from Italy, he was greeted at the airport by none other than Emperor Haile Selassie himself, who, in his soft-spoken manner, extended an invitation for the young physician to open his own practice in Addis and offered his choice of well-appointed offices from the royal family's holdings. Aware that an imperial invitation was really an order, Dr. Alazar abandoned his dream of setting up his practice back in Asmara, which was nearly eight hundred miles away from his new post.

After his brother's sudden death in 1957, the young Dr. Alazar, still a bachelor, assumed responsibility for his nieces and nephews and sent for them to be raised under his care. Manna, still reeling from her loss, didn't challenge his authority, hoping that her children, whether she had birthed them or not, would thrive under the watchful eye of their accomplished uncle. Elsa, however, was just teething and much too young to be separated from her mother. Dr. Alazar was adamant that her education not begin in Keren, so a compromise was made. When Elsa turned five, she would be sent to a Catholic boarding school in Asmara, where her mother could more easily manage the two-hour bus ride to visit. But when Elsa turned ten, she would have to join the rest of the family in Ethiopia.

The family was a family in name only. Elsa and her five older siblings, already separated by a distant ten years, had spent their entire lives apart. Elsa would only see them when they came back to Eritrea for brief visits in the summer, and even that time was short as they were off with their friends or occupied with their mother's family in Asmara. Elsa hoped for better in Addis, for her older sisters to take her under their wing and her brothers to escort her around the city's sprawl. Asmara, deemed Piccola Roma by Mussolini himself, could be explored in a day. Addis, on the other hand, was more than ten times the size of the Eritrean capital and seemed to shape-shift every day. But her siblings were in university, embarking on their own careers, and otherwise preoccupied with their own lives. She also didn't see Dr. Alazar often. He rarely came to the house he rented for his nieces and nephews or hosted family gatherings at his own, summoning them only to offer terse praise for perfect marks and promotions or voluble criticism for anything less.

When Elsa turned twelve, her mother braved the three-day

bus journey to visit them. Within earshot of the rest of the family, she marveled at Addis's size and exotic customs, but privately, while braiding Elsa's hair at night, she was overwhelmed by its chaos and filth, the murkiness sluicing through the open sewers and beggars banging on the gate. Dr. Alazar invited her to live there, a thoughtful offer, but one that her mother wouldn't accept. "Forgive me, my Elsa," she said, stifling her tears. "But I belong in my own home, not his."

To show her gratitude for all her brother-in-law had done, Manna hosted a feast in his honor. The preparations took her two days; she even ventured to the market to choose which sheep to slaughter, with the eldest in tow as translator. The maid, barely pubescent, with tattooed crosses rimming her neck, was scandalized by Manna's labor and fought her from entering the kitchen. That wasn't how things were done in Ethiopia, Elsa tried to explain. Hiwet and Hewan had gotten acclimated. On the rare occasions they cooked, the maid would prep the ingredients and do the cleaning afterward so that all they had to do was season and stir. Manna, however, would tolerate no such behavior and forced them back into the kitchen.

Manna served the lunch herself on a communal platter she brought as a gift from Keren, even feeding Dr. Alazar from her own hand. He picked his bones clean, cracking them and sucking out the marrow. Elsa would have liked to do the same; she could suck a bone drier than a dog, but she felt shy doing so in front of him.

During the course of the meal, Dr. Alazar gave his signature lecture on the Eritrean question: Is independence a legitimate cause?

"Ladies and gentlemen," he said, raising a gnawed chicken leg in the air, "that is not the right question to ask. Has our land been taken from us? Yes. Have our rights been violated? Absolutely. But we must consider where we are in history at the present moment, which is in the crosshairs of a voracious empire in the middle of a war between two global superpowers. Do you think our little ragtag bandits can take the Ethiopian empire on? They cannot. And the reason is not because we're facing the Conquering Lion of the Tribe of Judah, His Imperial Majesty, King of Kings, Lord of Lords, Elect of God—which, by the way, is the greatest fiction ever told. It's because that little man in his little cape has implanted himself in the imagination of people much more powerful than he is. The correct question is: Can we win this war? Since that answer is a resounding no, what we should be focusing on is how to make this unfortunate predicament work in our favor."

Manna kept her attention on the diminishing levels of food and drink, serving more helpings and replenishing Dr. Alazar's glass with the mead she had brewed. As he continued, she tore off bits of flesh from a braised chicken thigh and set them in front of Elsa.

"These people, who have *stumbled* into the opportunity of ruling us, are lucky and lazy. They are blessed with endless rainfall and lush plains, while our forefathers broke their backs on their lot from God, coaxing our dry land into yielding. But remember, we Eritreans, we have grit and honor. We make something out of nothing, every single time." Dr. Alazar thumped his fist on the table, and Manna flinched, her hands seizing momentarily before she regained her composure. "And while I'm not proud that we were colonized by the Italians," he went on, "we know how to keep the lights on and make the engines purr. Let them shut down our factories back home; we'll run them here. Let them pay for our education; we'll be their bosses. Let them set up their airlines; we'll fly the planes. Politics is a loud man's sport. But real power is a smart man's game."

Manna finally spoke after lunch, as she brewed the coffee. She blessed Dr. Alazar's name. She thanked him for being a father to her children and sighed about her dead husband. She recounted how on the morning of his last day, before he left for their fields, he complained about a sudden pain in his leg. Dr. Alazar then turned down the radio, which was playing a mournful Sudanese song, and Elsa's mother went on to say that he had wheezed, leaned against the door, and then sat on a flat stone until his breath steadied. When Manna paused, perhaps feeling she'd said too much, Dr. Alazar urged her to go on, and she described that ominous pain in her own thigh as he tapped his glasses.

In a display of physicality Elsa had never seen, Dr. Alazar jumped to his feet and directed Elsa's eldest brother to stand in front of the television. Sudden death, he said, was usually only caused by three things: a heart attack, a rupture in an artery in the brain, and the blockage of an artery in the lung. He tapped her brother's organs with each pronouncement and continued on, explaining that the most common cause of a blockage is a blood clot that forms in a deep vein in the leg and travels to the lungs, getting stuck in the smaller lung artery. Pulmonary embolism, he repeated, pointing at Manna. He sat back down, satisfied with his autopsy. She looked as if she had been accused of murder.

Elsa's mother never came back to Addis. Before she left, she told the older children to look out for their little sister, and Elsa to do what she was told.

"Pay attention to everything," she said. "But keep it to yourself."

June 1991

8

A WEEK AFTER ERITREA'S LIBERATION, EARLY ON A BRIGHT SATURday morning, Zewdi was feather-dusting the framed photos on her entertainment center when the phone rang.

"Does Ms. Zewdi still live at this residence?" the caller asked.

Zewdi chuckled. She recognized that sly voice. "They're allowing you to make international calls?"

"That's the least they can do for all the abuse I've suffered. Now I'm being told not to eat bananas. Can you imagine a Swede telling me what to eat? The bananas aren't even good here!"

Zewdi eased onto her loveseat. "I really miss you, Mama Minia. I can't believe we don't get to celebrate independence together."

"Let's celebrate now, my daughter." Mama Minia let out a shrill ululation that Zewdi echoed.

"I'm also calling to see if we have another reason to celebrate. Have you and Asgedom been in touch?"

"We've spoken a few times. He seems nice, very polite."

Mama Minia was quiet. Zewdi realized that she expected her to say more.

"And . . . I'm happy to be introduced to him."

"Of course you are. He's a good man. Why do you think I set you up? Let's talk about the next steps. When are you going to meet?"

"He's coming to D.C. next week for a work trip and asked if we could get together then."

Zewdi left out the fact that she and Asgedom would be attending the same independence celebration, which the community was holding the day after his conference; but they'd agreed to not meet at the party, as there would be too many distractions while catching up with family and friends. Left unsaid was the desire to avoid an awkward first encounter in public, an Eritrean public at that. They made plans to meet the next day for an early dinner in Georgetown before his flight back to Los Angeles.

"Excellent. I'm sure you'll like him even more face-to-face."

Zewdi nodded and picked at imaginary fuzz on the armrest, hoping Mama Minia was right.

"He comes from such a good family. In all the years I knew his father, Beyene, he always wore a three-piece suit, every single day. Can you imagine that? And Akhberet, his mother, kept a house like you wouldn't believe." Zewdi wondered who Asgedom was beyond the good breeding and education. She also wondered what he looked like. Mama Minia hadn't seen him since the '70s when he visited Asmara during summer vacation from his studies in Illinois, and only described him as nice-looking, which could be generous.

"You know I'm praying for you," she continued. "There is no one more deserving of a happy home."

"Amen."

"And since you gave me good news, I'll return the favor." Mama Minia paused before lowering her voice. "I think I found a relative of this Efrem Negash you asked me about. My daughter's brother-in-law and his wife came from Holland to visit, and the wife's best friend from high school happens to live here in Stockholm too. So, this friend came by the house, her name is Dahab, and it turns out that she is originally from Dekemhare."

Zewdi sat up straighter, feeling a warmth in her chest that she always trusted.

"Sooo . . ." Mama Minia continued with a dramatic flourish, "of course I told her who I was looking for. And she said that she had an older cousin named Efrem Negash who was martyred. Can you believe that? She was curious why I wanted to know, but I didn't want to tell her that her deceased cousin might have a child in America because, who knows, there could be more than one Efrem Negash. I told her that someone in D.C. was looking for his people, and that I wasn't sure why. I have her number—go get a pen. She's expecting your call."

Zewdi stood up as the heat intensified. "That's him. I know it is."

"Well, call her and find out. And let me get off this phone. This daughter of mine has set a limit for how many minutes I can talk. Can you believe that? The poverty of these people!"

Zewdi hung up quite satisfied with herself. This was exactly what family was supposed to do: get involved without waiting to be asked.

When Zewdi let herself into Elsa's apartment, Lydia was in the kitchen arguing with Elsa, who was still in her house dress, cutting the injera Zewdi had brought over the day before.

"You can't go in his room, Lydia," Elsa said with exasperation. "He's sleeping."

"But I need a book . . . and it's *my* room."

What Lydia needed to do was put on something halfway presentable. The child was dressed in jeans and a T-shirt, both oversized, even though Zewdi kept telling her that baggy clothes made her look bigger than she really was. The coarse hair at the nape of her neck stuck straight out, too short to stay in the high bun Zewdi was certain the poor girl struggled to form. The texture of Lydia's hair was a mystery. Elsa's hair was nearly as soft as Zewdi's, and Lydia's father's hair, silky and voluminous in the headshot that hung above the television, put their tresses to shame. Elsa should have made sure that Lydia got her hair done for the big weekend. With hair like hers, you had to plan.

"Didn't I tell you to put all the things you need in my room?"

"I can't fit all my books in your room. And I already finished the one I started yesterday."

"Why don't you keep the next few books you want to read in my room then?"

"Because I decide what I'm going to read next once I've finished the book I just read," Lydia said, as if her system were reasonable.

Elsa carefully considered the injera in her hands before straightening her compact frame. Her body always had the appearance of being wound up, as if at any moment more of her could spring out. Lydia looked over at Zewdi with pleading eyes, but she had the sense to remain unaligned.

"Elsiye, people will be here any minute." Zewdi stepped in between the mother and daughter. "Why don't you change? I'll warm up the food."

Zewdi had offered to host the welcome lunch for Berekhet, who was nearing his one-month anniversary in the States. Her home was better appointed for events like these. While their apartments had the same layout, they were opposite in both orientation and domestic philosophy. The entrance led to the living room on the right side and the kitchen on the other. The dining area lay just beyond the kitchen and opened up to the balcony, which, at Elsa's, was home to a dead tomato plant and a one-armed lawn chair. A long hallway—Zewdi's favorite feature, as it offered some measure of privacy that apartment dwellers were largely denied—distanced the two bedrooms from the rest of the home.

Elsa also initially resisted Zewdi's offer to make zigni, but not as strongly, which indicated her acceptance. Elsa still had to make tibsi; not having at least two meat dishes for an occasion like this would have been disrespectful. The tibsi was simple enough—cubes of beef sautéed with rosemary, onions, and clarified butter that tasted best if prepared right before eating. Zigni, on the other hand, took hours, and Elsa never wanted to put in the time.

"What's the most important ingredient when cooking, my dear?" Zewdi asked Lydia as she replaced the mismatched bowls and platters on the table with a more elegant serving set she'd gifted Elsa a few Christmases ago.

"Cleanliness," Lydia muttered.

"I can't hear you."

"*Cleanliness,*" she sang loudly in an operatic voice.

Zewdi always stressed this because children naturally wanted to take shortcuts, which became habits that were much harder to break. The other rule she taught her was patience. Vegetables won't cook evenly if they aren't cut the same size. Carrots won't caramelize if they crowd the pan. Red lentils lead to heartburn unless they are soaked raw overnight. Zigni was the most demanding of all. First, it required an obscene amount of finely diced onions. Elsa had picked up this trend of using a food processor, and once Zewdi even saw her use a blender. But the mindless blades turned the onions into a soggy mush that was impossible to strain and even more difficult to brown.

"Tomatoes, Lidu." Zewdi continued her line of questioning as she plated the curried lentils, garlicky mustard greens, and ground beef samosas she had also prepared. "What did I tell you about tomatoes?"

"Always chop them by hand."

An unenthusiastic response, but at least it was correct. Zewdi had also seen Elsa use the food processor to massacre tomatoes into a watery soup. She knew what Elsa had been thinking: the tomatoes were going to break down anyway, and zigni required a few cups of water. But that's not how it worked. The onions had to sweat out first. The garlic had to soften. Then the tomatoes, chopped finely, *by hand*, had to break down slowly, naturally, until the perfect base was created for the chicken.

Zewdi understood Elsa's impatience. She worked long hours in a stand smaller than the caves she used to hide in. Back in her fighting days, she ate only to survive and was served food prepared by men. The days of waiting for onions and tomatoes to reduce had long passed for Elsa and all the guerrilla fighters. They modernized, they liked to say, which just meant that they were looking for shortcuts. But that didn't mean Zewdi should have to eat a lunch she or anyone else for that matter wouldn't enjoy, which is why she always offered to cook, and Elsa knew to accept.

Zewdi did have hopes that Elsa would at least wear kidan habesha, as she had, but Elsa returned to the kitchen, clad instead in a gray cardigan and high-waisted slacks.

"I made lasagna, Zewdiye. Did you see?" Elsa asked as she cut serving portions in its dish.

While Elsa conceded that Zewdi was the better cook, she was convinced that her lasagna was the one dish she prepared better. Like most Eritreans who thought that food wasn't worth eating unless it was spicy, Elsa added heaps of berbere to the tomato sauce—so much that it might as well be eaten with injera. Real lasagna was made with béchamel and ricotta. But tell this to an Eritrean and they act like they know better than the Italians.

"With all this food, we certainly could have fed more," Zewdi responded with a smile.

Mengist and Genet were the first guests to arrive, along with their four children, a pair of ten-year old twins who waved shyly at Lydia, a six-year-old who'd defaced Zewdi's foyer table last Thanksgiving, and a darling toddler. Roma and Eyob, a younger couple from the tenth floor, made their entrance right as Berekhet emerged from his room, smoothing out the wrinkles from his rumpled dress shirt. Zewdi had suggested inviting others, but Elsa thought it best for the lunch to be more intimate. Weren't times like these when you needed people the most? Fifteen years ago, when Zewdi made the States her home, she would have been grateful to be welcomed by a houseful of people, even if they were strangers.

Elsa gave the salad another toss and called everyone to gather around the dining table, steering Berekhet to stand at its head.

"Wow, this is so much food, Elsa," Berekhet said with wide eyes.

"You should credit Zewdi. She's the chef in this family."

Berekhet thanked Zewdi, who had taken up a position to his left. Elsa handed him the first plate from the stack.

"No, no, please," he demurred, motioning for either Mengist or Zewdi to take it instead, uncertain if gender or age dominated the hierarchy.

"Today is in your honor, my son," Zewdi assured him. He accepted the plate and reached for the injera. "But first, we must say a prayer," she announced, and Berekhet hesitated before returning his plate and bowing his head.

"We must give thanks to God for bringing our Berekhet to us safely," Zewdi said with fervor. "God always gives us what we need: a brother for Lydia and a son for Elsa."

"Amen, Zewdi, my sister," Elsa said, motioning for Berekhet to help himself to the food. "Amen."

Zewdi went on in a louder voice, glancing pointedly to make sure that Berekhet did no such thing.

"We also thank God for his timing. As God brought Berekhet to us, he also brought the end of this war. We haven't seen peace for thirty years. We've been separated, our families flung all over the world, unable to celebrate together, raise our children together, bury our dead together. Why would God allow such suffering for as long as he did? As people of faith, that's not our business to answer. The task for us, the eternal task, is to find the blessing. It's always there."

Zewdi could see them all, Berekhet concentrating on the chicken, Lydia looking dreamily out of the balcony sliding door. She knew the younger generation thought people like her made too much of a fuss about things. Even Elsa was distracted, picking at her nails, hoping Zewdi would soon find her way to the end of the prayer when she really needed to be praying herself. There could be no shortcuts with either praying or parenting; whatever relief you gained in the moment wasn't worth the reckoning when God finally forced you to pay attention.

"Oh God. We thank you for Berekhet, which means 'blessing,' after all. And we humbly ask that you grant us the wishes in our hearts or free us from them forever more."

"Amen," they all replied.

Zewdi stepped back, directing their guests to make their plates and seat themselves in the living room.

Mengist claimed the space right next to Berekhet on the sofa and repositioned his two-year-old on his lap. With his protruding belly and half-tucked shirt, he looked like an overgrown version of his son.

"So! What do you think of America? Is it what you expected?"

"Some things I expected, and others I didn't. But I love it so far. And Lydia has been a great little sister helping me get adjusted," Berekhet said with a kind look in her direction. Lydia smiled wanly at Berekhet's knees from a dining chair she positioned across from the sofa.

"Listen," Mengist said, "this is a nice country, of course, but you have to be careful. People only look after themselves here, it's not like back home." He broke into the lasagna with his hands. Zewdi cringed. Injera was its own utensil, but lasagna wasn't meant to be disemboweled.

"There are forks right here," Zewdi said. Mengist waved her off.

"There's no place like Eritrea. None!" Genet declared loudly, as if they all weren't in earshot of each other. Zewdi vowed that this year she would convince her to get her hearing checked.

There were some Eritreans who should have never come to America. It wasn't their fault, of course; the war forced them out. Mengist and Genet, who had been pregnant with the twins at the time, left behind the small plot of land they farmed near Keren and trekked to Kassala. Zewdi wasn't even sure they had ever ridden in a car until they reached Sudan. There was no way Genet could handle a job in America; it took her six months to feel comfortable going to the grocery store by herself. And while Mengist made decent money driving a cab, he would never be anything else.

"Let's not scare our brother," Eyob said from the loveseat, smiling at Berekhet. "America isn't perfect, but there's more good than bad."

Zewdi beamed at Eyob as he spoke, taking a seat on a chair next to him and Roma. Even though Mengist was family, Zewdi wanted Berekhet to spend more time with Eyob, who had graduated from pharmacy school the year before, wore a white coat at his job at Safeway, and was the best example they had in that building of someone on his way to making it.

As soon as Zewdi sat down, she rose again to serve the drinks. "Berekhet might be the first one of us here to go to medical school," she said as she offered juice to the kids and Merlot and Heinekens to everyone else.

"Might? Of course he will," Mengist said. "He'll be just like his father. Lydia too. Is this all we're drinking today?" he asked Zewdi.

"Who knows about our Lydia," Elsa said, trying to smooth her daughter's hair. "These American kids change their minds every day."

"Her parents are heroes. Of course she'll do something great," Eyob said.

"Have you always been interested in medicine?" Roma asked Berekhet, covering her glass as Zewdi tried to pour her wine.

Berekhet was nineteen years old, likely a decade from marriage, but Zewdi already hoped that he would find a woman like Roma. She was almost finished with her nursing program, which meant that she and Eyob would soon be able to afford a detached house they would fill with children, the first of whom Zewdi sensed was likely already conceived, since Roma never refused wine. The "American Dream," Zewdi couldn't believe such an aspiration was called, as if everyone in the world didn't want a home of their own. They should have called it the "American Debt" since that was the only way to afford it.

"I'm actually not interested in medicine at all," Berekhet responded. "That was my father's calling, but I don't share the same passion."

Everyone stiffened, even the toddler, and stared wide-eyed at him. Just as quickly, they reanimated like pull-string dolls.

"What do you mean by 'calling'?" Mengist questioned.

"The son of a doctor must become a doctor!" Genet shouted.

"You can go into engineering," Eyob said, more so to Elsa, who was eyeing Berekhet as if meeting him for the first time. "Personal computing is also a growing field. Maybe you can work in software development."

"Hold on, guys," Roma said. Zewdi fixated on the mole in the center of her eyebrows that gave her the appearance of being as wise as she was. "Let him speak. Berekhet, what are you interested in?"

Berekhet set his plate down on the coffee table. "I've always been intrigued by history and philosophy . . . psychology as well. I'd like to better understand what it is we know and how we have come to know it."

Mengist and Genet wiped their hands and set their napkins on their plates. Eyob looked nervously at Elsa. "Maybe you can teach," he said.

"Yes, exactly!" Roma jumped in. "You can be a college professor."

"Whatever you end up doing, Berekhet, we're sure that you'll do better than all of us," Zewdi said in the hopes of uplifting the mood. "You can't imagine how hard it was when we first got here. We had to figure out what do to for work, where to live . . ."

"How to eat," Eyob said into his glass. "Some of us thought dog food was for humans."

"Ah, the famous dog food incident. I knew that food wasn't for humans."

"You can see my wife likes to show off."

"There are pictures of dogs on the package!"

"But there are pictures of dogs everywhere in this country!" Mengist said. "And they sell the food in the grocery store. Why would they do that?"

"Couldn't you tell by the smell?" Lydia looked horrified.

"We thought that's how food smelled here."

"Guys, it wasn't dog food," Elsa said. "It was cat food!"

Everyone yelled that she was wrong. Everyone but Zewdi because she hadn't been there, and if she had, she wouldn't have been confused.

"It was!" Elsa said. "I know because the cat on the label looked just like our neighbor's cat in Addis, Elizabeth Taylor."

Over another round of jeers, Genet leaned over to ask Zewdi who that was.

"Berekhet, let me tell you the story," Elsa said. "These guys"—she pointed at Mengist and Genet—"invited us for dinner."

"The dog food dinner wasn't at my house!" Genet shouted.

"Well, whoever's house it was told us they made pasta al tonno—pasta with tuna, with *fish*," she clarified for Genet. "We were so excited because we were sick of rice."

"Sick of it!" Mengist echoed.

"So everyone was eating the pasta, really tearing it up," Elsa went on.

"Not me," Genet said. "I knew as soon as they brought it out that something wasn't right."

"How could you know? Meat doesn't taste like meat here," Mengist said. "What do you think, Berekhet? Does this meat taste normal to you? These animals just sit in one place, getting fed God knows what. But back home? They are running around, eating grass and wheat, getting lean."

"One time I ate a chicken that had been on this Earth for five years. That's almost as old as our Helen." Genet pointed to their six-year-old.

"You guys are confusing him," Elsa said. "Let me finish the story. So, Almaz—you haven't met her yet, Berekhet."

"She lives downstairs," Zewdi interrupted. "She was really looking forward to meeting you today."

"Almaz went into the kitchen and started shouting when she saw the cans. I ran in behind her, saw Elizabeth Taylor, and tried to stop her from throwing up."

"I still don't understand why dogs need their own food. Why don't Americans just give them their scraps?" Mengist asked.

"It's probably a good business," Berekhet said with a shrug. "It's brilliant if you think about it."

"These Americans love their dogs more than they love you." Eyob pointed at Mengist. "Their food has grains and vitamins. You'd probably be healthier if you kept on eating it."

"I'll eat it if you do."

"What do you think we've been serving when you come over?" Roma said with a wink.

"Okay, okay. Enough." Eyob stood up. "It's time to make a toast. Berekhet, we toast to your success at whichever medical school you go to. Isn't that right, Elsa?"

"Absolutely." Elsa raised her glass in the air. Berekhet laughed good-naturedly as everyone clinked their glasses together.

"One more thing," Eyob said as they sat back down. Zewdi gestured for Lydia to clear their plates from the living room.

"Whenever we get together for holidays or special gatherings like this, we toast that by that time the next year, we will all be back home, raising our glasses in a free Eritrea. Well, brothers and sisters, that day has come. Who's going back?"

Mengist's glass lowered as he dropped his shoulders.

"These kids, Eyob, my brother, we have to educate these kids," Genet answered in the softest voice Zewdi had ever heard her use.

"I have to finish nursing school and then complete my clinical hours," Roma said to no one in particular.

"What do you think, Mom?" Lydia returned from the kitchen and stood at Zewdi's side.

"Yeah, Elsa. We want to go back with you and enter Asmara waving from a tank!" Mengist said.

Elsa cleared her throat and looked around the room. "Lydia's young, you know. Maybe one day we'll go for a visit but . . ." she said, trailing off.

"I'd like to share something that you all might find useful," Berekhet said. "It's from the teachings of the Buddha that I read in a book I came across in Addis. I don't remember the quote exactly, but the Buddha said not to get stuck in the past because the past is gone, and not to become obsessed with the future because the future is not yet here. There is only one moment for you to be alive, and that is in the present."

Genet leaned over to Zewdi. "Why is this boy talking about a budda?"

"No, he doesn't mean our budda. He's not talking about an evil spirit." Zewdi hesitated, trying to figure out the best way to explain who Berekhet was referring to. "The Buddha is like Jesus . . . but for Chinese people."

Genet sat back in even more distress, as if trying to determine whether a demon or Chinese Jesus was worse.

"Well said, Berekhet, my brother, well said," Zewdi said. "The messenger might be unfamiliar to some of us, but that doesn't mean we should dismiss the message. I think it's time for dessert."

9

IN THE OMNI SHOREHAM'S GRAND BALLROOM, A FEW HOURS BEFORE the independence celebration was set to begin, Elsa was watching Tekle, an Eritrean who worked at the hotel, have a tense discussion with his boss.

"Tek, I'm happy your people are finally free," the American said, pointing his walkie-talkie. "But that has nothing to do with D.C. fire code. If you want this dance floor bigger, you're gonna have to lose some tables."

Zewdi was standing on the dance floor in question, directing Lydia and Berekhet on where to place the foliage arrangements they'd hauled to the hotel. They had already set two planters of fake ferns on both sides of the Eritrean and American flags, stationed bouquets of ivory lilies and palm fronds, and strung garlands along the edge of the stage.

"Does that look right to you?" Zewdi called out to Elsa, who responded with two thumbs up.

Andat, the chair of the Eritrean Committee on Events and Holidays, rushed into the ballroom and gave Elsa a harried greeting, then stopped in his tracks at the sight of the stage.

"Zewdi," he said, like a doctor diagnosing a condition.

"Hi, Andiye," she said with great affection. "You're finally here."

"I've been here. What's all this?"

Zewdi waved casually at her creative vision. "I thought we should refresh our decorations. It's independence, after all."

"I'm aware, and as you know, Alganesh is in charge of decorations."

"Yes, yes. She's wonderful. Listen, Andat, my brother, that's too low." She pointed at the banner with the slogan of the Eritrean People's Liberation Front, "Victory to the Masses," printed in Tigrinya, Arabic, and English. "Does it need to be raised? What do you think?"

Andat looked up at the ceiling. Elsa was sure that he was deciding whether he had the energy to contest in this battle of wills. She felt a perverse satisfaction at someone else being subjected to her oppression.

"It needs to be raised," he said finally, with great sadness.

"Thank God you're here. Lydia, Berekhet! The banner needs to be raised. Baba Andat is going to help you." She patted him on the shoulder like a mother encouraging her child.

By eight o'clock, nearly a thousand Eritreans claimed seats at the scores of round tables that circled the dance floor, and the emcee finally quieted the crowd. Rows of children clad in T-shirts emblazoned with the Eritrean flag filed onto the stage, taking their position in front of the band. The chords of the national anthem began, and the children closest to the microphones edged away, until the audience overtook their cautious rendition. Elsa could see Zewdi eyeing the parents rushing forward with their cameras.

"Those parents must be so proud," Zewdi said wistfully from their table near the stage. "Lydia, I bet you would have liked to be up there too."

Elsa knew that Zewdi was really addressing her. Her lack of involvement in the community had long been a sore subject. Zewdi had pushed Elsa to join the D.C. chapters of every single organization there was—the National Union of Eritrean Women, Friends of Eritrean Orphans Association, Eritrean Relief Committee—and in a final, desperate appeal, to start her own. But what would that be? The Eritrean Hot Dog Vendors Politburo?

Andat appeared on the stage, smiling at the wild applause. Besides serving as the committee chair, he was a taxi driver beloved for convincing a passenger who was a *Nightline* producer into airing a four-minute segment on Eritrea's cause. After brief remarks, he introduced Osman Hussein, the lanky head of the EPLF's D.C. office, to even more raucous applause.

"Osman is a very capable leader and quite intelligent," Zewdi said to Berekhet. "Elsa knew him well in the field."

Elsa had known of Osman, but they didn't actually meet until she settled in Alexandria. Zewdi was well aware of that but preferred her version of the story.

Fifteen years ago, around the time that Elsa joined the EPLF, Osman had abandoned his undergraduate studies in Madison, Wisconsin, to serve as an EPLF community organizer in the States. The EPLF leadership had sent for him to tour the rebel-held areas in Eritrea, including Zager, where Elsa had been stationed, to observe her unit's efforts to create a model village. Elsa had been beyond excited to showcase their work, but she was summoned elsewhere at the last minute and missed his visit. She did leave Osman a letter, drafted painstakingly under the dim light of her kerosene lamp, urging him to persuade President Ford to support Eritrea's right to self-determination. She could see the humor in it now. Life in America had proved itself to be so narrowly focused; it was obvious why no one in this country cared the slightest about anyone in hers.

Osman took the microphone and stepped away from the podium. "How's everyone doing tonight?" he asked.

"Good," the crowd responded, over the din of people still chatting.

"Let's try this again. How's everyone doing tonight?"

This time, the crowd roared in response. Osman gestured for them to get louder, and they clapped and whistled and rose to their feet. The bass player started to strum a few chords. The keyboardist teased a melody. Elsa, along with everyone else, recognized the song, Wedi Zager's anthem for their country's liberation. A few people ran toward the stage, and once the percussion hit, even more surged onto the dance floor.

"Wait, wait. I had a speech." Osman waved sheets of paper in the air. "Can I share my remarks? Or should I sing instead?"

"Sing!" they yelled.

Osman replaced the mic in its holder at the podium and strode toward the mic stand in the middle of the stage. "Test, test . . . mic check one," he said with mock seriousness that Elsa couldn't help but laugh at.

The lead singer approached from behind and slung his electric lute forward on his chest. Osman looked him up and down and turned back to the crowd.

"Who do you want? This guy or me?"

"Him!" the crowd yelled.

The singer started the first verse. Before he could finish it, the dance floor was filled to capacity. People pressed themselves shoulder to shoulder, shuffling en masse like luggage on a conveyor belt. Those who couldn't find space created their own orbits in the aisles between the tables and along the walls.

"Let's show them how it's done!" Zewdi pulled Lydia and Berekhet up from their seats. Mengist and Genet, who were also at their table, rushed to their feet as well. Lydia looked back at Elsa, tilting her head toward the dance floor in an invitation to join.

"I'll join you for the next one. You all go ahead," Elsa said, waving them off.

She watched them disappear into the mass of bodies on the dance floor like trekkers entering a dense forest. At the chorus, the singer belted the poignant lyrics, "Asmara is finally at peace," and the crowd chanted them back. Instead of giving in to the rhythm, Elsa felt herself stiffen. She had only ever expected to celebrate independence with her comrades, far from the gilded ballroom she found herself in now. It felt as if the bass were thumping in her own chest. The chandeliers, with their glistening, tiered daggers, trembled to the beat, and for a frightful moment, Elsa imagined them, as if by design, crashing down onto the crowd. She stood up quickly and weaved to one of the rear exits, where Tekle's boss was standing with his arms crossed, shaking his head.

From the corner of her eye, she spotted a former neighbor—already tipsy, but no surprise there—zigzagging his way to her. She turned her head, hoping he didn't see her, but he rushed over and threw his arm over her shoulder, steering her to the bar.

"Just the person I've been looking for!" Tesfay planted a fat kiss on her cheek. "There are two kinds of people in the world. Those who run to the war and those who buy the drinks when the first kind returns!"

"There must be more kinds of people than that." Elsa tried to break from his grip.

"Let me have this honor, Elsa. This day would have never come without heroes like you."

A video camera surveilled the room, panning over to where they stood. Elsa squeezed her eyes shut, reminding herself to breathe.

"Look at our friends celebrating with us." He gestured at the somber Ethiopian bartenders, conferring to themselves in Amharic.

"Didn't you hear?" he said as they ignored his attempts at high-fives. "The war's over. Smile!"

Elsa asked for water and rummaged in her purse, stuffing $10 in the tip jar. Someone even more exuberant than Tesfay greeted him and dragged him off. Elsa stood to the side of the bar, planning her next move, when she saw Osman approaching her with a warm smile that she tried to reciprocate.

"Long time," he said. They tapped their opposite shoulders

together in the rebels' manner of greeting. The gesture required more effort of Osman, since he was nearly a foot taller.

"Long time, indeed," Elsa said. "Are you taking a break already? I thought you weren't allowed to leave the dance floor."

"I'm even worse at dancing than I am at singing. I've reached my quota for embarrassing myself tonight. What about you?"

"I'm just warming up," Elsa said, clutching a bar napkin in her hand.

"Listen—"

"So—"

Osman motioned for her to speak.

"I just wanted to ask if you know," she said, "when the names of the martyrs are going to be released?"

Osman didn't seem surprised by the question but considered her carefully with his hound-dog eyes before answering. "I don't know how any of that is going to be handled yet. But you know how the leadership does things. They already know who died but they're not going to announce the names until they demobilize everyone. And they can't demobilize everyone until they're certain it's safe to do so. Are you looking for someone?"

"Yeah, maybe," Elsa said.

"You should come by the office. It'll be easier to discuss there."

"Okay, I'll come." Elsa looked up at him, craning her neck. "And what were you going to ask me?"

"To come by the office sometime." He smiled warmly. "I need to make some more rounds. But it was good to see you, Elsa."

Even though Zewdi and Asgedom had agreed to not meet at the party, Zewdi was still anxious about running into him. She stalked the lobby, listening for his voice or someone calling his name. In the ballroom, she stood guard at the top of the wide flight of stairs that overlooked the dance floor. Possible Asgedoms were everywhere. Maybe someone had pointed her out to him, and he was looking at her. Almost everyone knew who she was; people needed injera more than they did pharmacologists.

While she was scanning the crowd, Ammanuel, a young restaurant owner, rushed up and engulfed her in an embrace, swaying her from side to side.

"Why aren't you up on that stage? You're the best decoration we got in here!"

She beamed and wrapped her arms around him, grateful for the confirmation that she did put herself together quite nicely. The burgundy embroidery on her dress was one-of-a-kind. Her natural hair dominated all three categories of competition: texture, thickness, and length. Ammanuel's flattery reminded her of the greatest compliment she ever received. "I see you in here all the time," a checkout woman at Giant once told her. "Your face belongs on money, Ms. Thing!"

Zewdi also felt her confidence buoyed by the beauty of her countrywomen. She looked out at them, all wearing every piece of real twenty-four-karat gold they had been given, bought, or borrowed: oversized orbs studding their ears; busts of Nefertiti, Lalibela crosses, and Greek coins dangling from sturdy chains; endless embellished bangles; and even a few waist-cinching belts. There were, of course, some misfires: mixed gold and silver jewelry, braids tiger-striped with blond weave, and arm flab exposed in Western ball gowns.

"Oh, please. That can't be true . . . not with all these younger women here." She tossed her hair. "Anyway, when are you going to put in your first order? Word on the street is that the injera at Asmara Restaurant is gummy."

"That's the least of my problems. Our cook is leaving to reunite with her kids in Frankfurt, and Robel wants to pull out and open his own restaurant in Atlanta."

Zewdi gave no response.

He cocked his head to the side, narrowing his eyes. "Zewdi."

"Yes," she said with feigned innocence.

"Forget the injera! Be the cook. There's no one who cooks better than you. You're going to have a line out the door!"

Zewdi shook her head demurely at his lack of vision.

"You're too kind, Aman. But it's more than food. It's efficient operations, good customer service, especially if you want Americans to come. Our people can eat just fine at their own homes, but Americans care more about the experience, don't you think?"

"Well, yes, of course."

"Asmara has such potential. This could be an opportunity for a bigger change." She paused, trying not to smirk. "And a new partner."

Ammanuel nodded and clutched her hands. "You're right, you're right. Why don't you come by the restaurant so we can talk more?"

Zewdi let him guide her to the dance floor and managed to forget about Asgedom altogether.

10

THE NEXT MORNING, AFTER SUNDAY BREAKFAST AT ZEWDI'S, ELSA asked Berekhet and Lydia to come outside to the parking lot. They followed her to the visitors' section along the chain-link fence and stopped in front of a four-door Honda Civic not much younger than Lydia, with a red hood darker than the rest of its body.

"This is for you." Elsa handed Berekhet a Washington Monument keychain with a single key.

"You bought him a car?" Lydia gaped, her eyes flicking back and forth between Elsa and the key now in Berekhet's hand.

Elsa knew Lydia was trying to make sense of where the money had come from. Their early years had been tight, but Elsa eventually started doing well, making $70,000 a year, untaxed and in cash. She kept their expenses low, maintained a sense of scarcity, and even used food stamps and low-income housing support for a few years to build up her savings. She never used the food stamps in front of Lydia, and only a few times with Zewdi, who would walk past her at the register and wait for her outside. They had made their own choices, and Elsa was satisfied with hers—pride wouldn't deposit funds in her bank account. She had seen enough to know that you couldn't predict what would happen. She could pull her back out, get hit by a truck, or even by one of those bike messengers who raced down Constitution Avenue. What would she do then? Who would she rely on?

Berekhet gave a subdued thank-you and walked around the car like a DMV inspector who took his job very seriously. Elsa didn't expect him to jump up and down like the people on that game show who guessed the price of toothpaste. But surely he could muster a hug. A real "Oh-my-God-I-can't-believe-this" would have been nice. Anything to dispel Elsa's suspicion that he was disappointed.

She was tempted to tell him that he didn't have to have a car, that he could do what everyone else had done when they first arrived: spend all their time waiting for the next bus or train, recalculating, as if the math had somehow changed, the hours of labor required to make the price of a car within reach, even one that was two-toned.

Berekhet completed his inspection with a solemn scan of the trunk, then walked back to Elsa with outstretched arms.

"Thank you." His face broke into a painful-looking smile, and he leaned in to wrap his arms around her shoulders. "I truly wasn't expecting you to buy me a car."

Elsa felt guilty in their embrace. "I wish I could do more," she said, trying to make up for her assumption of his ingratitude.

"Can you even drive?" Lydia asked with her arms crossed.

"Of course." Berekhet laughed. "Do you think I was riding lions around in Addis?"

"No. I thought you rode donkeys too."

"I'm going to see for myself if your cousin is telling the truth," Elsa said to Lydia. "Go upstairs, we'll be back soon."

Lydia left grudgingly. Elsa gestured to the driver's side, motioning for Berekhet to take his seat before settling into hers.

"Fasten your seat belt." Elsa did so in a theatrical manner, like flight attendants in the safety presentation. "And always check your mirrors, the rearview and sides."

Berekhet did as he was told, his eyebrows raised in expectation for the next set of instructions. Elsa instructed him to first drive within the complex. Southern Towers was on a massive lot with five high-rises, three that were parallel to the Seminary Road exit off of 395 and two that were in the back, encircling a pool, tennis court, and playground that had all seen better days.

Satisfied with Berekhet's skills, Elsa had him pull into the circular driveway of their building, the Sherwood, and then toward the end of the driveway that let out onto Seminary.

"Make sure you're careful here. Always look both ways. There's a blind spot for the cars coming down the road. Now, make this right."

Berekhet scanned the intersection carefully and followed Elsa's directions to Walter Reed Drive, which soon brought them into Arlington, the neighboring city.

"You don't like to drive," he said.

He, like her daughter, mistook her caution for fear. Elsa was careful because the activity required it.

"I don't like the way *other* people drive. Turn here, on Glebe."

In the vacant parking lot of Thomas Jefferson Middle School, only ten minutes away, and where Eritrean parents rented space for weekly Tigrinya classes for their kids, Elsa monitored Berekhet's parallel and back-end parking. Feeling more confident, Berekhet positioned his seat farther back.

"I'd heard that Americans stopped driving manual cars. They just want machines to do all of their work."

"The seat belt, Berekhet, my brother. Make sure you keep it on. I know no one bothers back home, but it's not a choice here."

"Well, that's what I mean. Good drivers are more important than a strap across your chest. Do we know for sure that seat belts are saving lives? Are there actually less accidents with all these traffic lights and regulations?"

The quiet young man Elsa had met in the airport was no longer. When Berekhet spoke, he lectured, pretending the audience mattered when he was just going to say what he wanted to anyway. It reminded Elsa of his father, and of the first and only time Dr. Alazar had driven her in his famed Mercedes-Benz. She had heard about the car even before she left Eritrea for Addis, with conflicting reports that the car was white, red, and Champagne-colored (gold to those who had never heard of the beverage). The most repeated detail was that Dr. Alazar had traveled to a place called Munich, which wasn't even in Italy, to buy the car himself.

None of it was accurate, consistent with the way stories were created in their family, layers of speculation and innuendo transforming the truth that only a few knew. In this case, the car was actually bluish-gray and medium-size, bigger than the Fiat 600s that were used as taxis and smaller than the Austins that were used to chauffeur officials to the Imperial Court. Dr. Alazar had bought the Mercedes at a discount from the head of a German medical mission who had been transferred from Ethiopia to Pakistan. The car looked distinguished, the only one of its class and color in Addis, and no one but Dr. Alazar ever rode in it, except for Elsa and only once.

"How am I doing?" Berekhet asked. "Have I passed the parking lot test?"

"You have. Let's see how well you do on the highway."

Berekhet pumped his fist in the air and turned on the radio. Elsa swatted his hand away and turned it off.

"We're not there yet." She directed Berekhet back down Glebe, where they merged onto 395. Thankfully, the highway traffic was light, and Elsa told Berekhet to stay in the far-right lane.

She thought of asking Berekhet about the Mercedes. Nearly twenty years had passed, but it was likely that Dr. Alazar still had it. Elsa sometimes imagined she saw the car cutting in front of her on the highway or turning a corner at the very intersection where she stationed her cart, opening a portal to Addis and the memories she tried not to conjure.

"I'm surprised your Tigrinya is so good. How did you learn it?"

"From Father," Berekhet said. "It was important to him that I knew our language. That's what we spoke in the house . . . when he was home."

Elsa shook her head in disbelief. Could they be talking about the same person?

"When I spoke to him in Tigrinya," she said, "he would pretend he couldn't understand me."

"I guess he just wanted to make sure that you would adjust to Addis. Did it work?"

"I suppose it did. Here's our exit." Elsa eyed the speedometer. "What does the speed limit sign say?"

"Thirty-five miles per hour."

"You're pushing forty." Elsa took her foot off her phantom brake once he slowed down.

"Do you remember when the Derg would announce on the radio who'd been captured?" he asked.

Elsa remembered it well. The Derg would broadcast an ominous jingle over the radio before announcing the names of rebels they'd captured and enumerating their treacherous deeds. It went without saying that the people named were never seen alive again.

"I was young and never really paid much attention to what they were talking about. One day, I was humming the tune and singing some silly lyrics I made up, when Father just up and slapped me . . . the only time he ever struck me in my life." Berekhet shook his head as if he still couldn't believe that had happened. "He told me never to sing it again, but he didn't explain why. The next time the tune aired, he was in his office with the door closed, but I could hear the radio playing and finally paid attention. I think he was worried they'd say your name."

Elsa felt her temples twitch. "Don't turn here, keep going."

Berekhet drove them past Southern Towers and made a right on Beauregard, then a sharp left on Fillmore, where they approached a sign that said NORTHERN VIRGINIA COMMUNITY COLLEGE—ALEXANDRIA CAMPUS. Elsa directed him to pull into the parking lot.

Berekhet took in the squat campus of two-story buildings. "What's this?"

"NOVA. This is where you'll start taking classes. I've already enrolled you in the second summer term, which starts in the beginning of July, about a month from now. You'll need to take your core classes and basics for pre-med . . . English composition, chemistry, biology . . . I'll show you the full list at home. You'll have two years here and then another two at a state university. Virginia has some great options, UVA, VCU, VTech, but George Mason University up the road is your best bet. Then medical school and residency, that's eight years altogether."

Bereket drummed his thumbs on the steering wheel, his eyes on the students going in and out of the buildings. "I already told you what I'm interested in . . . and it's not medicine."

"You did. But I'm here to help you, Berekhet. To get you to think more practically about your choices. What kind of job do you think you'll be able to get with your interests?"

"I'm more concerned with ideas than I am about jobs."

Elsa took a deep breath and clutched the grab handle, as if Berekhet were still speeding. She hadn't wanted to challenge him in front of everyone at his welcome lunch, but she needed to set him straight on a few things. Children of accomplished people generally became accomplished themselves. She never saw eye-to-eye with Dr. Alazar, but she wanted to meet the standard he had set. And now that it was her turn to be responsible for others, she had to compensate for the fact that her own life wasn't a good example.

"Why did you join the war?" Berekhet asked.

Elsa hesitated, unsure of his sudden curiosity. "Because it was a matter of life and death."

"Or was it instead because you believed in an idea?"

Elsa shook her head at how little Berekhet understood. The

audacity of comparing his intellectual curiosities to the war for Eritrea's very existence.

"Enough," she said quietly.

Berekhet was able to remember his way home without Elsa having to guide him. Before they turned into Southern Towers, she instructed him to pull into the 7-Eleven that was adjacent to their complex. She had one last stop in their tour of this new life.

"Lydia brought me here once. Nice concept. Are you hungry?" he asked.

"Not quite. I got you a job here. A distant relative of Zewdi's owns this franchise. Your first shift is tomorrow."

11

You Better Do the Job Right

BEFORE ELSA WAS SENT TO ETHIOPIA, HER SISTERS TOLD HER THAT Addis was Babylon, an unruly colossus of languages and people that made anonymity impossible to overcome. "You can get away with anything," they said. But Elsa found that while you could certainly keep secrets for longer, they would eventually be revealed.

In January 1975, Elsa waited in a seldom-used study room on the far end of the Commercial School's campus. She fiddled with her watch, anxious as the light outside began to die. If she didn't get home soon, the maid would call Dr. Alazar.

Finally, at six, three of her schoolmates burst into the room.

"Did you hear?" Girmai said, nearly out of breath.

"Hear that you're late again?"

"Okay, obviously you didn't." Girmai scanned the path outside the window, making sure that no one had followed them. He was a senior, like Elsa, and nearly as petite. To overcome his vertical shortcomings, he sported an immaculate Afro that added at least three inches to his height.

Temesgen, panting behind him, extracted a stack of pamphlets from his satchel and placed them down on the table.

"There's been another massacre," he said, tugging on his turtleneck. Inspired by the Beatles, his fashion idols, Temesgen wore a different color every day. His older sister, who was studying medicine in Beirut, sent him a new pack every season.

Kibreab, who they called White Boy because he was so pale, slumped in the chair next to Elsa.

"This time it was in Wekidiba, right outside of Asmara. My

mother's family is from there. Her parents, siblings, everyone." He put his elbows on the table and covered his face with his hands.

Elsa rubbed his back. She remembered passing through the village with her mother when they traveled between Keren and Asmara. "What happened?" she asked in a low voice.

"The terror isn't stopping." Girmai stood with his back against the door. "After all the bloodshed the Derg wreaked in Asmara last week, they just moved up the road. On Saturday, they stormed the village, looting homes, shooting and bayoneting men of any age right in front of their families. They said there were bodies just piled everywhere. The next morning, everyone who survived barricaded themselves in the church, thinking they'd be safe. But the soldiers stood at each corner of the church's compound and emptied their clips."

"Into the church?" Elsa was aghast, even though it hadn't been the first time. A few years earlier, the Ethiopian military massacred hundreds in Besikdira who sought refuge in a mosque.

Kibreab jumped to his feet, kicking his chair back so hard that it fell to the floor with a thud.

"What are we doing here? We've just been running our mouths in this stuffy room as our people, innocent civilians, have been killed in cold blood. I'm sick and tired of this!"

Kibreab picked up the chair, and for a moment, it looked as if he might sit in it; instead, he hurled it against the wall.

"Hey!" Temesgen rushed him. "Calm down, man!"

"Don't tell me what to do!"

Kibreab grabbed onto his sweater, stretching the fabric, and pushed him off. They were both juniors and alternated between scoring the first and second highest grades each year. Their academic rivalry often spilled over to their friendship.

Elsa exchanged a quick glance with Girmai. He also seemed unsure of how to respond.

For the past three years, they had been meeting secretly on

the grounds of their high school. Girmai had first approached her, having sussed out that she was also Eritrean. He asked if she was interested in joining a study group with other fellow Eritreans. Elsa happily agreed and discovered that the group's focus was on the revolution and not academics. Students at Haile Selassie I University were the most radical force in the country, championing the overthrowing of feudalism and redistribution of wealth. The Eritreans were also rallying for independence and organized separate cells of university and high school students to galvanize their movement.

To protect everyone's safety, only Girmai, their cell leader, knew their identities. He was in contact with an activist outside of their group who shared a study curriculum, updates about the revolution, and ways for them to get involved. As the Ethiopian emperor reigned, they covertly learned about the promise of socialism, the May '68 strikes in France, and the anticolonial movements across Africa. They distributed pamphlets about the revolution, surreptitiously leaving them in the school library and canteen. Every now and then, they were instructed to track the routines of men whose identities were never revealed, reporting their observations to Girmai, who then shared them with his point of contact. As students they were the perfect spies, ignored as they lingered at bus stops and trailed along quiet streets.

Last year, the unthinkable happened. The military toppled the empire, escorting His Majesty away from the palace in the back of a Volkswagen Beetle. Elsa and her crew hoped that the Derg, their Marxist brothers-in-arms, would support Eritrea's right to self-determination. But that dream soon proved to be delusional. Starting in November, Elsa's cell received regular reports of the bloodshed in Eritrea. Young people were dragged out of cafés and shot. Parents had to pay for the bullets used to kill their children if they wanted to lay their corpses to rest. And in Addis, the Derg was disappearing anyone suspected to be sympathetic.

Kibreab was standing with his arms at his sides, his expression calm and resolute. "You guys can play Che Guevara all you want. But I'm joining the rebels. The time for talking is over."

Night had come. Other than the distant sound of cars on Churchill Road just beyond the school gates, everything was quiet. Elsa looked at Girmai and Temesgen, who both appeared deflated. She knew that others, mostly Eritrean university students, were running off to join the guerrillas' ranks. Even Eritreans who were studying in Europe and the Soviet Union were flying to Khartoum, waiting to be shuttled across the border into rebel-held territory. But she never quite imagined that for herself. She still wanted to go to university, even though she was too ashamed to admit that now. Based on Girmai's and Temesgen's silence, she suspected they felt the same.

Kibreab picked up his bag and slung it over his shoulder.

"Listen, I mean no disrespect. I'm not judging you all . . . I swear. But I'm going to have to go home and face my mother." He exhaled and looked up at the ceiling, trying to regain his composure. "And the only way I can do that is by knowing that I'll avenge what they did to my family."

He walked to the door and looked back at them. "Take care of yourselves," he said as strode out.

A few days later, Elsa had another late night. Dr. Alazar had enrolled her in evening classes at Alliance Française. His response to her top ranking at the Commercial School, which was one of Addis's best, was that her French was still terrible. When she finally left the center, she was digging through her purse to see if she had enough money for a taxi, when a white Fiat Ritmo raced toward her and stopped, its left tire jumping the curb.

A man charged out of the passenger side, grabbed Elsa by the waist, and threw her into the backseat like a sack of dirty laundry. Elsa screamed and resisted as best she could, striking her knuckles on his front teeth. The man had better aim and more strength, landing punches on her face as the driver lurched the car forward. When Elsa felt him press a gun to her side, everything went silent.

Beside her was another man in the backseat. His split lips were swollen, doubled in size, and he tilted his head up to look at Elsa from under his bruised lids. It was Girmai.

"Aren't you going to greet your friend?" the monster asked Elsa.

She turned away, not to deny that she knew him—it was too late for that—but because she couldn't stand to see the shame in his eyes, the plea for forgiveness he couldn't ask with his bloody lips.

After a short drive south, just past Mexico Square, Elsa felt her stomach drop as they reached Alem Bekagne Jail, where their captors dragged them both into the compound before separating them. Elsa looked over her shoulder at Girmai, who shuffled and tripped toward a doorway that led to where she assumed the men were being held. He didn't look back at her.

Elsa was led to a narrow, windowless room, smelling of urine and sweat and lined with slumped-over, moaning women. After a while the monster from the car reappeared and dragged her into an empty room, then slapped her so hard that she fell from her chair. He started kicking her, his foot resisting the weak clamp her body tried to create around it. Her legs and torso jackknifed again and again, until Elsa saw another pair of shoes and then hands reach down to throw her back into the chair.

"I told him not to hurt you," the new visitor said. "He must have forgotten. Maybe it's because you're so pretty." He turned to the other man. "Why are you so rough with the pretty ones?"

Her abuser straightened his shirt and smiled at Elsa. He had two gold teeth. Elsa wished she had been able to knock them out of his mouth. The one who seemed to be in charge laughed.

"He won't hurt you anymore if you cooperate. It's Elsa, isn't it? Elsa Haddish. Did your comrade get that right?" He leaned in closer. "We know every crime you've committed against this country. Students like you pretend to be innocent, even though you're anything but. If you cooperate, tell us the names of everyone you've worked with, we'll spare you."

Elsa's breath slowed. She touched her jaw and recoiled, wondering if it was broken. The monster kept smiling at her. She didn't want to think about what they would do if she didn't cooperate.

"Listen, we know your uncle," the one in charge said pleasantly, as if he were a long-lost family friend. "He's a wise man, wise enough to know who he serves. We'll let you go home for now, but when we come back to get you, we expect names."

This was all a warning. The monster helped her up, dragged her back down the corridor and into a waiting car, and waved menacingly as the driver set off. As daylight broke over Addis, Elsa knew that when they returned for her, she would tell them whatever they wanted to know. She didn't have faith that she'd be able to withstand their depravity. So there was only one solution to avoid being a traitor.

Elsa stood at her front gate with her bag clutched to her chest, waiting for her captor to leave before going inside. As the faithful did on church facades, she rested her forehead on the door, yet instead of praising the Almighty, she wished the ground beneath her would swallow her up or, better yet, that she had never been born.

She knocked on the door and pushed past the maid who let her in, scolding her as if she were her mother even though they were nearly the same age. "Where have you been? What kind of girl stays out all night?" she hissed. Elsa ignored her, tucking her head down and hugging herself in an effort to hide the evidence of the horrors of the past ten hours, then locked herself in the bathroom. After catching her breath, she rummaged through the cabinets for something she could use. Under the sink, she found a small bottle of bleach and, without hesitating, removed the cap and drank as much as she could.

The smell alone was like taste, a physical force that triggered her eyes to water and throat to clamp. But that meant the taste was like something else—a hand of hot nails scraping the insides of her stomach. The coughing was only the beginning of her body's panic. The maid must have heard her; she knocked and then started banging on the door as Elsa swallowed the rest of the bottle, willing the back of her throat to relax, to let the fire down as her stomach heaved, desperate to protect itself. She vomited on her lap and then on the pink-and-white checkered tiles, her body lunging forward and face down to taste, for a second time, what she had done.

The maid yelled for someone to break down the door. Elsa eventually crawled to the door and opened it, staring at the tiles as the maid leaned her upright. She ran to the kitchen and returned with milk, forcing it down Elsa's scorched throat.

Dr. Alazar had come to the hospital, but Elsa had been sleeping—a coincidence that granted her only temporary relief. When she was released, the nurse walked her to his waiting car and the dreaded ride home.

Dr. Alazar didn't say anything when she got in the passenger seat. They drove in silence, a punishment nearly worse than his icy demeanor.

Addis had never looked more hostile. The grim skyline hung in low, uneven proportions. City blocks ended clumsily and careened into barren land. Paved roads shouldered the tentacles of rocky thoroughfares. In the silence of the car, Elsa felt the way she thought Addis looked—somehow incomplete.

"I am not interested," Dr. Alazar finally said, his hands never moving from their position on the steering wheel, "in how you got mixed up in politics. You deserve whatever you experienced for forgetting why you are here. And if you think that I brought you to this country to do anything but get an education and better yourself, as I have done, then you are dumber than I feared. The next time you decide to kill yourself in the name of Eritrea or socialism or any other big idea you have fallen for, you better do the job right."

His Mercedes was grand. She could still see that. Soft leather, and on the door panels, switches that powered the windows. Good for him, and his nice car, Elsa thought to herself. Maybe he'd find a way to be buried in it. But she was never going to see that day because she decided, right there at his side, to run away. She had to help liberate Eritrea.

12

ZEWDI ENTERED L'PORT AZURE AT FIVE PAST FIVE. ASGEDOM, THE only Eritrean visible, was already seated in the bistro's greenhouse-like extension shaded with lush foliage. As she neared, he looked up and stood.

"Hello, Zewdi."

His voice was less intimidating in person. Zewdi accepted his kiss and sat down, noting that in her two-inch wedges, they were the same height. He was a few shades darker than she was, and his hair was in abundant, graying waves. Unfortunately, his dental work overwhelmed his face, but it was a kind face—handsome, even—everything in pleasant symmetry. He dressed well, wearing a finely-knit, sky blue polo shirt tucked into creased khaki pants. On the post of his chair hung a pristine white baseball cap with "Lakeside" in navy blue lettering.

"I appreciate you making time to see me today," he said, settling back into his seat. "If I wasn't flying back to L.A. this evening, I would have suggested that we meet tomorrow so that you could have gotten your rest from last night's festivities."

"Not at all," Zewdi said. "I'm too overjoyed to be tired. After all these years we lost sleep with worry, I can handle losing sleep to celebrate."

"Ladies first," Asgedom said with a smile as the waiter approached.

This pleased her. She ordered steak frites, and when asked if she wanted anything substituted for the fries, a mixed green salad, steamed broccoli perhaps, she declined. Asgedom ordered trout amandine and requested salad instead of the mashed potatoes.

She knew about the California lifestyle and teased him about joining the club. He replied, in perfect seriousness, "I eat to live and not the other way around."

Zewdi started to recognize a pattern with him, a manner of speaking that didn't lend itself to an exchange, that was instead a presentation of declarative statements. It lessened his charm, which was a good thing, as it continued to make her more comfortable.

"Well, you chose California, and I chose Italy. La dolce vita," she responded with a wave of her hand. "Life is meant to be enjoyed. Good food, good coffee, but never in excess. Not like here in the States." Zewdi could have continued, but she was skilled in the art of conversation.

The food arrived, and Zewdi took small, infrequent bites, concealing what only her mother had known: she was a tremendous eater. She picked at her food in front of company, but when she was alone, she ate to her fill. It was always home-cooked—she didn't gorge on junk food, she couldn't even stand the sight of the stuff—but she had gotten so used to practically eating in hiding that she wasn't sure she could do it any other way. Suppose the unspoken happened? If she and Asgedom ended up making a life together, what would she do? She pondered this as he picked the onions out of his salad.

"Do you play golf?" she asked.

Asgedom looked surprised at the question.

She pointed at his cap, gloating inwardly at him not expecting her to be familiar with the L.A. golf club.

"Ah, of course." He set down his silverware and rested back against the chair. "Well, my colleagues invited me to join them a few times. It's more of a social sport than an active one. There's a decent bit of walking, but the point of it just seemed to be to chat at the holes and then back at the club. I much prefer tennis. I learned in Addis and continued when I got here."

He nodded at himself and took hold of his fork and knife again.

Zewdi didn't expect him to ask if she played any sports. She certainly didn't know Eritrean women her age who participated in any sort of athletic activity. Zewdi knew her greatest assets were her face and hair and that her body was thoroughly underprivileged. She was built like an inverted pyramid, with a huge bosom, fleshy, undefined waist, and spindly legs. Lydia would have been surprised to know that her preference for Eritrean and Arab-style dresses wasn't because she was conservative. Zewdi had once longed to wear midriffs and miniskirts, but they couldn't hide what traditional attire could.

The waiter came and took their plates and orders for tea. After he returned to serve them, she said a silent prayer to the Virgin Mary and looked down at her hands.

"If I may, what are you looking for at this point in your life?" she asked.

He seemed confused, and she faintly motioned to herself.

"Well," he said, clearing his throat, "I appreciate you asking. This is all quite new for me, and I assume for you, as well. My children are almost independent now. We got them through the really important years, set a good foundation and all, so I now have the time to be able to focus on myself. It would be good to have a partner for these years I have left . . . lots of years I hope," he said with an earnest smile. "My ex-wife and I were married for eighteen years. It didn't work out, obviously. I'm not sure if that makes me a failure or an expert . . . sometimes I think both. But I still want to try again."

There was a lot he wasn't saying about his first attempt at marriage, but Zewdi had done her research. When Asgedom was in graduate school in Illinois, a fellow Eritrean student wanted to set him up with his younger sister and asked Asgedom to call upon her when he returned to Asmara for a visit. They ended up marrying, and she joined him in California after he graduated. Some years later, her first love also turned up in the States, and they rekindled their relationship, the discovery of which led to her divorce. Zewdi's mother would have called for the death penalty. Zewdi would have been satisfied with a lashing. But what a gracious man he was for not saying anything negative about his ex-wife.

"And what about you?" he asked. "What are you looking for?"

Zewdi looked down into her teacup. It was the first time anyone had asked her that question. She didn't need to be asked to know what she wanted, but it sure felt good.

"Well, my experience is a bit different. When I was younger, I imagined the normal things for myself, marriage and children, a family. It didn't happen, at least not in the way that I thought, since I do have my Lydia, but that was God's will. I don't regret my years working . . . I was able to support my family back home. But I lost some time . . . a woman does have her time . . . and now . . . well . . . this is my life. And it's a good one, thanks be to God."

"Thanks be to God, indeed."

"But I've been thinking that it would be nice to have a partner." She said the word in English as he had. "To have some companionship. We weren't made to be alone, were we?"

There was one more thing they needed to discuss. She took a sip of her mint tea to steel herself. "Do you still want to have more children? Because . . . you know, it's no longer possible for me."

He set his cup down and smiled at her without any pity. "No, not at all, Zewdi. I'm quite happy with the children I have. I'm happy to hear that you are too."

Zewdi was touched by his kindness. She felt a sense of maternal care for him, a need to protect him from harm that might come his way. But she didn't feel much else.

Asgedom asked the waiter to call a taxi and retrieve his bag.

They exited the restaurant and idled in front until the cab arrived. Zewdi was relieved that the driver wasn't Eritrean.

"Can I drop you off at your car?" Asgedom put on his cap and looked like a much younger man.

"Thank you, but I have another errand to run in the neighborhood. I'm just going to walk there."

"Well, this was a pleasure," he said with a small bow. "I'll call you tomorrow to let you know that I arrived safely." He stepped forward for a chaste goodbye, pressing his cheeks to hers.

When he drove off, Zewdi walked toward M Street, heading eastward until it turned into Pennsylvania Avenue, leading her to the Four Seasons Hotel. She supposed she didn't end up there by accident. She stood across the street, watching the taxis and Lincoln Town Cars enter and exit the covered driveway. The doormen didn't seem so young anymore; a few were nearly as old as she was. She crossed Pennsylvania and entered the hotel. The air conditioning was a relief, and despite the healthy activity at reception, the lobby was as calm and quiet as she remembered, a study in discreet luxury with neutral furnishings in rich cream and chestnut, accented by spot-lit trumpet lilies.

In the spring of 1977, Zewdi and the Saudi princess came to D.C. for the same reason many tourists did: to see the cherry blossoms. Eritrean domestics were popular with the royal family, and while many suffered, Zewdi had lucked out with her placement. An Eritrean from Massawa who worked for one of the princess's good friends slept in a room the size of a broom closet, while ten other bedrooms in their palace lay vacant. Another young woman was tormented all day by the rowdy young children of the crown prince's favorite daughter and at night by the princess's husband. There were also rumors of what the male workers might be going through. While Zewdi couldn't be sure what was true, it was no secret that some Saudi men, more than one would think, liked it both ways.

Princess Rania was only aloof on her worst days. She was still unmarried and bounced between universities and vacations. That spring in D.C., while on an academic hiatus of undetermined length, all she wanted to do was spend her time under the cherry-blossom trees. So each morning, Zewdi packed dates they'd brought from Riyadh and followed the princess past the hotel doorman—who was Eritrean and always nodded politely, not the way one would acknowledge a fellow countryman, but Zewdi liked that he was professional—into the Lincoln Town Car that whisked them to the Tidal Basin.

The princess would lie on their blanket, and while Zewdi couldn't see her eyes behind her sunglasses, she assumed she was sleeping when her fingers stopped running along the jade prayer beads she clutched in her hand. Zewdi would walk by herself along the Potomac, winding through the bowed branches of the flowering trees. When there was a strong gust of wind, she'd stand still and let the petals fall all around her, creating a pink carpet at her feet.

That was Zewdi's third year with the princess. It felt like a turning point. She read in one of those magazines on the plane that a vacation can change your life, even change who you are. A stay-at-home mother who was interviewed said that strolling along the Seine inspired her to go back to school. An engineer from Vancouver was so awed by the pyramids in Giza that he quit his job to become a landscaper. A psychologist said that in addition to the obvious benefits of rest and relaxation, just physically leaving your normal environment was likely to make you reconsider other parts of your life.

Up until then, Zewdi was satisfied just to have stability. She had sought refuge from the war in Saudi, a country hostile to migrants but where she had managed to secure a job with a reasonable boss, a bit of savings, and the chance to see the world. But Zewdi started to feel like she wanted more. She wanted what she deserved, what was natural, what had eluded her—a life of her own, which meant a family of her own. But the consequence of leaving Eritrea wasn't just that she would never see her mother alive again. It was also that she had never gotten married. Like nearly every other Eritrean woman who had come before her, she was innocent about men and expected her husband to be chosen by her family. But she spent her eligible years separated from her family and at the side of a princess who had no interest in her marital prospects. While some of Zewdi's compatriots either came to Saudi already married or managed to find their spouses there, Zewdi hadn't been so lucky.

After splitting that summer between the hellish heat of Riyadh and serenity of Lake Geneva, Zewdi returned to D.C. in September; the princess was starting an international business certificate program at Georgetown University. With the princess's classes and the justification they presented for more naps, Zewdi could enjoy some more time to herself.

One afternoon, Zewdi returned to the hotel after lunch at an unassuming Italian restaurant in Foggy Bottom that put Café Firenze, a favorite of the princess's and D.C.'s jet-setting crowd, to shame. At the entrance, the doorman paused before pulling the oversized, gold-plated handle toward him.

"Good afternoon," he said. "I've been meaning to introduce myself. I'm Daniel. You're Eritrean, yes?"

"Yes, I am," Zewdi said.

"Nice to meet you," he said in Tigrinya, extending his hand. "I noticed you when you visited a few months ago but didn't get the chance to say hello."

Zewdi shook his hand, trying to ignore that they were in an entranceway and on full display, at his job no less. Daniel didn't seem bothered.

"How long are you with us for this time?"

His voice was higher than she expected, but he was sturdy and broad-shouldered, rare for an Eritrean.

"We're here until December."

Zewdi wanted to say more so that she could have time to examine him—exiting and entering with the princess had robbed her of opportunities to look closer—but she suddenly felt self-conscious under his studious gaze.

"Well, I'd like to make sure this place feels like home. Let me know if you need anything."

He gestured for her to enter. While she was sure that to an observer their exchange couldn't have looked more than just courteous, it felt as if a force other than her own momentum were propelling her forward.

Zewdi resolved to get to know Daniel better. Between two and four o'clock, while the princess napped and the lobby tended to be less crowded, Zewdi stationed herself in the sun-drenched atrium, within sight of the hotel's entrance. She also strategized that she'd have more to talk about with Daniel if she paid attention to local affairs and started flipping through *The Washington Post*. While she couldn't be sure, she thought that Daniel began to appear in the lobby before his shift.

He would come over to chat, and they soon learned more about each other. Daniel was an Asmarino and the only son left behind in his family after his two older brothers made their way to America to study medicine and engineering. After boarding school in Ethiopia, six months in Sudan, and a year on a workers' program cleaning toilets in West Germany, he finally made it to D.C.

He was one semester away from graduating from pharmacy school, that much closer to being able to quit his job at the hotel and finally get some sleep, he told Zewdi as he straightened his collar. He wore his blazer with military-style brocading as if he'd chosen the uniform for himself.

That's what Zewdi liked most about him—the fact that he was a man. He moved deliberately, spoke to his boss and guests politely but not with excessive deference, unlike his colleague who smiled as if his salary would be deposited directly into his mouth. When he asked Zewdi how the princess was treating her, with his hands clasped behind his back, feet hip-distance apart, she was convinced that he would be able to intervene if she reported negatively.

In October, while the princess was studying for her mid-term exams, Daniel passed by the atrium to give Zewdi a stuffed panda with a map of the National Zoo tucked behind its clasped, furry hands.

"I went with my brother's kids this past weekend," he said. "Jie-Jie hasn't given birth yet."

Zewdi had read the news of the panda's pregnancy. She and the princess had laughed about the American fixation on whether an animal would produce an heir in a man-made cage.

Daniel started his shift, and Zewdi tucked the toy into a corner of the armchair, waiting just long enough before she rushed back to her room and curled up with the panda on the bed. The next day brought another surprise: an invitation.

"Why don't we go for a walk later?" Daniel asked, standing tall in his military stance. "I get off early tonight."

If King Abdullah bin Abdulaziz himself had needed Zewdi, she would have found a way out of it. At eight thirty, she waited just past the hotel driveway, as they had agreed, to grant Daniel some privacy from his colleagues.

It was the first time she had seen him in regular clothes. He wore a gray polo shirt tucked into khaki pants, and a crucifix pendant hung from a thin gold chain around his neck. He leaned in to kiss her on the cheek, and she breathed in his cologne, pleased even though she was certain its use was a daily habit. They walked to the nearby bridge on the old canal, a narrow space of still water that ran parallel to M Street. He leaned against the wooden rail and turned to face her. She could see, as if she were someone else, how perfect the scene looked.

The next month felt like a fairy tale. On Sunday afternoons, they would escape the city in his Toyota Corolla and sightsee in Mount Vernon, Baltimore, and Annapolis, places he also hadn't been. Now, when Zewdi watched American movies with Lydia, full of men and women racing to get their clothes off, she always wanted to tell her that you can have more intimacy, the real kind, just by riding in a car with a man, his hand on the gearshift near your thigh, Tewelde Redda playing from the speakers.

On what would be their last drive, with the slowly approaching winter turning the trees barren, Daniel said he wanted to introduce Zewdi to his older brother.

"Dinner," he asked, "would that be okay?"

Of course it was okay. It was what Zewdi had been waiting for. They weren't back home, where someone in his family would've gone to someone in hers to ask for her hand. Who was his brother going to talk to anyway? The princess?

Daniel suggested Amalfi, an upscale restaurant near the hotel whose offerings bore little resemblance to that of the charmed destination. His brother greeted her warmly and led her to her seat with a firm hand that reminded her of Daniel's. They had barely ordered before the questions started.

The brother wanted to know about her family, birthplace, and schooling, even her whereabouts when the emperor had been overthrown three years prior. Zewdi had questions, too, about how he liked America, if he knew a cousin of hers who had also studied engineering in the Midwest. But he didn't spend much time on himself, answering her inquiries with more of his own.

Daniel was mostly quiet, nodding when his brother spoke and motioning for the waitress when they needed more water or wine. She tried to keep up with the last round of questions about her migration to Saudi when it dawned on her that his brother was trying to figure out her age without asking directly.

She was thirty-six. It hadn't come up with Daniel, but Zewdi assumed he could tell they were close in age and that she, obviously, was not in her twenties. She looked over at Daniel. It occurred to her that he hadn't once spoken on her behalf, leaving her to make her case, as if it were him and not her who was being pursued. She disengaged from the conversation, offering the most perfunctory of responses, understanding that there was no reason to be hopeful and that her last chance at marriage was disappearing as unexpectedly as it had arrived.

Daniel was distant after that dinner. So was Zewdi. The day before she was scheduled to return to Riyadh, she packed her jewelry and clothes, divided $15,000, all the cash she had, among her bags and each cup of her bra, and left the hotel, not saying goodbye to him or the princess.

The furniture in the Four Seasons atrium was different now, the armchair Zewdi used to sit in no longer there. She took a seat in the corner by the bar. She had never run into Daniel or his brother again, which had always surprised her. Every now and then she wondered if he was still in the area. She was certain that he married and started a family. Maybe his wife bought injera from her, and she didn't even know.

She imagined herself fourteen years ago, sitting under the skylights, looking up at Daniel as he spoke to her. She marveled at the certainty of that younger woman's heart. There would have been no hesitation to give up whatever life she had then for that man, to start a new life however or wherever he wanted.

That was the closest she had come to marriage, and now, at the cusp of turning fifty, came her second chance. But she didn't feel the same for Asgedom—and this made her feel very tired. Did she really expect a sweeping romance? Her heart to beat out of her chest? No, not at this age.

She sucked her teeth so loudly that the man sitting nearest to her turned to look at her. What a disappointment she was. All at her own hands.

13

IT WAS THE LAST DAY OF SCHOOL, AND THANKFULLY, LYDIA'S LAST mass. She fidgeted in a rear pew, where she sat with some other non-Catholics enrolled at St. Francis of Assisi, wishing she had anything but the Bible to read.

She fixed her attention on her classmates ahead of her, namely on three matching hair bows, their silky fabric catching the light streaming from the stained-glass window of Jesus on Via Dolorosa. The owner of the first bow was Lindsay Teller, a former friend who dumped Lydia in the fifth grade for Jordyn and Megyn Forsyth, the petite twin gymnasts sitting on either side of her, who, despite their vertical disadvantages, still managed to look Lydia up and down. Lydia watched as they received communion. She imagined herself as they were, walking with reverence to the altar, raising her head as the priest dipped the wafer in the chalice and rays of light rippled over her shiny tresses before floating back to her seat as the host dissolved on her tongue.

Lydia could have been Catholic like her mother, but her father was Orthodox Christian, and she had been baptized the same. Mama Zewdi, who was a much more devout Catholic than Elsa, hadn't known this when she scouted St. Francis for Lydia before her second birthday. Tuition was already discounted by half for Catholic students, but Mama Zewdi had been attending mass there once a month, angling for a full scholarship. It wasn't until after Mama Zewdi started the enrollment application that she discovered Lydia's actual faith. Elsa refused to convert Lydia, countering Mama Zewdi's plea to spend less on tuition with the firm response that if Lydia's father was Orthodox, then she would be as well. Mama Zewdi lost the fight and focused her energy on the school administrators instead, whom she managed to harangue into awarding Lydia that scholarship.

Lydia was too young to remember all of this but had heard the story countless times. She had also gathered that there wasn't much difference between Catholics and Orthodox Christians. According to Mama Genet, the Catholics abandoned the Orthodox faith of their forefathers for ham sandwiches. Mama Zewdi corrected that it was for opportunities instead. Boys could either rock back and forth on the ground reciting the Bible or sit at a desk and learn something that could change their status. What bothered Lydia most was that it was Mama Zewdi who told her that she wasn't Catholic. "It just never came up" was the best defense Elsa could offer when Lydia confronted her about it. "Besides, your father and I weren't very religious anyway."

At the end of mass, Lydia watched the sisters in their swishing robes shepherd the elementary schoolers into the center aisle and her classmates make their way toward the exit. Lindsay was walking with a new switch in her hips. Joel Ramirez, who in the first grade bragged to Lydia that communion wafers tasted liked the best sugar cookies in the world, looked over at the sisters to make sure their attention was elsewhere before tugging on Lindsay's ponytail. She rolled her eyes at him in a way that expressed more pleasure than annoyance. His face flashed with joy, and just as quickly, hardened once he realized Lydia was watching him.

Lydia walked out of school to find Berekhet waiting for her, leaned against his car that he parked in the emergency lane. He straightened when he saw her and waved as if they hadn't just seen each other in the morning.

"Check out Lydia's boyfriend," Lydia heard Joel say to Matthew Flannigan. "It must be the car." Matthew extended the string of his yo-yo vertically, making the plastic discs spin up its length before accidentally smacking himself in the face.

Lydia rushed over to Berekhet. "What are you doing here?"

"I see you with your book bag, but how do I know you are actually going to school?"

He jabbed her upper arm. She jabbed him back.

"I always come to school. See? I'm here."

"I'm joking, Lidu." He smiled. "I just wanted to get out of the house."

The two-toned car, his weird face. Her family really wasn't doing her any favors. Lydia was always self-conscious when her mother or Mama Zewdi came to school to pick her up or meet with a teacher, and she didn't need another reason. Elsa dressed casually but not in a stylish way like the other moms in their puffer vests and slim-cut jeans. She usually wore souvenir T-shirts bought at a discount on the Mall, in colors and styles the tourists didn't want, along with dress slacks and fat, off-brand white sneakers. Mama Zewdi had the opposite problem, looking like an extra from *Lifestyles of the Rich and Arab*, clad in floor-grazing caftans with garish detailing.

"Let's go inside," Berekhet said. "I'd like to see this institution of American learning."

A glance over her shoulder confirmed that Joel and Matthew were still smirking at her.

"It's a school like every other school. Can we go now?" she asked, hearing her own desperation.

Berekhet opened her door and, after walking around to the driver's side, instead of entering the car, thrust his head eagerly through the open window. "Do you want to wait for any of your friends? I can give them rides."

"You're a stranger, Berekhet."

"I'm your cousin."

"You can't just give people rides here. It's weird. Can we please just go?"

Berekhet got in the car. He strapped his seat belt with a dramatic gesture, checked Lydia's to make sure that it was secure, and adjusted his rearview mirror.

"Safety first," he said.

Then he inserted a cassette in the player. As soon as she heard the first melancholy guitar chords, Lydia recognized the song. Every Eritrean loved Tracy Chapman's "Fast Car."

Berekhet pulled off and turned right on Seminary, away from Southern Towers.

"Our house is the other way."

"I know. I thought we could drive around a bit."

Lydia could see that Berekhet was already looking a little more American. He was wearing the light blue polo shirt she had picked out for him at Marshalls, a real Ralph Lauren, with the player in the tiny logo raising his club, unlike the empty-handed player in a knock-off Elsa had once bought for Lydia. It was the same shirt he wore when he asked Lydia to take a picture of him in front of his new car. After he and Elsa had gone for his first drive, he came back upstairs, changed into the shirt, and asked Lydia to bring her Polaroid to the parking lot. "How's this?" he asked, leaning against the hood and crossing his arms. He watched over Lydia's shoulder as she shook the exposed film and smiled as his own image appeared.

"Where do you want to go?" Lydia asked in her attempt at a sweeter tone.

"You choose. It's your city."

Lydia had never shown anyone around by herself. She, her mother, and Mama Zewdi had already taken him to the National Mall and a grassy lot off of GW Parkway to watch the planes land at National Airport. She considered directing him to the McDonald's on Columbia Pike, to join the other Eritreans happy to be in the States but confused as to why it was so hard to find a place to sit and have a cup of tea. She wasn't feeling that charitable, so she suggested they go to Burke Library instead. Berekhet drummed the steering wheel in excitement and followed her directions there.

When they entered, he solemnly bowed at the librarian behind the circulation desk. "Hello, madame."

"The library will be closing in thirty minutes," she said without looking up.

Lydia pointed out the children's nook, the periodicals and reference section, the card catalog, and the two computers set up to eventually replace it. There were the regulars, a man hunched over a mammoth binder, erasing lines and lines of writing from yellowed paper. At another table, the homeless doppelgänger of Mama Zewdi's favorite weatherman from the *Today* show sat snoring with his head in his hands.

Berekhet took it all in and pressed his hands to his chest.

"I have been in the desert, and now, at last, I have found water."

"Take it easy, Prince Akeem," Lydia said under her breath.

"I'm sorry?"

"Nothing. Library voice." Lydia pressed her index finger to her lips. "Why don't you look around? Take my card."

She watched Berekhet set off, the chest-level shelves providing an unobstructed view of his browsing. He gathered books and, when he couldn't hold any more in his arms, piled them at the circulation desk. The librarian, eyeing the growing collection, announced in the opposite of a library voice that it was the last chance for patrons to check out their items.

Lydia sorted through his selection: *Gandhi Through Western Eyes*, *Model Speeches for All Occasions*, *The 7 Habits of Highly Effective People*, and plenty of other titles, each less appealing than the last.

He presented Lydia's card to the librarian with a flourish. "To the keeper of the flame."

Lydia cradled the checked-out books Berekhet saddled into her arms and rushed out of the building without waiting for him to catch up.

"Do you know the joke about how Italians give directions when their hands are full?" he called out behind her. "Ask me how Italians give directions."

"How do Italians give directions?" Lydia muttered.

"No, talk to me like *I'm* the Italian and ask me for directions."

Lydia stopped and slowly turned around to face Berekhet.

"All right, signore. How do I get to the library?"

Berekhet made a big show of setting down his books on the ground, throwing up his hands, and saying, "Non lo so!" He laughed heartily. "Do you understand, Lidu? They can't talk without their hands!"

"I get it."

"They could just say they don't know without putting down what's in their hands!"

"I got it!"

When they got back home, Berekhet went straight to Lydia's room and began removing books from her shelf. "So! This is what an American teenager reads, huh?"

Lydia watched from the doorway as he ruined her very thoughtful organization system. The *Baby-Sitters Club* series was on the top shelf, *Nancy Drew* on the next, and *Sweet Valley High* followed, sharing space with *The Hardy Boys*, which she read more out of obligation than interest. Farther down was nearly everything by Judy Blume and Roald Dahl, and on the last shelf were school binders and all the Bibles that Mama Zewdi had bought her, which included a few children's versions, one written in Ge'ez that Lydia couldn't even read ("our Latin," Mama Zewdi declared), and a large-print edition for sight-impaired readers since Lydia read too much in the dark.

"These books are for children. And it's never too early to learn about Stalin's Great Purge." He waved a library book at her. "How else can you understand the Derg? They were copycats, all of them."

Elsa appeared next to Lydia in the doorway. While she greeted them cheerfully, her eyes betrayed her fatigue.

"Do you see how much Lydia likes to read?" she said, resting her hands on Lydia's shoulders. "She's been crazy about it since she was a little girl, even before she started school. That's why she has to wear glasses. It must run in the family . . . I know you like to read as well."

"The man who does not read has no advantage over the man who cannot read. Mark Twain. One of this country's greats," he said while piling his books on the shelf.

Elsa shifted her attention to Lydia.

"Didn't you read one of his books? You two should go to the library together."

"We just did." Lydia shrugged her mother's hands off of her.

"Okay, okay." Elsa threw up her hands defensively. "I'm going to take a shower and let you guys continue. Lydia, make Berekhet some tea," she said as she walked out of the room.

"I don't see any Mark Twain here," he continued. "Aren't you thirteen? You should be getting a real education, thinking about real ideas, not whether some boy is going to ask some girl to the dance."

"This is what people my age read," Lydia replied while making a silent pledge to never make him tea. "And I read more than anyone else I know."

Berekhet sat on the floor and leaned back against the bed.

"Do you know that at age thirteen Renoir was painting flowers on plates? That Joan of Arc first heard the angels, and Jodie Foster had already written and directed a film? You are smart, okay, but your education should be preparing you to be great, not just literate."

"Wait." Lydia joined him on the floor, sitting cross-legged, and narrowed her eyes. "Say education."

"I just did."

"Say it again."

"*Edukayseeyon*," he said slowly.

"It's *edjukayshun*."

Berekhet pressed his lips and looked to the side, as if Lydia were looking for an issue that wasn't there.

"Say '*eh*.' Just say it. I'm trying to help you out."

"*Eh*."

"*Dju*."

"*Dju*."

"*Kay*."

"*Kay*."

"*Shun*."

"*Shun*."

"*Edjukayshun*," Lydia enunciated with great effort.

"*Edukayseeyon*. What's so funny?"

"You can't hear the difference?"

"Does it matter? The point of communication is to be understood, is it not? I might pronounce some words differently in English, but you still understand what I'm saying. And at least I can speak English. I speak three languages, which is two more than you."

"English is the only one that counts."

"Oh really?" Berekhet sat up straighter and rolled his shoulders back. "Everyone in the world should learn English. Go."

"Go what?"

"We are going to have a debate. A formal presentation of two opposing sides."

"I know what a debate is."

"Then go!"

"Fine," Lydia said, straightening herself as well. "Everyone in the world should learn English. The most powerful country in the world speaks English, and if you want to get ahead, you should know it."

"Anything else?" Berekhet cupped his chin with his hand, making him look boyish. Lydia tried not to smile.

"If people know English, they can learn from the best books and become really smart and talented in their jobs. Like, you wouldn't want a doctor who didn't know English because he might not be able to understand really important information that could save your life. Go."

"Are you sure you've made the strongest case you can?"

"Go!" Lydia snapped her fingers.

"I've been taught English since I was six years old. That's thirteen years, my entire education in a language not my own. *Edukayseeyon.* Did I say it right?"

"Nope."

Berekhet looked up at the ceiling and continued. "But isn't how we're taught to think more important than just the language we speak? Do you think you're smarter just because you're a native English-speaker? Shouldn't we also be encouraged to think critically and develop our own theories? Has everything been discovered, proven true or false? If so, what's the point of the whole educational system? The point is to conform, Lydia, which is the death of real knowledge and the rise of memorization."

Lydia wasn't following where Berekhet was going. Plus, spit was starting to collect in the corner of his mouth.

"Everyone wants me to be a doctor; there's no higher status, right? But that's just mastery of a certain skill set. I'm interested in creating new ideas, not just faithfully executing someone else's."

"Sooo, what exactly are you going to be studying?"

Berekhet rested his mouth on his clasped hands, as if he were posing for an author headshot in one of the books on the floor.

"The question, Lidu, is what am I going to be exploring?

Maybe I'll write a book . . . a big one . . . a sociological study of the United States . . . the same way these people traipsed around Africa and Asia, defining and categorizing and judging, but reversed. I can travel to all fifty states and put them under the microscope and chronicle how they live and eat and worship. Or I can do something else entirely, like invent a new color. The point is that I can dream bigger than what our family thinks is possible."

Lydia snorted but stopped herself at the sight of Berekhet's sober expression.

"You don't think I can do it," he said with some satisfaction. "It's because we're family. Einstein's a genius because you never saw him in his pajamas."

Lydia hadn't thought about it that way before, but it made sense. Everyone called her parents heroes, and while she couldn't imagine her mother as one, her father seemed a more likely candidate only because she didn't know him.

"What do you want to know, Lydia? What have you been told is out of your reach?"

Berekhet was asking earnestly, as if her response was the most important thing in the world. No one had ever looked at her like that before. No one had ever asked what she wanted most.

Lydia left the room and retrieved the photo of her parents from Elsa's room, grateful that her mother was occupied in the bathroom and therefore didn't present an obstacle. She returned to Berekhet and took a deep breath before pressing it into her cousin's hands.

"My dear Lidu," he said, holding the photo like it was a precious artifact. "I hope you find what you're looking for. You must be brave in your pursuit. And I will be right by your side."

14

ZEWDI CHECKED THE CLOCK ON THE MICROWAVE. BECAUSE OF THE time difference, she kept missing her window to call Efrem's cousin. Thankfully, it was only three p.m. on the East Coast, which was still a reasonable time to call Stockholm.

Zewdi also needed to call today, as it was Lydia's last day of school. Lydia's summer plans usually consisted of her loafing around Zewdi's apartment and reading, which would have made it hard for Zewdi to have some privacy. For the first time, Zewdi wondered if she should have pushed her into sports. The child had all that height and wasn't doing anything with it. She was positive that Asgedom's daughter was doing something active in the summer.

Zewdi moved to the living room and set a bowl of freshly rinsed cherries next to the telephone. After thumbing through her address book, she dialed the eleven-digit number.

A woman answered with a greeting in Swedish.

"Good evening," Zewdi said in Tigrinya. "May I please speak to Dahab?"

"This is Dahab."

Zewdi hesitated. With all the activity of independence and her introduction to Asgedom, she hadn't really thought carefully about how to approach this.

"My name is Zewdi Naizghi. I'm calling from Alexandria, Virginia, in America, it's right outside of D.C. Mama Minia should have told—"

"Zewdi! Yes, I've been waiting for your call. Mama Minia told me that you were looking for the family of my dear martyred Efrem." Her voice cracked. "There's not a day that goes by when I don't think of him. And then with independence, there's just been so much joy and grief and . . . I don't have to tell you. But please, tell me, why are you looking for Efrem's people?"

Zewdi felt her heart rate quicken with Dahab's rapid-fire manner of speaking.

"Yes, it's been such an emotional time for all of us. And I can imagine how knowing that someone is looking for Efrem's family spurs all sorts of feelings." Zewdi fiddled with a cherry stem, hoping to God that her hunch was right.

"Just to make sure we're talking about the same person, I'm looking for an Efrem who is the son of Negash."

"Yes, Negash and my grandfather were brothers. There's only one Efrem Negash who would have been of age to fight in the war. Dekemhare isn't big; we know everyone."

"Okay, well, there's no right way to say this, especially not over the phone . . . but I think that my niece is your Efrem's daughter."

The line went quiet. Zewdi waited for what she thought was an appropriate time. "Dahab. Are you still—"

Dahab let out a shriek so loud and shrill that Zewdi had to pull the receiver away.

"Efrem," the woman sobbed. "My Efrem!"

Zewdi tried to calm her down; after a few more moments of crying, Dahab's voice softened.

"I'm sorry," she said. "I don't mean to be so hysterical. It's just . . ." She paused again to blow her nose. "Please, tell me everything."

"My cousin Elsa lives here with me in Alexandria," Zewdi said slowly. "She was a freedom fighter and came when her daughter was barely one year old; this was in 1978. All she told me was that her daughter's father's name was Efrem Negash and that he was originally from Dekemhare. She said that she tried to track your family down but she wasn't successful."

"Well, who did she ask? Dekemhare is only but so big. All these years, and she wasn't able to find us?" Somehow, Dahab's rate of words per second accelerated.

"She tried, of course . . ." Zewdi started to say in Elsa's defense. She shared Dahab's skepticism but wouldn't dare echo it.

"Why did she leave the front? Did something happen? Does she have other children? Is it just this one she thinks is Efrem's?"

"Listen, Dahab." Zewdi sat up straighter, injecting a hint of steel into her tone. "Elsa is a wonderful, dedicated mother of one who has sacrificed a lot to raise up this child. And like most of us, her leaving Eritrea wasn't a decision she made lightly."

"Of course not," Dahab said after a pause, her voice turning soft again. "How old is this girl? What's her name?"

"Lydia. She's thirteen. And she's a wonderful child."

Dahab let out a deep sigh and said something in Swedish. "God is good," she said in Tigrinya. "Despite everything we've gone through, He is still good."

Zewdi murmured her agreement while resting her head in the hand that wasn't holding the phone. "I need to talk to Elsa. I just wanted to make sure that I found the right family before saying anything to her."

"I'll talk to her myself," Dahab said.

"I'm sorry?"

"It's another miracle, Zewdi. My husband and I are coming to D.C. in the beginning of August to visit his sisters. I'll call you when we're in town so that we can meet properly in person."

Zewdi pressed a finger to her mouth. How was she going to explain this to Elsa?

"Wow, that is a miracle. Okay . . . please call so that we can coordinate everything. Take my number."

"Zewdi, thank you for being my blessing. I really must lie down now . . . I'm so overwhelmed by this unexpected news. But I can't wait to see you all soon."

They said their goodbyes. Zewdi hung up the phone and said a silent prayer to God, asking him to give her wisdom on how to reunite this family. Then she pushed the cherries aside and made her way to the Entenmann's coffee crumb cake in the kitchen cupboard. She was going to need a lot more than fruit.

15

ELSA STEPPED OVER THE TELEPHONE BOOKS STACKED AT THE entrance of the EPLF's office and into the waiting room. The secretary was on the phone and politely motioned for her to take a seat. When Elsa was in the field, she had always imagined the rebels' offices in D.C. and Rome to be housed in sleek towers and buzzing with well-oiled efficiency. In reality, the EPLF office occupied half of a duplex a few blocks from Scott Circle, among the neglected row homes and liquor stores off P Street. Despite the office's humble appearance, the EPLF being recognized by the State Department as the legitimate representative for the Eritrean people was a monumental feat.

Elsa hadn't called ahead to make sure that Osman was available to meet or even at the office. As she picked at the frayed seam on her purse strap, waiting for the secretary to end her call, the stairs behind the secretary's desk, which faced the rear of the office, groaned under the weight of someone descending. Elsa leaned over and spotted Osman walking down the hallway toward the back door.

"Osman!" she called out, hurrying toward him.

He turned around and smiled in pleasant surprise. "You showed up."

"I showed up," she repeated, craning her neck to meet his eyes.

"I'm happy you did. Can you give me a few minutes though?" He tapped the bulge of Marlboros in his shirt pocket. "I won't be long."

Elsa watched him exit and returned to the front lobby. After watching the wall clock tick for one minute, she lurched across the room and out the back door, surprised by her own impatience. Osman was smoking on the shaded side of the alley and waved her over.

"Terrible habit." He flicked his cigarette. "Unless . . ." He extended the pack toward her.

"No, I don't smoke," Elsa said, even though she felt tempted for the very first time. "I mentioned to you at the party that I'm looking for someone . . . a comrade of mine."

"You're in good company. Everyone's trying to track their people down. And for everyone who's called back home and gotten good news, there'll be plenty more who won't be so lucky. Who are you looking for?"

"When you came to Zager, do you remember meeting a fighter who looked like me? Well, what I would have looked like fifteen years ago." Elsa wished she had brought the photo she'd kept hidden to show him.

Osman tilted his head and studied her carefully. "I do, actually. I don't think I could have forgotten her. Sharp as hell . . . and I see the resemblance. Is she your sister?"

"No. I mean, she is my sister, yes, but not by blood. We were very close. We met at training and then we were stationed together in Zager. Her name is Lydia Tekeste." Elsa paused, realizing that she hadn't said her name out loud before. "You know what happened in '78. It was chaos, a complete nightmare losing all the territory we had gained. I lost track of her and . . . I'd like to know . . . maybe you can ask around . . . figure out where she is or what happened to her?"

It wasn't even eleven o'clock, but Elsa felt her T-shirt start to stick to her back. The sun was shifting. She moved to the other side of Osman to occupy more of the shade. There was a long scar running up his forearm and another starting from his collarbone. If she had actually paid attention to him in their previous encounters, she would have noticed them. She wondered if he had been injured in the field.

Osman stubbed out his cigarette against the brick facade and tossed the butt into an empty bin. He lit another. "Sure, I'd be happy to ask around." After a slight hesitation, he asked, "Are you thinking of going back?"

Elsa looked down at her shadow. The sun seemed to be inching closer to her, but she wasn't sure if it was just her imagination.

"I have a child. This is all she knows."

"No, not to live but to visit. To see your family, your comrades. At least one carrier will start flying to Asmara by December at the latest."

It was all everyone was talking about, the rumors that Lufthansa and Alitalia were finally starting service. Ethiopian Airlines was also supposed to be resuming its flights, but that meant connecting through Addis. Some, Zewdi included, said they'd rather fly through Khartoum on Inshallah Airlines. There was still plenty of gossip about the group who just chartered a cargo plane to fly to Asmara. Some of them hadn't been very active during the war, or even doubted the struggle for independence altogether, but when independence came they were the first to go. "It should be you on that flight," Zewdi had said. "Not the ones who can put up the money."

"Do you mind if we go up to my office?" Osman asked abruptly. "I want to show you something."

Elsa followed him back inside and up one flight of stairs to a spacious yet shabby room with a cozy bay window facing Fifteenth Street. He motioned for her to take a seat while he opened a drawer in a standing filing cabinet and extracted a single sheet of paper from one of the color-coded hanging folders.

"'March 1976,'" he said, easing into his chair. "'Dear Comrade Osman. Greetings from Zager, Eritrea's first model village. I regret that I am not able to be there to present, along with my comrades, our efforts to lay the groundwork for a peaceful, just, and prosperous Eritrea. Our work is the struggle within the struggle. We are fighting the Ethiopians for our land but we are also fighting to uproot the enemies of inequality, factionalism, and sexism from our society. What you'll find in Zager is the practical application of our ideals: land reform, education for all, and the empowerment of women. I hope that you are encouraged by what you see and share our work with our brothers and sisters in the United States of America. As the esteemed representative of the EPLF's North American office, I also urge you to use your position to educate President Gerald Ford on the legacy of the United States' hegemonic and reactionary foreign policy. You must make him understand that his unwillingness to condemn Ethiopia's barbaric war on Eritrea's right to self-determination means that the blood of many is on his hands. Remind him of his own nation's history, of its noble pursuit of freedom, and the same noble pursuit of ours.' "

Elsa closed her eyes, ever so briefly, as if to switch the scene from Fifteenth and P to the dark house on the hill in Zager. She tried to imagine herself perched on the woven seat of the stool she'd sat on to scribe those words. Things were very clear to that young woman. Right was very far from wrong. And she believed that if she wanted something enough and fought for it, that it would be realized.

He continued: " 'I hope our paths will one day cross. Victory to the masses! Signed, your comrade, Elsa.' "

Osman put the letter down and looked at her with awe. "I always hoped I'd meet the author of that letter. Didn't think she would be here though. You still think America is the evil empire?"

Elsa laughed dryly. "I don't even know what any of that means anymore. Consciousness, class struggle, what are we supposed to do with all that in this country?"

"Plenty! The work has just begun! But if you've let America dampen your revolutionary spirit, that's fine. Keep on being a capitalist cog here and donate your riches to the cause."

Elsa marveled at people like him, all the activists who joined the cause from the States and whose lives were split between the West and back home. It was easy to join the guerrillas while in Eritrea or Ethiopia. But if she had been a student in Wisconsin the way Osman had, she wouldn't have abandoned her studies and job prospects. She certainly would have been involved in some way, making lasagna for fundraisers, but she would have wanted to make something of herself as well. She probably would have gotten some flak for that too. People kept tabs on how others spent their time and money, long absences from community events were noted, and romances with Ethiopians were disparaged. Buying a house was seen as diverting money from the cause and, even worse, proof of a desire to put down roots when life in America was supposed to be temporary. A year after Elsa had arrived, an activist couple held a wedding reception that many refused to attend. The thought of eating cake while their people were being bombed was just too much to bear.

Elsa leaned over the desk and took the letter, rubbing her fingers over the precious paper they'd once had to ration. She started to put the letter in her purse, but Osman reached over and held her wrist.

"That's mine. You gave it to me." He gently extracted the letter from her hand.

"But I wrote it! Why should you be the one to keep it?"

"This is history, Elsa. I can tell by how you were going to stuff it in your purse like chewing gum that you don't get that." He smoothed the letter on his desk and placed it back in the filing cabinet.

"Don't you ever visit those museums you work in front of? Haven't you seen all the documents and artifacts they protect like gold? We have to do the same. Our history is just as important."

He sat back down and fiddled with his shirt pocket. Elsa wondered if he was already in need of another cigarette.

"About your sister. I can try to get a letter to her . . . since you're such a writer. Fitsum downstairs is heading there soon, flying to Khartoum and then going on land via Kassala. You'll have to give me the letter pretty quickly. But if you're just going to tell her that America isn't so evil after all, I might not try as hard."

They both laughed. Elsa started to see what Zewdi saw in him. She used to beg Elsa to snatch him up, which of course made Elsa avoid him. It surprised her that Zewdi could look past the fact that he was Muslim, considering how traditional she was. According to Zewdi, a Muslim could be your dearest friend or neighbor but never your spouse. Elsa supposed she had grown desperate on her behalf.

"By the way," Osman said, "there was a guy with her in Zager. I don't remember his name, but he was tall and skinny and well liked. I met a lot of fighters on that trip, but for some reason he and your sister really stood out to me."

Elsa gave a slight nod. "Efrem; his name was Efrem. He died."

Osman bowed his head. "I'm sorry to hear that. I'll be waiting for that letter though. And don't disappear after you drop it off, okay?"

Elsa nodded again, this time to appease him. He stood up to walk her out, but she held out her arm, making her way to the door. "I can let myself out," she said. "Thanks for your help today."

She trudged down the narrow staircase and exited out the back, pondering just how to put in writing all that she had been avoiding for the past thirteen years.

16

From Girls to Guerrillas

WHEN ELSA TURNED UP AT THE EPLF TRAINING CAMP IN RI'SEE ADI in February 1975, she was directed to a hidden dugout, where she sat facing an administrator with an amputated leg and gray in his beard. From a battered metal filing cabinet, he withdrew a notebook and, without looking up, registered her details.

"First name?"

"Elsabet."

"Father's name?"

"Haddish."

"Grandfather's name?"

"Ghebrealfa."

"Mother's name?"

"Letemariam."

"Place of birth?"

"Keren."

"Date of birth, if known?"

"The third of Yekatit, 1949. Or February tenth, 1957, in the Western calendar."

"Western's fine. Marital status?"

"Unmarried."

"Level of education?"

"High school."

"Did you complete?"

"Yes."

"Special skills?"

"French."

He finally made eye contact.

"I'm not one hundred percent fluent," Elsa said, "but I can communicate well enough."

The man closed his notebook and studied her as if he'd just realized she had entered his office.

"French. Okay. When De Gaulle shows up, we'll make sure to find you. Until then, here are the rules: There is no tolerance of regionalism. You are Eritrean and that's it. There is no tolerance of religious factionalism. You can pray to whoever you want to, but keep it to yourself. There is no fraternization between members of the opposite sex. None. Last, but not least, if we catch you spying, may your God help you." He offered a small, sincere smile. "Welcome, Elsa."

There were nearly eighty young women at the training camp. Elsa gathered with the newer recruits, making small talk as they waited for what would come next. They sat in a clearing surrounded by a chain of mountains and hills, unevenly covered with low scrub that barely hid the dry soil and rocky earth. Elsa was still getting adjusted to being back in Eritrea after nearly ten years away. The lushness of Addis and its surrounding villages had the effect of making her homeland seem more arid than she remembered.

The training camp used to be for both men and women, but since so many youth were flocking to join, the male volunteers were sent off in rounds to the Sahel Mountains far in the north. The women had been outfitted with a drab-colored button-down shirt and pants, two pairs of underwear, one bra, rubber sandals, and a long white scarf they would be buried in when they died. Scissors were passed around, and as each girl cut their hair into an Afro, the rest clapped and whooped.

"We still know who's nappy though!" called out a young boy hauling stones. Someone threw a rock in his direction, and the women cheered.

Elsa saw a plume of smoke rising up from a gentle slope a few steps away. She walked over to discover a tall, well-built man fanning a mound of charcoal in the clearing below. The man set a large stone on top of the charcoal and spread dough on its smooth surface, careful to keep the thickness even. The task was familiar to Elsa and every woman she had ever known, but men didn't do that kind of work. Even more shockingly, a few female rebels crouched at his side, idly watching.

"Hey, city girl. Do you know who that is?"

The girl who asked the question appeared at Elsa's side, her face partially shielded by a faded green scarf that covered her hair.

"That's Andemichael Kahsai, the pilot who—"

"Who commandeered a fighter jet and landed it in Aden." Elsa finished the girl's sentence, staring at him in disbelief. She heard about his daring feat back in Addis: The Eritrean-born Ethiopian Air Force pilot commandeered his B-57 during a training operation and landed it at the port in Yemen. While he couldn't fly the jet into rebel-held territory in Eritrea, as the Ethiopian military wouldn't have hesitated to shoot him down, the whole point was to publicly humiliate them and create a global news event. Elsa had exercised great self-control to not gloat about the incident to her uncle. And now, this hero was not even a hundred feet from her, baking bread.

"I can't believe he's here," Elsa said, turning to the girl.

The girl smiled as she turned in response, her scarf falling to her shoulders. Then came the next shock: she and Elsa looked just alike. What a strange thing it was to recognize your face in someone else's. The girl was just as petite and well-proportioned as Elsa, and her hair, which curled tighter, was also cut short.

"Yes, he is, city girl. And so are you."

The girl went off to join three older fighters who were washing linens. When the young boy who was hauling stones passed her, she tripped him, nearly upsetting his load. They both laughed as he gently wrestled her to the ground. Elsa could tell she was from a village, and like the other village girls, she was more at ease in the camp. They were used to rougher conditions and had long been interacting with fighters in the liberated areas. The city girls from Asmara and Addis, on the other hand, were as wide-eyed as Elsa was.

Every day at four in the morning, the women were shouted awake and given just enough time to wash their faces and relieve themselves. Then they lined up, jogged in place, jogged in laps, and did jumping jacks. They marched and saluted and dropped to the ground and crawled on their bellies. They disassembled and reassembled their Kalashnikovs. They scurried up and down mountains and collected water and firewood. Elsa would return with much less water than she started with, and when her ineffective knotting of the wood on her back unraveled, spilling her haul to the ground, she fought back tears. It was Little Goat, the girl with whom she shared a face, called such because of the way she could so easily find her footing, who showed her how to secure the wood and firmly strap the bucket of water to her back.

Real names weren't always shared. Most people went by nicknames that were either insults or praise. One girl was called "Jerry" because she was shaped like a jerry can. Another they called "I Can't Do It" after she collapsed on a brutal midday hike and had to be carried back to the camp. Elsa was just referred to as "Hey You," and while she would have liked something more meaningful, she was grateful to not be ridiculed anytime someone addressed her.

Breakfast was at eight—tea without sugar and bread that crumbled like cork. Political education classes followed. The recruits gathered in the same plain they slept in and were lectured on issues that had consumed Elsa's study cell in Addis: the real history of Eritrea, centuries of foreign occupation, and the most dangerous enemy of all—capitalism. Marx was referenced, as was the Little Red Book. The People's Republic of China was identified on a map, a picture of Mao Zedong and a sickle and hammer centered on its great mass. There was also a delicate matter: Imperial Ethiopia had been an unambiguous foe. But between the Ethiopian Marxists who ousted the emperor and the Eritrean Marxists who didn't want to be ruled by them, it was no longer so clear whose struggle was progressive and whose was reactionary.

Next were literacy classes. The recruits were paired off, and it was the city girls' turn to share their expertise. Elsa and Little Goat were paired together, since the joke around camp was that they were twins separated at birth. Little Goat always laughed in response—she laughed easily at everything—but Elsa felt somehow that it was true, that she had finally found her kin. They had even been rechristened with their new shared name: "Twin."

Literacy classes were one of the few times they were guaranteed to spend alone. Twin had already learned to read from the fighters in her village, so she and Elsa sat together under a sparse acacia tree, discussing the booklets they had been assigned on the French in Algeria and Vietnam and the treachery of the Kuomintang in China. Elsa preferred to hear Twin tell her about her childhood and family in Adi Grotto, but Twin had no time for reminiscing, instead bemoaning their discovery that the Algerian mujahidat returned behind the veil when the French were defeated. That certainly wouldn't happen to them, she railed. Eritrean women wouldn't return to the kitchen when their war was won.

Elsa agreed heartily, but in private she had never anticipated the physical and material demands her political beliefs would make of her. She hadn't even really processed that she would be expected to handle a weapon. Yet there she was—dehydrated, hungry, at least ten pounds skinnier, hauling herself and her weapon over daunting terrain. Very quickly, her motivation to liberate her country stopped being the force getting her through those long and miserable days. Instead, she found herself deep in the realm of something much more elemental: the need to save face. Elsa soon understood what all the other women did: if she showed any weakness or fear, proved herself to be incapable in any way, it would reflect on her entire gender and undermine the endeavor of allowing women to fight in the first place.

Elsa was also desperate to keep up with Twin. She was tireless, running faster and harder than any man or woman. She could carry gallons of water on her back without so much as spilling a drop. She never complained of hunger and thirst, and she always had a smile on her face. Everyone wanted to be around her, and it was Elsa's luck that their resemblance secured her place by her side. Twin even changed a childhood game they all knew, a song of gibberish words recited while pointing in succession at everyone playing. When the last word landed, instead of that girl being "it," she would be the first to be martyred. Whenever Twin won, she would leap in the air as if she'd scored a championship goal.

Every evening at five, the trainees dined on lentils and bread, and at sundown, they were ordered to sleep. The twins slept together, with one of their scarves laid on the bare earth and the other used as a cover. Wednesday was the only day of rest, a compromise between Christianity and Islam. That was their life together for three months.

Every now and then, people would come looking for their loved ones, hoping to convince them to return home. The director of the electricity authority showed up looking for his son but found his neighbor's daughter instead, who refused to go back with him. An overeager ninth grader, dressed in his Eagle Scout uniform, was turned away by his older sister, who was supposed to be in her last year at university in Addis. "Why should I leave? You're the girl!" he complained as she twisted his ear.

Even Twin got a visitor. Twin had come to Ri'see Adi at

the age of seventeen, one year younger than Elsa, fleeing her impending marriage. Her father was the more sympathetic of her parents, enrolling her in elementary school, a hard-fought victory, but he lost the battle with her mother to send her to the nearest junior high school ten miles away. He knew his teenage daughter had been secretly helping the rebels, passing details on the activity of the nearby military garrison. Twin's mother would have none of it; when she discovered her daughter's secret affiliation, she began grinding grains and brewing beer for the wedding that would stop all that nonsense.

Twin ran away to the rebel camp the week before her nuptials. Her mother turned up soon after, yelling that she knew her daughter, *a bride*, was hiding there, and that if they had any decency, the rebels would release her. The administrator explained that they had no control over the matter—Little Goat had come on her own and would have to leave the same way.

"Who is Little Goat?" the mother demanded to know. "My child's name is Lydia!" Twin eventually faced her poor mother, and at the sight of her daughter, whose formerly long hair was supposed to have been in bridal braids, she collapsed, screaming, "This is not my daughter! What have you done with my daughter?"

Twin laughed easily when recounting the drama, as did Elsa, who didn't expect her mother or anyone else in her family to come for her. Twin volunteered to help send word—it was her family, too, she joked—but Elsa changed the subject. Once the war ended, Elsa told her, she would complete her bachelor's degree and apply for medical school in America.

Twin laughed as if someone had announced that capretto would be served for dinner.

"I can make it to America," Elsa said, punching her shoulder. "All you'll do is get married. And to someone with even less teeth than the man you jilted."

Twin became even more hysterical, nearly falling off the tree stump she was sitting on. "You want to talk about your plans for after the war?" she asked. "I came to die, my sister. I'm not planning for anything else." She looked at Elsa and broke out in laughter all over again. That was the right answer.

In their last week of training, their commanders warned that an attack was close. They couldn't say when exactly, but their intelligence revealed that the 9th Brigade of the Ethiopian Army had discovered the camp's location and would strike sometime in the middle of the night. The trainees were given strict orders to stay put and not pick up their arms and shoot, no matter what they heard. There was a plan to defend the rebel camp, and if the girls did anything but keep still and not make a sound, they could undermine it.

A few nights later, Elsa awoke with a start. It was too dark to see anything, and she grabbed at Twin's body, forcing her awake. "Do you hear something?" she asked.

"Stop breathing so hard and maybe I can," Twin replied.

Elsa tried to steady her breathing, but shots started to ring out. She shrieked and made to get up, but Twin threw herself on top of her and pinned her down.

"Shut up!" she hissed.

Elsa held her breath, but the shots grew louder. She imagined Ethiopian soldiers scaling the hills and descending into the valley to kill them all. She wanted desperately to go home. She didn't want to die in the dark, lying there on her back. She screamed until Twin pressed her hand to her mouth. Then she began to cry.

"Shut up!" Twin whispered. "You're going to get us killed!"

No one around them made a sound. Elsa wondered if only she and Twin were in that valley, if everyone else had run to safety while they had been sleeping. It was hard to catch her breath with Twin's hand clamped down so tightly. Her heartbeat soared with the new fear that instead of dying valiantly in battle, she would suffocate here, at her twin's hand.

All at once, the shots quieted. There was a shaky flash of light, and then the unsteady illumination of kerosene lamps widened around them. Elsa could make out a few of the women on their bellies with their weapons pointed ahead.

"Did you all survive the attack?" the head trainer called out. "Who was scared?"

All the other trainers gathered around the girls and started cheering, in what now appeared to be a training exercise and their de facto graduation ceremony. After that night, they'd be separated and assigned to different units across the country.

Twin rolled off Elsa and jumped up to join the high-fiving and back-slapping. Elsa stayed on the ground, hugging her knees to her chest. What was she doing there? What had possessed her to think that she belonged, that she was made of the same stuff they were? She was grateful for the dark that hid her terror, hoping that Twin wouldn't see her in the sporadic flashes of light.

July 1991

17

IT WAS THE FIRST DAY OF JULY, AND THE SUMMER STILL FELT ENDless. Lydia managed to get invited to the "I scream, you scream, we all scream for Lindsay Teller" ice cream–themed birthday party, which felt like an auspicious start. The note on the invitation read, "We look forward to seeing you there!" in the hand of Mrs. Teller, but most likely at the behest of her husband, Lieutenant Colonel Teller. When the lieutenant colonel was a child, his father did a tour of duty at Kagnew Station, the U.S. military base in Asmara. Even though he was too young to remember much, he took a special interest in Lydia and her family and was overly demonstrative about how much he liked spicy food. In elementary school, Lydia and Lindsay had spent countless afternoons hula-hooping in the Tellers' backyard; but Lydia's stock had mysteriously gone down, and he seemed the most hurt by it. Lydia wasn't sure what he hoped her presence in his daughter's life would do, but she was at that party, whether the birthday girl wanted her there or not.

One round of sundaes seemed plenty for the other guests crowded in the kitchen, but Lydia stayed close to the elaborate spread of Breyers cartons nestled in Tupperware filled with ice. Ryan Lowry, whose pants even Berekhet would agree were too short, wanted to debate her on the superiority of butter pecan over cookies and cream.

Lieutenant Colonel Teller appeared, thankfully directing Ryan to try caramel swirl, only to corner Lydia into a conversation about the blistering temperatures of the Danakil Depression, a region of Eritrea she knew nothing about.

"The Afar nomads would cross into Ethiopia via this route," he said with great confidence, using Popsicle sticks to diagram his point. "They are a Cushitic-speaking people, that's just one branch of the Afroasiatic language family, as you well know." He was blocking her view of the rest of the kitchen as the other kids started to trickle out. "While your ethnic group, the Tigrinya, speak a Semitic language, which is just a hop, skip, and a jump over in the same tree."

Once the ice cream lost its firmness, Mrs. Teller came to the rescue and directed Lydia to a bean bag in the basement. Everyone else had already moved down there and was sifting through Lindsay's massive collection of board games.

"I will crush you all in Battleship," Matthew said.

"Anyone up for Scrabble?" Ryan asked.

"I've got a better idea," one of the Forsyth twins said with a mischievous look that Lydia was sure she practiced in the mirror. She whispered it to Lindsay, who whispered it to Joel, who whispered it to the other Forsyth twin, and so on and so forth, until everyone heard the brilliant idea—everyone but Lydia. They all started giggling their way into the laundry room.

Lydia wanted to disappear. If her suspicions were correct, she would enter as someone who had never been kissed and exit as someone who had finally crossed over to the other side. Her fantasy of how this would happen was like how she used to long for communion. A light would shine, and a boy (she was ambivalent about which one) would choose her from all the other girls, cup her face, and gently press his lips to hers. That wouldn't happen if she stayed enveloped in the bean bag, so she hoisted herself up, freed the bit of T-shirt trapped between her belly rolls, and followed her classmates in.

As soon as Lydia entered, someone closed the door behind her and darkness fell in the windowless room. She could sense people adjusting, bodies hoisting themselves onto the washing machine and dryer, someone moving things from a worktable. The only physical contact she felt was with elbows and backsides being repositioned, all inadvertent. Then came the sounds. Light murmurs and moans. Lips and tongues smacking. Lydia slowly turned herself in a half-circle around the beaded chain that hung long from the lightbulb and gulped down the Downy-scented air. A tentative hand caressed her hip—it was finally happening. She tensed in anticipation, only to feel herself being nudged out of the way.

Even though it was dark, she felt completely exposed, as if everyone knew that she was the only one not wanted. Then came a desperate idea: it shouldn't take much to turn a breath into a moan. She tried it, faintly at first and then a bit louder. Just a few more times, enough to realize that faking it felt worse. A wristwatch thankfully beeped, and one nervous giggle sparked a round of laughter. Lydia was the last to leave the room.

After Lindsay passed out goodie bags filled with Ring Pops and Hubba Bubba Bubble Tape, Ryan's mother shuttled Lydia back to Southern Towers in the early evening. The apartment was quiet, except for Berekhet's snores, which boomed down the hallway. Lydia approached her bedroom door and rested her head against it, reliving the darkness of the Tellers' laundry room. She needed a distraction, and a debate with Berekhet would suffice. After a moment's hesitation, in which she heard her mother's warning to never enter her room without Berekhet's permission, she turned the doorknob slowly and crept into the room. Carefully stepping over the layers of clothing and CDs on the floor, she approached the bed. Berekhet was sleeping on his stomach with one arm folded above his head and the other flopped over the side of the bed. His eyes were open: not in a just-a-bit-of-the-whites-are-showing way but in an I-might-not-be-breathing way. Lydia held the back of her hand in front of his nose just to be sure.

Elsa had been worried about Berekhet sleeping through his

shifts and community college classes, which just started that Monday. A few weeks earlier, she'd dragged Lydia to Radio Shack and Circuit City, where they tested alarm clocks with their arms crossed like laboratory scientists. None had been loud enough, until, at the Indian store where they bought their spices, they found a brick of a clock whose alarm Lydia could feel in her teeth. Elsa and the man behind the counter shook hands as if they had discovered a very important cure.

Lydia hovered over Berekhet and nudged him with increasing levels of aggression. But it was hopeless. She left her room and went up to the thirteenth floor, where Mama Zewdi and her mother were laid out on the sofas, watching the TV chef Nicoletta Farinelli make ravioli.

"Sit, Lidu," Mama Zewdi said without shifting her eyes from the screen. "Learn something from this woman."

Mama Zewdi and Elsa loved to analyze cooking shows together. Mama Zewdi focused on unsanitary handling, while Elsa took a stand against premature or excessive self-praise. According to these two critics, Nicoletta Farinelli was the standard-bearer, representing the nontheatrical ways women have always cooked, unlike the obnoxious male TV chefs who had something to prove.

Lydia tucked herself into the armchair, determined to gain control of the television. The show's credits rolled, and Mama Zewdi and Elsa groaned when Henri Augustin appeared on the screen.

"Can we change it?" Lydia asked.

"No, no, no. We have to see what this good-for-nothing is up to," Elsa said. "Did you have dinner, Liduye? Go help yourself to some shiro."

"And make us some tea while you're at it. Extra-special tea so we can survive this guy," Mama Zewdi said. "Maybe today he'll actually clean the chick—Oh God, look at him! What is this 'just pat the chicken down' business? Clean the damn chicken, Frenchie!"

Lydia got up and made her way into the kitchen, pulling out the Lipton tea bags, sugar holder, and mason jar of cloves, cardamom, and cinnamon, slamming as many drawers and cabinets as she could in the process. She decided she wasn't hungry and tapped her fingernails on the counter as the boiling water in the teapot began to sing and then shriek, turning off the heat only after her mother and Mama Zewdi shouted at her to do so.

"And bring us a few cookies too!" Mama Zewdi called out. "The ones on top of the fridge!"

Lydia returned, bearing a tray with their demands, and sat stiffly. "Has Berekhet been sleeping all day?"

Henri lifted a lid and waved his other hand toward his face. "Mmm . . . smells heavenly," he said to the camera.

"They're just onions!" Elsa snapped back at him.

"*Mom.* Hello?"

"This guy acts like he never smelled sautéed onions. What did you say?"

"Forget it." Lydia slumped back down in the chair. She wondered if Berekhet had woken up; perhaps he was continuing his assessment of her home. He had already pointed out the dining chair with the wobbly leg and how the showerhead fired errant missiles of water. She didn't know the lifestyle he was used to, but she generally didn't trust Eritreans' recollections of how great back home was: the air, the food, real leather shoes. If it was so great, then what were they all doing in America?

He probably liked Mama Zewdi's home more. She had the walls repainted a warm orange and had made the building management replace her carpet. Framed scenes of aristocratic life, with richly furnished sitting rooms and castles in expanses of green, were hung throughout. Her cream sofa set rested high upon gold claws, which matched the tasseled gold pillows and curtains ("typical Arab style," Elsa had told Lydia privately).

They had the same televisions, but while Lydia's sat on a low stand, Mama Zewdi's was housed in a console taller than she was. The compartments were filled with photos from her travels, pictures of saints, miniature Eritrean flags, and wedding favors (Jordan almonds wrapped in tulle, all identical and never to be consumed).

Lydia stood up. She was bored and irritated by how terribly her summer was already going. "I'm going back home," she said, heading to the door.

"Lydia!" Mama Zewdi brushed the crumbs from her hand. "Bring the whole box over here, will you?"

Back downstairs, Lydia ran into Berekhet as he was leaving their apartment.

"Going to sell some Slurpees. Don't get into any trouble!" he said, patting her cheek.

Lydia threw herself on the sofa. She ended up watching Henri complete the chicken fricassee, as well as a PBS documentary on the Army Corps of Engineers that Berekhet would have loved. Then she walked aimlessly around the apartment and reclaimed some territory on her bookshelf before getting back on her knees in her mother's closet and retrieving the photo of her father.

Locked in the bathroom, just in case her mother returned, she sat on the edge of the tub and inspected the photo, hoping to discover something new. She looked very much like her father; they shared small, almost sad eyes, a long face and nose, and an upper lip that disappeared when they smiled. Elsa and the mysterious woman were like two dolls on either side of him, their perfect faces making it seem like they were just pretending to be fighting in a war.

Lydia faced the mirror and tucked the photo in the edge of the frame. There was a brightness about pretty women—their faces held a light—and as Lydia studied herself, she thought that she looked a bit dim. Was it her bone structure? The proportions of her features? Her skin color? It was a strange feeling to be raised by women who were more beautiful than she was; in her family, age had nothing to do with beauty. She had once asked her mother if she was ugly. Elsa made a face and swatted Lydia's question away. She told Lydia that she was beautiful but that looks mattered little; her abilities were all she needed to worry about. Lydia wasn't appeased. She wanted her mother to convince her that she, too, had the light.

There was another question the photo introduced: between two equally and identically beautiful women, what made one more appealing than the other? Even through the two-dimensional surface of a photo, Lydia could see that there was something special about her mother's friend. Shoulders back, head high, she looked head-on at the camera lens, communicating to the photographer and everyone else who might see that image that they got it wrong: she was the one who was looking at them. Lydia stood as tall as she could in front of the mirror, trying to summon that same energy.

She fell asleep before Elsa came home. Sometime in the middle of the night, she was awakened by clattering, followed by a muffled curse. She rose and stumbled down the hall toward the light in the kitchen. When she entered the kitchen, Berekhet turned to face her.

"You're up? Good!" He motioned at his getup, an apron decorated with I LOVE MY MOTHER finger-painted in bright, childish script that Lydia had made for a third-grade art class assignment and gifted to Elsa.

"Would madame care to join me?"

He pulled out a chair and gestured for her to sit down. Lydia collapsed into it and rested her head on her bent arm, feeling her eyes starting to droop. "What time is it?" she asked.

"Past your bedtime. But everything tastes better this late."

"Aren't you supposed to be at work?"

"They let me leave early."

Berekhet's frenetic energy was making Lydia feel even more tired. With one hand, he whisked eggs and milk in a shallow dish and with the other, handed her a plate of French toast.

"How are you not exhausted?" Lydia yawned into the toast. "Shouldn't you be reserving your energy for studying? . . . How was your first week of class?"

"Wait, wait. I forgot the powdered sugar." He rummaged through the drawers for a fine mesh tea strainer and tapped it over her plate as Henri Augustin would have.

"You want to talk about my classes when I just presented you this work of art? Hurry and taste it. I need to know if it needs more vanilla."

Lydia sat up to take a bite. The French toast was perfect. "Wait. How do you know about French toast?" she asked in disbelief. "Don't tell me this was your regular breakfast in Addis?"

"Of course not," Berekhet said as he sautéed chopped franks in butter. "I found this American cookbook at my school library and practically memorized it. I was obsessed with the breakfast recipes and vowed to try them if I ever made it to the States."

He served her the franks and garnished their plates with strawberries. "To secret breakfasts with my Lidu." He raised his glass of orange juice. "Now, tell me all about your adventures. What truths have you discovered?"

Lydia looked down at her plate uncertainly. "Nothing. My mother is the only person who knows what I want to know, but I can't get anything out of her."

Berekhet nodded as if that were the response he had been expecting.

"Listen, Lidu. Let me tell you the rules of exploration and discovery. Number one: Question everything you're told. Nothing is true just because someone says it is. Number two: Gather information from as many sources as you can. Your mom isn't offering much . . . fine. But where else can you dig? Your terrain is much bigger than you think. And number three: You could be wrong. Do you know that Darwin was shockingly wrong about heredity? Everyone can come to the wrong conclusion. And if you do, you'll be in good company."

Berekhet plopped another piece of toast onto her plate.

"Any questions?"

18

THERE WEREN'T MANY PLACES IN D.C. BUSIER THAN THE NATIONAL Mall on Fourth of July weekend. Herds of humans trod up and down the space between Constitution and Independence Avenues, looking up at buildings they had been told to regard with reverence, down at marked-up maps, and across the wide expanse of grass and gravel for any shade from the blistering D.C. sun. They also needed refreshments, and their thirst and hunger drove them to Elsa and her kind.

By three o'clock, Elsa had already met her goal for the day. She took out her notebook to log the inventory she needed to replenish—mustard and Andy Capp's Hot Fries. Flipping through the pages, she thought it a good time to determine whether stocking a more premium brand of honeybuns was worth the additional expense. She jotted down the calculations, redoing them three times before she had to stop and admit to herself what she was avoiding.

Closing her eyes to summon her strength, she slowly turned to a new page. *Dear Twin,* she wrote. *I hope this letter finds you well.*

How could she say what she wanted to, which was, of course, that she hoped the letter found her alive and well, but also not upset. Upset that Elsa left her behind and had taken thirteen years to finally make contact.

I don't know where to start, so let me start here. There is not a day that has gone by when I don't think about you. I will have to explain why this message has come so late. But first, I need to know that you're okay. And second, I want you to know that I have kept my promise. Everything else will come after.

"Earth to Elsa!" Ricky popped his face through the opening in her cart.

Elsa gasped and clutched her notebook to her chest.

"My bad, boss lady. I've been calling your name."

Elsa smoothed the pages and placed the notebook back in her bag. "I was just so focused . . . doing inventory."

"You need to be focused on making up for Memorial Day. Left all that money on the table."

Elsa came out of the cart and handed him an iced tea from the cooler. "Sometimes I think you care more about my business than I do. Are you hoping I'll give you a cut?"

Ricky downed nearly half of the bottle in one swallow and then wiped his brow. "My only reward is to see a strong Black woman be successful."

Elsa raised her fist in the air like she was back in the field. "Amen, my brother."

Ricky raised his as well. "Right back at you, sis."

"Yoo-hoo! Are your hot dogs any good?"

Elsa was startled at the sight of Zewdi somehow materializing from behind the cart. "What are you doing here?" she blurted.

"I hope this beautiful young lady isn't coming to take you away. You've got work to do," Ricky said with an outreached hand to Zewdi. "Richard Richmond. It's a pleasure to make your acquaintance."

"I'm Zewdi Naizghi. Lovely to meet you as well." She took his hand like a starlet would in an old Hollywood movie.

Elsa took the stool out of her cart so that Zewdi could sit down, rolling her eyes as her back was turned.

"Oh, I just couldn't." Zewdi motioned at Ricky, who was leaning with both hands on his cane.

"No, please. This cane is just for show." Ricky took Zewdi's hand and gently eased her onto the stool.

"You are too kind." Zewdi set her purse on her lap. "You

know, I was just in the area and wanted to check up on you," she said to Elsa. "I haven't been down here in a while, and it looks like I've been missing so much fun." She smiled at Ricky.

"You certainly have. You should come by more often and check us out. In the meantime, I'll let you two catch up." Ricky raised his iced tea and made to leave.

"I hope you're not leaving because of me!"

"I just stopped by to make sure Elsa was working hard. Something tells me you'll be able to do that better than me. You all take care!" Ricky waved and set off toward the Capitol.

"You were just in the area, huh?" Elsa crossed her arms.

"Mmm-hmm. Prices still the same?" Zewdi asked, peering over her Chanel sunglasses.

As Zewdi selected a bag of Famous Amos cookies and made herself comfortable, Elsa tried to discern the motivation for her visit; Zewdi could either make you forget your troubles or remember them all.

"I heard you stopped by the EPLF office recently," Zewdi said. "The secretary told me that you and Osman had a meeting."

There it was.

"How's he doing? He's such a nice guy. Did you know that he started a weekend soccer league for the kids? What kind of man does that? A single one too."

Elsa reached through the opening for her dishrag and began wiping the front counter down.

"Yeah, we spoke briefly. He seems to be doing just fine."

"You just went there to chat?"

"Yep. I just happened to be in the area," Elsa said with a big smile.

"Oh, how lovely," Zewdi said with a bigger one. "You should visit him more often. Did I ever tell you that his auntie was with me in Riyadh? Such a sweet woman; it must run in the family. I really should give her a call. And *you* should really try to spend more time with him, Elsa. You're not getting younger, and I don't know why you insist on being alone."

"I'm not alone," Elsa said, wiping the counter more vigorously. "I have you and Lydia."

"That's not the same, and you know it."

Zewdi was looking at her sternly. The good cheer had dropped.

"I really don't want to talk about this today." Elsa tossed the rag back inside the cart. "Can you not?"

"Can I not what? Care about you? Is that what you want? You know, at this rate, I'll get married before you do."

Elsa let out a deep belly laugh but stopped when she saw how wounded Zewdi looked.

"You don't think I can? You think that because you want to be alone that all of us do?"

Elsa didn't know what to say. Of course she knew that Zewdi would have wanted a husband and her own family. They never discussed it, but she thought that Zewdi had accepted that life had turned out differently for her, as Elsa had for herself. At this age, she couldn't imagine Zewdi settling down with some stranger. Elsa could only see Zewdi as part of her own family, but living two floors up at a nice, healthy distance.

"Do you think Lydia can't handle seeing you with someone else? She needs to see her mother happy and fulfilled. She needs a father figure, Elsa, a man around the house. It's good that Berekhet is here, God help him, but he'll leave eventually, and so will Lydia when she grows up. And suppose something happens to me, or heaven forbid I find someone?" she said, tilting her head. "Who will you have then?"

Zewdi straightened her pale yellow linen skirt over her legs with just enough force for Elsa to know that she was upset. Elsa pursed her lips and let out a deep breath.

"Anyone would be lucky to have you in their life, as we are. But I know what I need and what's best for me and Lydia."

Zewdi nodded slowly but not in agreement. “That’s the sad part. You think you do. Maybe I talk too much, so much that you don’t even hear me at all. But God has a way of making us listen. Just wait.”

She adjusted her sunglasses and turned her face away from Elsa, in the direction that Ricky had walked off in. Elsa turned to face the other way, too irritated to try to decipher Zewdi’s veiled threat.

A red-faced tourist with one of those silly umbrella hats approached cautiously, as if he could sense the tension.

“Please, come on up,” Elsa said, pasting a smile on her face. Zewdi did the same.

“Can I get two franks with everything on them?” the man asked.

“Of course, of course.” Elsa hurried inside the cart and prepared the order, saying a silent thank-you for the interruption.

“Don’t worry, I’ll let you work,” Zewdi said. She got up and took another bag of cookies. “But don’t take anything for granted, me included. See you at home.”

19

IN BUSINESS, IT IS ALWAYS GOOD TO CATCH PEOPLE BEFORE THEY are expecting you. Zewdi strode into Asmara Restaurant twenty minutes early for her ten o'clock appointment with Ammanuel. The restaurant was empty. If it wasn't for the door being unlocked and a cup of steaming 7-Eleven coffee on the bar, she would have thought no one was there.

"Hello!" she called out. "Ammanuel!"

Zewdi circled slowly, eyeing the space. It was the standard mediocre and unimaginative Eritrean establishment. Mismatched chairs, cheap plywood tables with smudged glass tops. She pressed a finger on the table closest to her, certain that it would wobble. Her suspicions were correct.

The menu was a one-pager slipped under each table's removable glass tabletop. What was the point of the menu anyway? All these places served the exact same things: beef and lamb tibsi and pasta with either chicken or fish cotoletta. Let her run a restaurant and show people what could be done. Sizzling filet cuts served on clay platters, accompanied with saucers of awaze pooled into perfect circles. Tuna tartare set on injera no bigger than chocolate-chip cookies. The vegetarian options wouldn't be an afterthought but prepared as thoughtfully as they were at home, since observant Christians regularly abstained from animal products. Velvety red lentils braised with tomatoes and ginger. Bright greens with heaps of onion and garlic. A proper salad that wasn't doused in "Italian" dressing that came out of a bottle.

It was Monday morning, but the restaurant still smelled like

Saturday night, the odors of beer and cigarette smoke trapped in the air. Zewdi made her way to the windows that faced U Street and opened the blinds. Now she could see the future. Sturdier furniture, fresh flowers on every table, outdoor seating barricaded with planters of jacaranda. Let people sit outside like they did in Asmara so the place could be deserving of its name.

Along the bar, Zewdi felt the mottled wood and checked for gum underneath. The bar could stay. Different stools were needed, of course, but if they opened in the morning, people could stop by on their way to work and grab an espresso, even drink it standing like they did at Tre Stelle back home. No, she had a better idea. The bar would go and instead of people drinking coffee like the Italians, they would stick to tradition. A proper coffee ceremony with low stools, a clay jebena brewing on a charcoal grill, and a pretty girl dressed in kidan habesha studding the popcorn, the traditional accompaniment, with dates and candies. They could start just doing it on Sundays, but there was no reason they couldn't do it every day the restaurant was open. Americans would love it. They would want to sit on the stools and watch, ask about the roasting process and the significance of brewing three rounds. Zewdi would be happy to field their questions, let them shake the pan of roasting beans and pose for pictures with their children and wide smiles.

How would Asgedom fit into this fantasy? Faster than they had materialized, the awestruck Americans disappeared, then the stools, and finally the pretty girl vanished, leaving Zewdi tapping on the sticky surface of the bar. She had to remind herself to factor him in. They'd spoken a few times since their first date, and on their last call he offered an invitation for her to visit him in L.A. He said he would take care of everything, send a ticket, and book a hotel.

It was the right thing for him to ask; they couldn't keep breathing at each other on the phone like American teenagers. If they were going to make a life together, it would have to be in L.A. or wherever his career took him, not the other way around. She accepted his invitation, agreeing to come at the end of July, when both of his kids would be traveling with their mother. Zewdi would have loved to commiserate with Elsa about the trip, share her nervousness and review her wardrobe and jewelry selections. But she was reluctant to tell her about Asgedom altogether, their exchange at her cart over the weekend proving her instincts right. Elsa felt more comfortable standing still.

If Zewdi's mother were alive, God rest her soul, she would have dragged Zewdi out of that restaurant and onto the plane herself. Her greatest wish was for Zewdi to get married and have children, as all women were supposed to do, but life had other plans.

When Zewdi was of marrying age, she was training to be a nurse. During her first delivery in Haikota Hospital, a bomb blasted through the operating theater down the hall, collapsing the ceiling. Despite the chaos and destruction, the baby wailed in her arms, and they all survived. Zewdi's mother said it was a sign for her to stop working and settle down, always fearful that her own divorce would hurt Zewdi's prospects. Eligible girls were judged based on their mothers' fertility and homemaking skills, and as the mother of one, she labored to demonstrate her good standing. But as much as she accused Zewdi of being too proud, she had also been guilty. When Zewdi's father had started a trucking business in Ethiopia, she stayed behind, unwilling to live somewhere foreign. He divorced her, and she never remarried, making Zewdi an only child.

Zewdi saw her survival of the bomb attack as proof that children were her guardian angels, something she still believed even though none had been her own. She wasn't naïve enough, however, to think that they could keep her safe from the war; they were getting killed themselves. She also didn't think her mother and uncles had many suitors for her to choose from. Young men were disappearing daily in Eritrea. If they were in their twenties and still hanging around, they were on their way to being conscripted into the Ethiopian military or joining the rebels, both of which likely led to death.

Zewdi also faced those options. As certain as she was that Eritrea would one day be free, she was just as certain that she didn't have the courage to join the independence movement. So she decided to leave, as many were, making her way to Sudan. As she wandered around Kassala, exhausted and afraid, a man dressed in white emerged from behind a hut and gestured at her. She had been warned not to trust Sudanese men—they were said to try it with anything that moved—but when he handed her a tin cup and led her to a covered trough of water, she dropped to her knees and drank. At the first sip, she felt certain that she was going to make it. She didn't know exactly where that "it" was, but she just knew she would.

Some contacts from her hospital got her a job in a pharmacy in Port Sudan and found a home where she could stay. The house was next to an Eritrean family that sold injera, and four months later she happened to hear a familiar laugh over the shared compound wall. When she entered the courtyard, she saw one of her uncles, who had disappeared from Eritrea a few years earlier, sipping a cup of tea. Zewdi's mother had feared the worst, so she hugged and kissed him the way her mother would have if she had been there.

Last spring, Lydia had written this whole story down for a class project called "History All Around Us." She came to Zewdi with a notebook, even though she knew the story as well as Zewdi did, and begged to borrow some of her pictures, which she glued onto a yellow poster with "Zewdi Naizghi Weldegebriel" written in the middle. When she came home after the presentation, she told Zewdi that her teacher asked how all those things could have happened to one person.

" 'She walks to another country and then hears her long-lost uncle from the house next door'?" Lydia repeated. "She said that 'maybe your neighbor is trying to play a trick on you.' "

Neighbor? Is that what Zewdi was? Lydia still didn't understand the difference between lying to Americans and using words differently. Zewdi could imagine Lydia describing her as her aunt, getting flustered when her teacher asked if Zewdi was her father or mother's sister, and then dropping it altogether. And once her teacher thought there were too many coincidences, a word Zewdi didn't learn until she came to America, Lydia dared to question what Zewdi had taught her: that God doesn't just let things happen. Life was more purposeful than that. People were at the mercy of something greater. Zewdi had so much taken away from her, but she still wanted and she still had faith. Those who didn't were weak. Those who wasted were worse.

There were parts of the story Zewdi never told Lydia. Lots of Eritreans passed through that house in Port Sudan. When there was space, Zewdi shared a cramped room in the main house, but more often she slept in the courtyard. In the day, there would be a few chairs, clothes hanging, and chilies set out to dry. But at night, people Zewdi never saw when the sun was out—Eritreans who worked as maids, drivers, errand boys, and store clerks—dragged cots from the service quarters and created a maze of burlap-covered beds they had to step on to pass through. Zewdi wanted to believe that the worst the men did was just rub themselves against the girls. It had only happened to her a few times; a young man whose face she never saw would lie down and then leave her with his wetness. But when a girl got pregnant by the son of the woman of the house, she was forced to give up her child and then disappeared soon after. So when Zewdi's uncle told her that he was visiting from Saudi and could get her a work visa, that wasn't a coincidence, that was God getting her out.

Zewdi made her way to the billiards table in the back of the restaurant, approaching it deliberately like a butcher who had made his choice. Pins lay scattered on the battered table, and she fired a striped ball at the white one near the corner pocket. The space in the back was narrow, and when the men played at night, the smoke hovered thick and heavy. A few years ago, she, Elsa, and Lydia had come for dinner on a Saturday night. They didn't often eat at Eritrean restaurants, and Lydia, instead of just burying herself in a book, kept looking around, eyeing everyone with curiosity. On her way back from the bathroom, she'd lingered at the boisterous cluster of men playing boccette, then rushed back to their table with a look of relief, as if she had finally figured out what had been bothering her. "Where are all the women?" she asked.

Zewdi knew for certain that she was the reason Lydia had noticed that. Since Lydia could eat solid food, Zewdi had been taking her to bakeries and nice restaurants, even treating her to high tea at the Mayflower every Easter. When Lydia got her period last year, Zewdi took her to the Alexandria Hilton for London broil. She wanted her to see families sitting together, couples out on dates, girlfriends catching up over glasses of wine. All the things that Eritrean women wouldn't or couldn't do because of their kids and husbands, or fear of what people would say. What were the men doing? Drinking beers and throwing balls in a dark corner.

The child could see for herself that a place run by men and for men was no place at all. Zewdi banged her hand on the billiards table like a judge with his gavel. Asmara needed her, Ammanuel needed her, case closed.

A distant door opened, and Zewdi could hear voices coming from the kitchen. She walked in to see Ammanuel setting a box on the counter, shouting at a man in the other doorway that led to the back alley.

"What am I going to do with cherry tomatoes, Oscar? I've ordered regular tomatoes every week for three years. How did you get this wrong?"

"Keep them, Aman," she said, smiling as they both turned to her. She handed Aman the coffee he had left on the bar. "You can make a simple pasta with basil and garlic. Everyone will love it. Hello, Oscar. I'm Zewdi, nice to meet you."

Oscar nodded at her gratefully.

"Why don't you come by tomorrow and tell Yodit what to do?" Ammanuel said, stroking his chin.

Zewdi laughed and shook her head. "You think I was born yesterday? If I come here tomorrow, you're going to have me slicing these tomatoes!"

As Ammanuel claimed his innocence, Zewdi took note of the kitchen—it was much cleaner and well-appointed than she had imagined. The range was well worn but spotless, there was no stickiness or visible debris on the floor, and each pot, pan, and cooking utensil had a dedicated storage space. Zewdi nodded approvingly and went back to the dining area, waiting for Ammanuel to finish up with Oscar.

"Soooo," he said, strolling in. "What do you think?"

"What I think depends on what you need. How do you plan on working with whoever buys Robel's share? Who makes the decisions?"

"I focus on the finances and permits, paying rent, keeping the books, et cetera. And I'd like for my partner to take charge of running the restaurant."

Zewdi imagined what that would mean. Setting the menu, having a strong team in the kitchen, managing supplies.

"Would you know how to handle that?" he asked. "It's different from cooking in the house."

Zewdi set her bag on the bar and clasped her hands together. She wasn't offended by his skepticism. He thought she was just a nice lady who made injera. But she catered events with over four hundred people a few times each year. And while she had never run a restaurant, she had a knack for numbers and had visited more restaurants in more countries than he could probably name.

"The restaurant seats forty, plus these seats at the bar. On a good night, you'll serve thirty-five parties, so you'll need enough food to feed around 160 people. One order of tibsi requires about half a pound of meat, so it would be safe to have forty pounds of meat on any given day. Onions and tomatoes, that's all easy to figure out. I have some ideas about tuna, but I'm sure you're only offering fried flounder or tilapia now. And as we discussed at the party, Ammanuel, my brother, restaurants don't just offer food, they offer a feeling. What's the experience your diners are getting here?"

Ammanuel stammered in an attempt to answer, but Zewdi just continued on. "Imagine if you let the light in a bit more," she said. "Imagine if it's not just a place where taxi drivers come to drink. This place could feel like home. Flowers, good food, whole families eating together. It has the potential. What are you selling Robel's share for?"

"Twenty thousand."

"What about yours?"

Ammanuel nearly choked on his coffee.

"I'm joking, Ammanuel!" Zewdi said with a slap to his back. "Just waking you up in case that coffee isn't."

"Oh, I'm up! Let me ask you this." He set his cup down and pointed at her with both index fingers. "Are you ready for this restaurant to be your new home? You've been lucky, working out of your apartment all these years, making money right from your kitchen. But you take this on and the only thing you'll do at Southern Towers is sleep. You won't be going to people's houses for coffee, no more weddings, baptisms, baby showers. Why do you think I haven't married yet? This place is my wife and kids."

As he spoke, Zewdi was mentally writing the profile that would appear in *The Washington Post* entitled "Zewdi Naizghi Knows Food." That might be overselling. "Zewdi Naizghi Brings the Flavor of Asmara to U Street." That was good. She'd be wearing a chef coat in the photo, her arms crossed and a sage expression on her face, the jacaranda peeking through in the background.

Could she imagine a new life where home was the restaurant and not Unit #1341? If this offer had come when Lydia was younger, Zewdi wouldn't even have considered it. But the girl was growing more independent and would be leaving for college faster than Zewdi and Elsa could imagine. Zewdi also knew her own life would change as a result and that she was bigger than her apartment and the buckets of injera batter at her feet.

Zewdi ran her hand over the bar again, breathing in the lingering yeasty scent of beer. "Twenty thousand, eh?"

"Twenty thousand."

"Anyone else interested?"

"My sister's husband, but that man will drive this place into the ground and blame me for it. I prefer you. You've got until the middle of August to decide; that's five weeks, plenty of time."

Plenty of time it was not. Especially with her impending trip to L.A., which gave her a sinking feeling. But she threw her shoulders back, returning her attention to the buzz she felt in the restaurant. "I'd like to see the books first. And I'll be back on a Saturday night to see how the kitchen flows."

Zewdi held out her hand. Ammanuel reached out to shake it. "Just give me a call, Zewdi. I'm not going anywhere."

20

IN THE FOURTH GRADE, BACK WHEN LINDSAY TELLER USED TO actually invite Lydia over, Lindsay once called her mother stupid and old, *to the woman's face*, and slammed her bedroom door shut, *in the woman's face*. Lydia expected Mrs. Teller to tear down the locked door with bionic arms, hoist Lindsay up by the neck, and throw her against the wall. Instead, Mrs. Teller retreated and served the girls Oreos and milk when they returned downstairs, not saying a word as Lindsay chattered and licked the cream from the insides.

Lydia had always assumed that the showdowns between mother and daughter on television were exaggerated, never thinking that real children had the power to put real mothers in their place. She could try to confront Elsa the way she'd fantasized: declare in a shrill voice that her mother denied her the only thing she had ever asked for and throw herself on her bed as Elsa hung her head in shame. But this wasn't TV; the scene wouldn't just transition seamlessly to a fast-forwarded happier time, and her mother would never be Mrs. Teller, with a plate of cookies in hand. Lydia still had options, however, and she headed up to Mama Zewdi's with Berekhet's rules for discovering the truth guiding her way.

Lydia walked into the apartment, finding her potential source for information brewing coffee in the living room as Mama Genet squinted at the television. The topic of conversation was familiar: the royals. The women talked about that family as if they were Eritrean and lived in their building. Lydia didn't get it. What could they possibly have in common with the British royal family, loaded with castles and money?

Mama Zewdi always waved that away. "Material things," she said, "all irrelevant. There are families with more wealth than the royals have, filthy rich Saudis whose grandparents were camel drivers fifty years ago. It's not money, Lydia, it's tradition. They *have* to do things a certain way. What's more Eritrean than that?"

Today, the television was blaring news coverage of Princess Diana's recent trip to Brazil. Lydia curled into the armchair as the conversation predictably shifted to Lady Di's wedding, which was still referred to as if it was a milestone in their own family history. Mama Genet flipped through a collector's wedding photobook that occupied prime real estate on the coffee table, and Mama Zewdi recounted the details that even Lydia had committed to memory. The world's royals were all in attendance (even the queen of Lesotho, whoever she was), save for the Saudis, a mystery Mama Zewdi had never solved. The twenty-five-foot train was made of ivory taffeta and antique lace, and of course, the ring—fourteen solitaire diamonds encircling a twelve-carat blue Ceylon sapphire set in eighteen-karat white gold.

"Eighteen karats," Mama Genet scoffed, handing her cup back to Zewdi in anticipation of the next round. "Even I was given twenty-four-karat gold."

Mama Zewdi looked like she was in pain.

"My God, Genet. It's white gold. And did you forget about the fourteen solitaire diamonds?" she said through clenched teeth.

Somewhere in Rio de Janeiro, Princess Diana touched the cheek of a toddler poking her head out from in between her mother's legs. The crowd swooned. Lydia could see the princess's appeal, the light in her eyes, the innocent set of her face, and for the first time, could see that her mother had a similar allure, as did the mystery woman in that photo. What would it feel like to look that way? To have such an effect on people without even saying a word?

"Something isn't right." Mama Zewdi passed a platter of popcorn to Mama Genet, who then handed it to Lydia. "They're not even looking at each other."

Prince Charles seemed like a forgettable figure who faded into the background when he was with Princess Diana, but not to Mama Zewdi. She said that their marriage was in trouble, and that he was seeing another woman.

"You mean that old lady in the magazines?" Mama Genet barked.

"Well, she is his age," Mama Zewdi said with a sniff.

"You think he's going to leave this beautiful flower for that dried-up lady? You don't know what men want, my dear."

"What do you know about men? All you know is your husband," Mama Zewdi said with a sharp tilt of her neck.

"If you know one, you know them all." Mama Genet took a stiff sip of her coffee. Her eyes were still trained on Princess Diana. "This one is damaged though. Women like her are doomed. They want too much, and that's their downfall, not the man. Look at her eyes. There's trouble there."

Lydia tried to find the trouble. But the princess looked full of life, the entire scene transformed by her presence, like when Cinderella's fairy godmother would wave her hand and transform the mundane into something spectacular. Was that power dangerous in some way?

Mama Zewdi was also studying the scene, her hands slack in her lap. She looked tired. There were bags under her eyes and the skin on her cheeks seemed looser. For the first time, Lydia saw her as a much older woman.

"Go ahead and change the channel, Lidu." She handed over the remote. Lydia flipped through and was forced by both women to stop on a slow-moving western that soon relieved their tension. After three rounds of coffee, Mama Genet excused herself, declaring that she had to get started on dinner before Mengist left her for a younger woman.

Mama Zewdi heaved herself from the stool and stretched out on the sofa, covering her face with the crook of her arm.

"Are you okay?" Lydia asked.

"I'm just tired, Liduye. One of those days."

Lydia pulled the stool up to the sofa and leaned toward Mama Zewdi. It definitely wasn't a good time, but she was committed to her mission.

"We haven't talked about this in a while . . . but I just wanted to know if my mom has mentioned anything to you about reaching out to my father's family or to any of her friends?"

Mama Zewdi shifted her arm just enough to glance at Lydia with a mysterious expression. "Be patient, little one. Something tells me that you'll find what you're looking for . . . and that it might show up right at your door." With that, she covered her eyes again.

Lydia trudged back downstairs to a still-empty apartment, wondering what Mama Zewdi meant. The light on the answering machine was blinking, and she pushed the Message button. An unfamiliar voice urgently introduced himself as Osman from the EPLF office and asked that Elsa call him immediately about what she was looking for. He left his phone number. Lydia wrote the number down and deleted the message. There was no rule about having to share her sources.

21

ELSA ENTERED HER APARTMENT AS DUSK BEGAN TO DESCEND, THE sky beyond the balcony door revealing hints of purple. She kicked her shoes off onto the pile by the door and trailed down the hallway, checking to see if anyone was home. Instead of peeling off her clothes and taking a shower, as she normally did when she returned from work, she collapsed onto her bed.

Elsa was certain that Osman's contact had already made it to Eritrea. She was surprised that he hadn't called to remind her to drop off the letter, even though it worked out in her favor, as she couldn't bring herself to give it to him. Elsa sniffed her underarms. The dried sweat on her body made her skin feel tight and dry. She willed herself to sit up, making eye contact with her reflection in the mirror on the dresser. She walked toward it as she removed her watch and earrings, then set them down on the surface. The brochure from Northern Virginia Community College had somehow made its way from Lydia's room to hers. Elsa browsed through it, noting the dates of the summer term that Berekhet was enrolled in: July 1 to August 9. Two weeks had passed since the start, yet she still hadn't seen him sitting in front of a textbook. Granted, their schedules weren't aligned—by the time Elsa got home, he was either at the library (so he claimed) or working. But she had a feeling he wasn't on top of his studies.

Elsa left the brochure on her dresser and went into Lydia's room, surveying its chaos from the door's threshold. She started kicking through the clothes on the floor, unsure of how to find proof that her suspicions about Berekhet were correct. She walked over to the bed, where she got on her knees and thrust her arm underneath it, toward the balled-up paper and orphaned socks.

"What are you doing?" she heard Lydia ask.

Elsa jerked back, banging her finger against an unforgiving bolt on the frame. She cursed and sucked her knuckle as Lydia stood in the doorway with her arms crossed. Elsa wasn't sure if her child was trying to intimidate her, which was impossible since this was her home.

"Does Berekhet have a printout of his class schedule somewhere?" Elsa used her other arm to extract a crumpled Wendy's bag that still had fries in it.

Lydia shrugged. Elsa heaved herself up and looked right back at her as if to say that if she didn't drop the attitude and start helping, Berekhet wasn't going to be the only one with problems.

"Go look through those papers," Elsa said, motioning to the bookshelf. Lydia didn't move fast enough for Elsa's liking. Elsa cocked her neck until her pace picked up.

Last weekend, she'd overheard Berekhet telling Lydia that when adults ask young people what they want to do when they grow up, they only want to hear what they think matters. "Adults want to know your profession so they can label you. 'She's a lawyer—she's successful. He's a musician—he's not a serious person,'" he had said with a mocking tone. His advice: "Do what you love. If you have a passion for baking, then bake. And if you stop being passionate about it, then do something else." God help her child if she was going to believe that nonsense.

Elsa spotted a few notebooks under the nightstand and flipped through them, finding exactly what she was looking for.

"Got it!" She waved the schedule triumphantly.

"Good for you." Lydia offered two thumbs up and turned to leave.

"Wait," Elsa said. She straightened the rumpled blanket over the sheets and sat on the bed, motioning for Lydia to join her.

Maybe she could diffuse their friction and also glean some intelligence on her cousin. "How is everything going, Lidu? Having a fun summer with Berekhet?"

Lydia eyed the bed as if it were covered with spikes and left the room without a word.

Elsa watched her leave, so taken aback by her child's brazenness that she didn't know how to respond. One thing at a time though. First, she needed to get Berekhet on the right track.

The next morning, Berekhet was sleeping when Elsa left for work. But at 3:50 p.m., having packed up her cart before her normal close time, she stationed herself in the Bisdorf Building at NOVA's campus, pacing in front of Room 205. Berekhet was glaringly absent from the students who shuffled into the class with their weary expressions and bulging book bags. Elsa intercepted the stern-looking professor, an East Asian woman with bobbed hair that barely moved, before she could enter.

"I'm sorry to bother you. I'm looking for a student of yours named Berekhet Alazar. He's my cousin." Elsa held up a Polaroid of him that she brought just in case.

"I know him." The professor barely glanced at the picture. "He's hard to forget," she said, raising her eyebrows.

"How's he doing in the class?"

"Well, he's very opinionated, which might be helpful in other subjects but doesn't serve him in chemistry. Is he still sick?"

"Sick?"

"He missed last week's class and lab, as well as a test. We're on a compressed calendar in the summer, so based on that zero, it's impossible for him to pass. I'm sorry."

Elsa watched the professor enter the room. Once the door closed, she turned herself around in a tight circle, then peeked into the glass strip of the door to witness the education that Berekhet had abandoned.

"Impossible for him to pass," she muttered to herself as she exited the building and walked back to her car. "Impossible for him to pass. *Impossibleforhimtopass.*"

With her hands on the wheel precisely at 10 and 2, she drove to the 7-Eleven, repeating her mantra. He wasn't at the register, and the man who was told Elsa that Berekhet wasn't on the schedule for the day. On the drive home, she clutched the wheel at 11 and 1, imagining that it was Berekhet's neck. When she barged into the apartment, at the sight of Lydia, who was curled up on the sofa reading a book, for one fleeting, shameful moment, she imagined hitting *her* instead.

"Is Berekhet here?"

Lydia shook her head.

"Where is he?"

"I don't know," she said, sitting up with alarm.

Elsa slowly walked closer to Lydia, trying to show her that she was calm, that she wasn't mad at her.

"Your cousin is supposed to be focused on school right now, but he's not. And I . . . we," she said, gesturing to herself and Lydia to generate solidarity, "need to make sure that he does what he's supposed to."

"He seems pretty focused to me," Lydia said, a little too pointedly.

Great, Elsa thought. Hostilities were increasing on all fronts. She pulled her hair back from her face until she could feel her eyelids strain from the pressure. "Impossible for him to pass," she whispered.

"What was that?" Lydia looked concerned and set her book down on the sofa cushion.

Elsa mumbled that it was nothing and headed toward her room, too tired to do anything else. She didn't hear Berekhet come home that night. But when she rose for work at 4:30 the next morning, she barged into his room and shook him awake.

"What happened?" he said, jolting up. "Is everything okay?"

"Everything is not okay," Elsa said. "Get dressed. You're coming with me."

Berekhet did just as he was told. He filled two thermoses with tea, prepared cream cheese and jelly sandwiches, and sat in silence as Elsa drove them to the depot.

"My first job in America was at the same 7-Eleven you're working in now," she began once they crossed into D.C. "I left that job to work the register at Giant from six a.m. to three, and after my shift, I'd cross Route 50 to clean rooms at the Holiday Inn from four till ten. I wanted to be a doctor like your father, but I didn't have the time or money to continue my education. I had a child to raise. But you don't have those problems, Berekhet. Things are much easier for you . . . just do what I'm telling you to do and your life is going to look very different. You hear me?"

Berekhet pressed his lips together before speaking. "I hear you, Elsa, but—"

"No, you don't. I went to your chemistry class yesterday. Your professor said that based on what you've missed, it's *impossible for you to pass*." Elsa slammed her hand on the wheel. "I don't want to hear about your curiosities or your . . ." Elsa said, searching for how he liked to phrase it, "or your passions."

"You are not who I thought you would be!" Berekhet turned to face her and shook his head. "Everyone said that you were the freethinker in the family, that you did just what you wanted to. Father disagreed with the decision you made, of course. But I thought it was so cool that my cousin was a freedom fighter. I used to brag to my friends who sat around debating politics that my own flesh and blood was a hero on the front lines. You of all people should be able to understand me."

Elsa steadied her breathing, thinking carefully about how to make him understand how things really were. But they had already reached the garage. "Let's go," she said, turning off the ignition.

She introduced him to her fellow vendors and showed him how to help the porter hitch her cart to his truck. When they reached her spot on the Mall, she walked through how to turn the burners on, heat up the franks, prepare the condiment stations, hang the metal rods with their branches of chips, and fill the coolers with ice. He was quiet with customers, talking only when he needed to, and stared off toward the Washington Monument or jotted things down in his little notebook.

Nineteen years old. He had his whole life ahead of him and didn't believe a thing Elsa said.

"I know what it's like to be young and passionate," Elsa finally said to Berekhet as they packed up at the end of the day. "I was that way too. But sometimes you have to trust us older people because we're trying to protect you from making the mistakes that we did."

"But I have a plan . . ." Berekhet started.

Elsa held her hand up to silence him.

"As long as you're in my house, Berekhet, my brother, you have my plan. I am here to guide you. And that's not up for negotiation. I promised your father I'd look out for you, and that's what I'm going to do."

Elsa got the silence she asked for. Berekhet didn't say another word.

22

The Nation's Daughters

"DO YOU THINK THEY'LL SEPARATE US?" ELSA WHISPERED INTO Twin's neck. After three months of training, she still wasn't used to the frigid nights and lay curled up against Twin, whose arm was flung over her face.

"If they do, I'll finally be able to get some sleep," Twin mumbled.

Elsa huffed and turned over, taking the majority of the threadbare scarf they were sharing with her. Unable to sleep, she watched as the rising sun leisurely revealed the craggy mountains that stood guard over her and her comrades. On that morning in May 1975, the training commanders assigned them to their new units. Elsa was sent to the fighting forces. Twin was not—a decision that baffled Elsa until she thought that maybe the least talented were sent to the front line.

The company Elsa was assigned to had been ordered on a secret mission to Asmara. For days, they hid in the city's southern outskirts, giddy with the prospects of liberating the capital. Instead, their company leader revealed that they would be stealing a recent shipment of hoes from a government storehouse.

"Is there a problem, Twin?" he asked, noting Elsa's disappointment. "These hoes aren't for your father's fields. They're to build trenches to keep your head on your neck. And if we get word there's a shipment of underwear, we'll steal that too."

For months, they snuck in and out of the city, stealing government supplies identified by the rebel movement's network of urban agents. Rubber sandals, clothes, pharmaceuticals—they took it all without a single shot being fired. In October, the entire company gathered for a big announcement. Elsa was hoping to hear that they'd finally be sent to battle. Her shameful performance at the training graduation still haunted her and she was desperate to prove to herself that she was as brave as her comrades. But the company leader just shared staffing changes. A former leather craftsman was being sent to a workshop to construct rifle cartridge holders from a supply of hides the unit had just raided. Three men and one woman were selected to train as foot doctors near Keren. Elsa was transferred to Zager, a liberated village twenty miles northwest of Asmara, to join the public administration unit. Elsa didn't know much about her new unit, only that being stationed in a liberated area meant that she'd be far from any action.

Before sunrise the next morning, she hopped on a truck with a unit of medics, and after a three-hour journey was given vague instructions to walk toward the escarpment in the distance and then through a narrow break in the range. As the sun grew hotter, she cleared the break and began her descent to Zager, cursing the village, even though there was something charming about its patchwork plots of farmland and homes built out of stone and mud that spiraled the abundant hills.

She stopped to sit on a rock and take in her new home. At the highest point stood the Orthodox church, painted a brilliant marine blue, and at the other end of the village was a smaller stone chapel built by Lutherans who had long left the area. As she scanned back toward the blue church, she spotted the back of a fighter walking along a path that wound down a hill. Elsa stood up immediately, recognizing how the woman stepped on the balls of her feet. Elsa rushed in her direction, watching as the woman made her way toward another fighter who was sitting under a low acacia tree. When she reached him, he jumped up and exaggeratedly brushed off the stone he was sitting on before bowing deeply. The young man was tall, all limbs and no torso.

Once he made sure she was seated comfortably, he eased himself onto the ground and threw his arms behind his head. He said something to make the woman laugh, and Elsa quickened her pace, ignoring the children who'd stopped their games to shout in her direction and the mothers who'd straightened their backs to peer at this new freedom fighter in pants and wild hair.

Twin turned around abruptly, as if she could sense that Elsa was approaching. She whooped when she saw her, her face beaming.

Elsa raced toward her, and when their bodies finally made contact, she held Twin tightly, relieved that their embrace felt the same. She pulled back and let Twin press her palms to her cheeks. There was so much information to take in. Only six months had passed, and yet Twin seemed more mature, her facial expression both serene and expectant, indicating that she could handle whatever did and would happen.

"You won't believe what I've been up to." Elsa took great care to avoid the eyes of the man, who now rested on his elbows watching them both. "I was stationed right outside of Asmara, and we cleaned the Derg out! Equipment, shoes, enough batteries to keep our radios chirping for the next year. I might not have fired this baby yet," she said, swinging her rifle over her shoulder, "but my time has been much rougher than this cute village you're playing house in."

Twin stuck her chin out good-naturedly but offered no retort.

"You know," Elsa continued, "we weren't far from where Black Friday happened. I'm sure you heard."

One month prior, an entire rebel battalion had spent two weeks hiding along the road from Asmara to Afabet, waiting to sabotage the Derg's supply line. But despite the rebels' solid intelligence, the convoy never materialized. On the Friday that had since been given the dark moniker, the elders from the closest village invited the rebels to join in their Saint's Day celebration. The fateful decision was made, and the majority of the battalion trekked up into the hills for a day off. As soon as they did, Ethiopian troops hurtled down the road, slaughtering the few fighters who had been left behind.

"A spy had to have tipped them off," Elsa said conspiratorially to Twin, as if that weren't obvious. The rebels heard the shots and raced back as soon as they could, but it was too late. Among those killed was a woman known as Gazelle, the first female guerrilla to be martyred. The men wailed as they buried her, gripping their heads in grief.

Elsa's recounting wasn't going quite as she expected. Twin didn't seem the least bit enthusiastic, and when Elsa finally stopped talking, waiting for something from her friend, all she said was, "I did hear about her death, yes."

"Oh, I get it," Elsa said with a playful nudge, too eager to heed the rebels' code: they accepted the inevitability of their deaths yet didn't divulge details of their comrades' martyrdom. "You're mad it wasn't you!"

The man finally stood up to join the conversation, his head nearly touching the branches of the tree. He threw a protective arm over Twin's shoulder.

"This is the twin you told me about." He looked down at Elsa from his great height. "She's ready for blood. But does she know this war has to be fought with more than guns?"

His direct gaze made Elsa feel uneasy, though she was happy to hear that Twin had talked about her.

"I know that the only way to drive the enemy out is to kill him." Elsa stood as straight as she could. "And the only way to kill him is to be prepared to die yourself."

"Did you come to die?" He widened his eyes in mock horror.

"And what about you?" he said to Twin, who smiled and shrugged knowingly, as if this was a routine they regularly put on, he the wise man and she the silent affirmer. His huge hands covered Twin's shoulders. Was she leaning into him?

"Why have we joined this struggle?" he asked, turning his attention back to Elsa. "Is it because we are bloodthirsty? Absolutely not. We have joined because we have a vision of what our country should be like. And while that vision might be defended by guns, it won't be won that way."

He released Twin and reached toward the tree, tearing off a small, thin branch, carefully removing the bone-colored thorns, and then clenching it between his teeth. Elsa watched as it dangled from his mouth.

"Only a change in consciousness can bring liberation," he said. "People have to mentally unshackle themselves from centuries of occupation and backwards traditions in order to cultivate a new and just society. We must first free the people, then the land."

"Introducing Comrade Efrem," Twin said with a wry smile.

He was beautiful. Once Elsa was sure she hated him, she could admit that. He wasn't cute though. He resembled those busts of Greek philosophers Elsa had studied in high school, with perfectly coiled curls and wise expressions, one of those people who was hard to imagine as a child.

"Careful, Efrem," Twin said. "My sister likes to fight."

"Oh, like you? Then how am I supposed to tell you two apart?" he asked, leaning in closer to inspect Elsa's face. "I see it now. One of you smiles and the other doesn't."

He tapped Elsa sweetly on the cheek. Would she just give him a smile, he seemed to be saying with those sad, ponderous eyes. She took a step back and tried to make her expression inscrutable, waiting for the heat on her face to subside.

A soldier had to respect her orders. Elsa took to her new assignment in Zager's public administration unit with revolutionary zeal. Her unit's goals were ambitious: teach the illiterate how to read, institute a serious political education program, establish democratic people's assemblies, and set up economic cooperatives.

Their most radical goal was land reform. Rich farmers would have to give landless farmers their fair share and, most controversially, unmarried women would be allowed to own land as well.

All of this couldn't happen overnight. As Tedros, Elsa's unit leader, repeated, they had to be like the people to lead the people. Their four-person team quietly integrated themselves into Zager, living and working together in a humble three-room cement house, proving that they could be trusted.

As graciously as the guerrillas had been welcomed, it was also impossible for them not to stand out. Elsa and Twin walking around in pants and Afros were as unbelievable as a donkey parading around in a dress. Tedros, an Addis-born lawyer with accented Tigrinya, was nearly as exotic. Efrem, however, who had been raised in Dekemhare, was a more familiar entity and clearly beloved. Watching him interact with the inhabitants of Zager, Elsa understood the true value of his gifts: his emotional intelligence, powers of persuasion, and ability to explain complicated ideas to any audience.

Elsa was also impressed by Twin. In the time they had been apart, Twin had transformed into a civic leader who had overseen the creation of political study groups and the village militia, a spirited group of civilian volunteers who at first chafed at being mobilized by a baby-faced eighteen-year-old girl but now saluted her when she walked by. Her next task, which Elsa was to help her with, was to organize residents into separate associations of men, women, and youth, which would elect representatives to the village's first people's assembly.

After a few months of visiting these women in their homes and listening to their problems, Twin and Elsa gathered over a hundred of them in the village meeting hall to explain their political program. Elsa felt confident; to an outsider, the village women might have looked beleaguered and impoverished, but she saw warriors.

The open-air hall was perched up on a hill, with wood columns supporting a wide and sturdy thatched roof. The villagers had constructed the space themselves under the guidance of the unit before Elsa had joined them. As the women settled on the freshly swept earth, Elsa welcomed them and launched into her remarks before Twin could speak.

"You are all victims of double oppression," she said with a booming voice she had never used before. "Not only have you been subjected to exploitative and capitalistic rule, you have also been subjected to a patriarchal culture that has suppressed you, forcing you to work as the property of your parents and then your husbands. Eritrea will never be free with half of our people still in chains. You, the nation's daughters, will fight, just as the sons are, for the right to finally call ourselves Eritreans."

The women were impassive, even to the bold flies that made homes of their faces, only moving to adjust the babies on their backs. Elsa spoke louder, looking past them out to the farmland and barefoot children chasing after sheep, to the twitching dry shrubs and snub-nosed mountains. Eritrea was transforming before her eyes, the plotted terraces lush, happy men and women with flushed cheeks and fat on their bellies, gourds filled with milk and butter, schools full of bright-eyed students and gleaming supplies, the scene replicated over miles and miles so that the whole nation was conscious and prosperous.

"I think this is the right time to go over Mao Zedong's strategy of a protracted people's war." Twin gave Elsa a look that said she didn't think it was, but Elsa continued on.

"In the first stage, the strategic defensive, a liberation army wages hit-and-run guerrilla warfare until popular support and military strength becomes developed enough for them to establish a secure base area. Then, in the strategic stalemate, the guerrilla units merge into a broader army that can engage in fixed-position warfare to defend the base against the enemy.

Finally, in the strategic offensive, the phase we are in now, the liberation forces encircle cities and towns and liberate them one by one. This strategy will deliver us to victory. Do you hear that?" Elsa raised her hand up to her ear. "Shout if you are ready to fight until Eritrea is finally free!"

A pleasant breeze rippled through the hall. The babies, for the first time, were all quiet, their heads lolling on their mothers' backs. In the silence that shouldn't have been, Twin cleared her throat, the sound bringing Elsa back to Earth, to a hundred pairs of eyes regarding her with polite skepticism.

"Thank you, comrade." Twin rested her hand on Elsa's shoulder and stepped forward. "We've been tackling some of these issues in our study groups. But we gathered you all today to tell you about our new women's association and what it'll be offering. Based on what we've heard from you, we'll start with building a mill that will spare you all those hours grinding grains by hand. How does that sound?"

There was a murmur of assent, and the women became more animated. Twin went on to explain that once the mill was operational, they'd offer literacy classes. The women asked for more information and agreed to join. Then they rearranged their scarves and babies and went back to their homes.

At their team meeting that night, the public administration unit gathered in the living room of the home they shared, lit by a single lamp. Twin reported that their meeting was a success.

"Any items of criticism either about yourself or your comrade?" Tedros asked, keeping with the EPLF's meeting protocol.

"I have some constructive criticism," Twin said gently. "Twin was passionate in her remarks, but I'd like to remind her of our training to meet people where they are. Speaking in plain language as opposed to lecturing on more sophisticated concepts is how we can make sure that we are understood and also understand our audience."

"Anything else?" Tedros asked.

"Smile. It helps to smile when giving presentations," Twin said, offering one to Elsa.

"Do you have a response?"

"No," Elsa said, watching the shadows flicker on her comrades' faces. "I accept this criticism and will work to improve."

But word of Elsa's intensity had spread. In their next team meeting, Efrem raised his hand to ask when Elsa would be organizing the donkeys into a class-based association, according to the 1930 Chinese Communist model. It was a joke, of course, but when he gave her a playful nudge after the meeting, she shrugged him off and started a conversation with Tedros.

It was hard to avoid him—Zager wasn't Addis. If they weren't working on something together, he was always within reach, trudging up and down the hills to help farmers with their fields, making up new songs to entertain the women who washed their laundry in the stream behind the rebels' house.

They did manage to find common ground in the middle of the night. Overall, Elsa slept better on the woven cot she shared with Twin than on the rocky earth in Ri'see Adi. But on some nights, sleep evaded her, and she would shuffle to the courtyard to feel the night's breeze. The first night she did, she found Efrem there, slung over a rickety wooden chair that barely contained his lanky frame. Her instinct was to return to bed, but there was something in the way that he tilted his head, motioning that she join him, that compelled her to stay. She perched in the chair next to him and watched the lights in Asmara glimmer over the low courtyard wall. On the nights Elsa found him there, they never spoke, their private silence lulling her into an easy peace. But in the light of day, among their comrades and constituents, she couldn't help but feel confrontational toward him.

Their longest-running debate was about the rumor that marriage would soon be allowed among the rebels. In February 1977, a year and a half since Elsa was stationed in Zager, and the night before Tedros set off to attend the EPLF's first Organizational Congress in Nakfa, Elsa shared her outrage, once again.

"We are outnumbered six to one against the greatest modern army in Africa. We can't afford to have the women tucked away nursing babies. Women need to fight. Sex and childbirth can wait until after we win the war."

"It's been years, Elsa," Efrem said wearily. "This war started in 1961. Is it that impossible for you to understand how freedom fighters, who are still human beings, after all, could be dedicated to the war and still get married? Are you that unfeeling?"

Tedros returned a week later with news that marriage was finally permitted. Coed relations were still restricted, but if a man and woman wanted to be together, in any way, they had to tell their unit leader and formally request permission to get married.

"Are you happy now?" Elsa confronted Efrem as if he had introduced the resolution himself. "It's better for us to get out of the way and get married than to fight for our independence, right?"

"Was I at the meeting?" He threw up his hands. "Did I pass the resolution? Go yell at Tedros!"

"Don't yell at me," Tedros said, raising a finger. "I'm just reporting what happened."

"Did I say it was your fault?" Elsa said to Efrem. He made a face at Twin, who tousled his hair in response.

"Actually, it is your fault!" Elsa heard her voice get shrill. "You're thinking with the wrong head. If us women were the only ones fighting, Eritrea would be free by now!"

Later that evening, Elsa found Twin in the bedroom they shared, writing her weekly report under the dim light of the lamp. Elsa watched her for a bit. Two years had passed since they first met, but she still wasn't used to seeing herself. Villagers got them confused all the time, wondering why Elsa couldn't remember something they had actually told Twin. One had even asked Elsa if she was the mean one or the nice one. It must be nice to put people at ease, Elsa thought, to always say and do the right thing.

"Why didn't you back me up earlier?" Elsa said quietly.

Twin looked up in surprise and then laughed. "When you and Efrem get started, it's impossible to get a word in. And good evening to you too." She returned to her report.

"I'm serious, Twin. Do you support this?"

"It's already done, Elsa. The congress has ruled on it."

"Do you want to get married? Is that why you didn't say anything?"

Twin hesitated before putting her pen down. "I understand why marriage and relationships were banned at first, and I also understand why they overturned that ban now. This war is going on for longer than anyone thought it would, and people naturally want to have partners and families, so if they do, why not let—"

"I'm asking you about you. Do *you* want to get married?" Elsa didn't want a lecture. She wanted to know what was in her best friend's heart. That was easier than sharing what was in hers.

"Elsa," Twin started to say, but then trailed off.

"Do you want to get married to Efrem?" Elsa asked. "Has he put these ideas in your head? All you used to talk about in training was how you couldn't wait to have the glory of being martyred. I'm concerned, you know."

"You're concerned? That's funny because I'm concerned, too, Elsa. I'm concerned that you assumed Efrem convinced *me* of something. I'm concerned that you think I'm different now because of him. You can't even imagine that maybe it's the other way around, that I'm responsible for the thoughts in his head, that I've changed since training, and that he's trying to keep up with me," she said, pounding her chest.

Elsa felt her face flush and held her tongue.

"When you're ready to talk about what's actually bothering you, let me know," Twin said. "But until then, my sister, don't bring this up again."

23

ZEWDI'S FIRST AND LAST TRIP TO L.A. WAS WITH THE PRINCESS over fifteen years ago. Up until then, they usually traveled to Europe for holidays. While the United States had cheaper shopping, its sheer newness, measured not in centuries but in decades, was too reminiscent of Saudi for the princess's taste. Europe, in contrast, represented the ideal. Real history was everywhere, the cities dense and walkable, stores small and unique, and the nearly hostile indifference to tourists proof of a superior consciousness. But in the summer of '76, the princess's brothers and their families occupied everywhere on her short list: Costa de Azul, Amalfi, and Majorca. Europe wasn't big enough for all of them—the princess called her sisters-in-law the killer whales. So she and Zewdi spent the season in Malibu.

This time, California didn't feel like a consolation prize. The plane's descent into L.A. was cinematic, with a triumphant score playing only in Zewdi's head. Waiting for her at the baggage claim stood Dr. Asgedom Beyene, as alert and professional as a black-capped driver.

They greeted each other warmly, with kisses on each cheek. Zewdi couldn't help but wonder how they appeared to others. Siblings, possibly, or family members of some kind. He took her luggage and, with his other hand lightly on her back, directed her to the exit. She relaxed when he dropped his hand and followed his lead through the crowds in LAX.

After helping her into his black Volvo, he reappeared in the driver's seat holding cream hydrangeas sheathed in tissue wrap.

"From my garden," he said.

Zewdi held them up to her nose. They smelled like nothing, but a man had never given her flowers before.

"These are beautiful. This was so sweet of you, Asgedom."

"It's a thank-you for coming all this way. Wait, there is something else."

He thrust toward her to reach around his seat, grasping for something on the floor. Zewdi drew back to avoid his face. He straightened up, holding up an expensive-looking crystal vase.

"So they won't die. You can put them in water at the hotel."

He placed the vase back on the floor and the flowers on the middle seat behind her. What a thoughtful man he was. Zewdi looked down at her now-empty hands and set them primly on her lap. She felt like a teenage girl.

"This is a lovely car," she said. His Volvo seemed brand-new and in pristine condition, but she had expected that he'd have a Mercedes or some other luxury car.

"The 850 is Volvo's safest car to date and superior to any other car on the market. I flew to Gothenburg to choose it." He looked over at her briefly as he reversed out of their parking spot. "It seems a bit ridiculous, I know, going all the way to Sweden, but it was actually cheaper to purchase it directly from the factory. The dealer suggested it."

Zewdi was impressed, but if she were going to fly to Europe to buy a car, it would only be for a Mercedes or BMW.

Asgedom had something to say about everything: the traffic, the condition of the 405, the demise of a city councilman. He explained the geography of the city, pointing out neighborhoods and orienting them by their cardinal directions. They were headed north to what was known as South Central L.A., and farther northeast, in Sierra Madre, was where last month's earthquake had struck. Zewdi couldn't keep up, the sprawl of the city illegible in her mind. She really just wanted him to be quiet for a bit, raise the volume on the faint classical music playing so they could settle into a comfortable silence.

From La Cienega Boulevard, they ascended into a charming neighborhood with spacious homes tucked into the hills. He stopped in front of one with a terra-cotta roof flanked by two palm trees and well-maintained flowering bushes. Asgedom confirmed that the house was his and accepted her praise with the right combination of humility and pride. Zewdi didn't say much else, because she wasn't sure if she would or even should be invited into his home. This whole trip was already so suggestive. What exactly were they supposed to do if he invited her in? Thankfully, he didn't and continued to drive, explaining that they were now heading west to where she'd be staying in Santa Monica.

Villa Lucia, the hotel he'd booked for her, resembled a wealthy Spanish landowner's estate. It took up half a block, and its inner courtyard echoed with the gentle sound of water trickling in a tiled fountain. Asgedom checked her in and suggested that she relax before he returned to pick her up for lunch.

"Thank you for this." She gestured around her. "All of this is so—"

"You're not going to spend the whole weekend saying thank you, are you? It's my pleasure, really." He smiled and bowed his head.

Zewdi beamed at him, as if he were her son who had done something to make her proud. He ushered her and the bellhop to the elevator and waved goodbye. The bellhop let her into the room and refused the five-dollar bill that she offered him. Apparently, Asgedom had already given him a tip. How had she missed that?

The room decor was simple but elegant, a rustic wood bed frame, sprigs of lavender in a jar on the bathroom countertop, miniature bars of soap bundled with twine, the kind of country chic the princess never appreciated. She ran the water in the shower and disrobed, avoiding her naked body in the mirror. It wasn't the luxury that awed her, she thought as she lathered herself. She had seen much more extravagant accommodations. But her presence in those spaces had been incidental, years of her life in which anyone else could have stood in her place. The difference was that all this had been done just for her.

She hung up as many of her clothes as she could and called for more hangers—packing light had been impossible. After careful deliberation, she chose to wear her second-best outfit for the rest of the day, a flowing, lime-colored linen tunic with a long matching skirt.

Asgedom called to say that he'd returned, and when they reunited in the lobby, she presented him with two loaves of hambasha.

"These are for you," she said. "I made them right before I came."

Zewdi knew she was a fantastic gift-giver, and she knew it was because she listened to people, actually paid attention to what they wanted. Her generosity wasn't regulated by the holiday calendar. If someone complained about cold weather, she bought them thicker gloves. If a guest gushed over her tea set, she gifted them the identical kind. Zewdi certainly had an appreciation for frivolous and expensive things—thin scarves, decorative plates, candle holders—but her real skill was in sourcing practical goods that made everyday life better, like garlic presses and heating pads. She often bought extras (she purchased so many olive oil and vinegar cruets from an infomercial that they sent her three more for free) and kept them boxed in her closet, all the easier to present to someone in need.

She struggled, however, with what to give Asgedom. A proper home-cooked meal—a feast, really—would have been ideal. In her estimation, there was no greater gift a woman could give anyone (the equivalent the other way around was gold). But for logistical reasons, she obviously couldn't cook for him. The practicality of a shirt and necktie seemed more appropriate for intimates. She did briefly consider engraving a pen or business-card holder with his name. She was certain that she had introduced the entire Eritrean community to the Things Engraved store at Pentagon City Fashion Centre, as well as the kiosk that sold mugs and plates personalized with photos and names. But nothing was more personal than something she made with her own hands, and so the bread it was.

"Oh my . . . you shouldn't have, really," Asgedom said.

He held the round, flat loaves with both hands and looked at them almost bemusedly.

"I can't think of the last time I had hambasha. Thank you."

Why hadn't he had hambasha recently? Did he not have relatives around? Wasn't he invited to people's homes? Surely his ex-wife must have baked it often. He'd been divorced for years, though, so why, Zewdi chided herself, would she still be making it for him? The diet, it's his strange diet! Zewdi almost clapped her hands. Who in this world didn't eat bread?

"Do you not eat bread?" she asked.

Asgedom looked surprised and then somewhat embarrassed. "Well, it's for my health. You see—"

"Oh, dear. Are you ill? Do you have a condition?"

"No, no, no. You see, I try not to eat anything overprocessed, and that includes white bread, anything made with white flour, really. But this was so thoughtful of you. My kids will love it."

Zewdi blinked. She brought her arms in and held her hands together under her bust as Queen Elizabeth often did at receptions.

"And I'll try it . . . of course," he said, clutching the hambasha to his chest. "I'll definitely have some."

"Wonderful! Shall we head out?"

"Yes, I thought it would be nice for us to walk to lunch. The restaurant isn't too far away."

Zewdi waited while Asgedom put the hambasha in his car, and together they walked down the Third Street Promenade, near her hotel. She could already feel her new sandals pinch, but she smiled through it, taking in the happy Californians who filled the outdoor mall. The sun was bright and warm and, without the humidity of D.C., a delight on her skin. She window-shopped, ignoring Asgedom as he pointed out things that were obvious: a fine art gallery, used book shop, specialty cookware. Lunch was at an upscale Mexican restaurant within sight of the hotel.

Asgedom went over the menu, suggesting dishes she might like, even though she already knew she wanted steak fajitas with all the fixings. She predicted that he would order one of the fish options without the rice. When the waiter came, Asgedom proved her right. She lost her nerve, ordering the red snapper as well. How would she enjoy food with this man?

When they finished their meal, Asgedom said, "I hope you saved some space for dessert." He folded the napkin that was on his lap and set it on the table. "There's a place nearby I think you'll like."

He ushered her out of the restaurant, and after a few blocks, just as Zewdi's feet started to hurt again, he stopped at a storefront and pointed to the sign.

"La Dolce Vita," he said with a smile.

There were two round tables on either side of the door and, inside the shop, a gleaming fortress of gelato in frosted steel tubs. A teenage couple rose from one of the outdoor tables and walked away holding hands. Zewdi raced to it and motioned for Asgedom to sit down.

"You wait here, and I'll get the gelato!" she said.

Asgedom refused, and they began to participate in the oldest of Eritrean pastimes: fighting over who'll pay the bill. Asgedom grabbed her purse, she grabbed his hand, he grabbed her forearm, until she finally threatened to not eat a single thing if he paid—all while the family at the other table quieted with concern. Asgedom finally relented and told her his order. Once inside, Zewdi gave herself permission to get what she wanted, a scoop each of hazelnut and biscotti, and doubled his single-scoop order of mango sorbetto.

From the window, she could see Asgedom check the table's stability, extract some napkins from the canister on the table, fold and wedge them between one of the table legs and the ground, check the stability, extract more napkins, and repeat the process.

"Ecco," she said, setting the gelato before him.

"Ecco," he repeated, and turned his chair to better face the street. "When I was in grad school in Boulder, there was this guy who claimed to be *puro asmarino,* always talking about *certo* this, *allora* that. One day, I pointed him out to this Italian graduate student, a very pretty woman actually, and told her that he was homesick and desperate to find someone to speak Italian with. She tried to talk to him, but he could barely carry a conversation. So she reported back to me with a 'niente.' I've called him Niente since."

He laughed at the memory and looked over at Zewdi. She laughed politely in response and took another minuscule bite of her gelato.

"It's just a funny story," he said.

Zewdi shifted the conversation to their plans for the rest of the day. It was already three thirty, and Asgedom had made dinner reservations for seven in Malibu. Instead of more walking, he thankfully suggested that Zewdi relax back at the hotel until he returned to pick her up. Zewdi tried her best to take a nap, but she was still feeling anxious. She called her apartment to make sure that Lydia was there selling the injera she'd baked before her departure. Lydia reported that she had sold out of everything at noon, which was a record. Zewdi then reorganized her clothes in the closet, a habit from her days of traveling with the princess. She would usually create different outfits from the princess's abundant selection and present options with jewelry and shoe pairings. However, the task didn't take nearly as much time with her own more modest wardrobe.

On the drive to Malibu, both she and Asgedom were quiet, the classical music the only sound in the car. Asgedom didn't even once clear his throat. She wondered if he were running out of things to say. She felt like she was. At the restaurant, they were greeted by an ecstatic hostess.

"You must be the Ashers. Happy anniversary!" she cheered.

"No, we're not," Asgedom said. "Our reservation is under the name Beyene."

The hostess laid her hand on her chest and apologized just as exuberantly.

"I'm sooo sorry. They booked for the same time as you . . . thirty years of marriage! Can you believe that? And you look sooo lovely, so I assumed it was a special occasion."

That comment seemed to be for Zewdi; she was now wearing her best outfit, a white chiffon dress patterned with teal flowers. They followed the hostess to a table on the far end of the huge terrace, next to a table that had a RESERVED sign on it.

"Well, you two seem like you're on the way to thirty! I hope you come back and celebrate with us then. Enjoy your dinner!"

The Ashers, tan and fit, soon appeared. Mr. Asher wore a polo shirt with a pink sweater draped around his shoulders, and Mrs. Asher wore a coral dress that left much of her neck and arms exposed. Asgedom busied himself with reviewing the wine list while Zewdi watched Mr. Asher pull the chair out for his wife and then kiss her neck. A flutter of embarrassment ran though Zewdi as she tried to imagine Asgedom doing such a thing, even in a private setting.

It was back to more practical matters. The wine was ordered—two glasses of Chardonnay—and then their dinner—fish, fish,

fish. For Saturday's activities, Asgedom thought Zewdi might like to get on one of those double-decker tour buses; they could see all the sights and get off wherever she might like to explore a bit more, the Chinese Theater, celebrity homes, maybe even Universal Studios. They could also hike Runyon or take a day trip to San Bernardino. Zewdi nodded at all the options, realizing that she finally had to alert Asgedom to one important item on her agenda: she had to visit family.

Before her trip, she wasn't sure how to explain to Elsa why she was visiting California, so Samrawit, her distant cousin on her mother's side, became a convenient excuse. She considered not actually visiting her cousin, but that kind of deceit was always uncovered. Elsa and this cousin, who weren't even related themselves, would somehow cross paths, and the truth that Zewdi never saw her would be revealed.

However, there was a silver lining to this interruption to their itinerary. When Zewdi accepted Asgedom's invitation, she worried about how they were going to spend so much time with each other. Four days and three nights with a man she barely knew was a situation she wasn't prepared for. So why not orchestrate a little escape plan? A way to get some relief from obsessing over what Asgedom might expect of a woman who had never given a man anything at all. Zewdi called Samrawit, who rejoiced in the auspicious timing, as it was their family's Saint's Day, and demanded that Zewdi stop by on Saturday.

Zewdi offered Asgedom the edited version: she had a cousin who would be terribly offended if she didn't call on her. He said that he understood and seemed like he meant it. Asgedom faced the sunset with a content expression, while Zewdi confronted her racing thoughts. Did Asgedom think ill of her for making other plans? He'd paid for her entire trip, and here she was using it for personal ends.

"You don't see sunsets like that in D.C. I really recommend

you wake up to catch the sunrise too. Is your room eastward-facing?" he asked. "When you look out of your balcony, do you see the bank in front of you or the parking lot? Because if you see the bank then you are facing east. But if you see the parking lot, you can still see it, but you'll have to—"

"I don't have to meet my cousin tomorrow," Zewdi interrupted.

"What? You should if you want to."

"But I don't have to. I just felt bad because I came all this way and I didn't want her to find out, you know? L.A. is big, and there aren't even that many of us here, but I have that kind of luck. I can never get away with anything. Not that I try to, but you know what I mean. It's the people who feel guilty who get caught. My mother used to say that all the time." Zewdi clutched her fork and then put it down.

"Zewdi, I understand . . . I do. It would have been nice to know earlier, only in terms of preparing the itinerary, but it's not that serious. Really."

Zewdi nodded and smiled. She took another bite of her sea bass and pledged that once she left California, she wouldn't consume another bite of fish until 1992.

24

LYDIA SAT FACING THE RECEPTIONIST AT THE EPLF OFFICE, CLUTCHing her book bag to her chest. Although she had never met Osman, she thought he would be more cooperative if she showed up to his office instead of calling him on the phone. She had needed Berekhet to accompany her into D.C. for her secret investigative mission, which he was all too eager to do, the only condition being that they visit the National Air and Space Museum afterward.

Berekhet paced around the reception area, which was only slightly larger than their own living room and looked as if it was used as such before the row home was converted for its revolutionary purposes. After thumbing through the journals and magazines on display, he reclaimed his seat next to Lydia and pulled out a city map from his pocket that he had diligently marked up.

Lydia held her breath as she heard someone bounding down the stairs, then jolted to her feet as Osman came toward them with a warm smile.

"How can I help you?" he asked Berekhet.

Berekhet put his arm around Lydia and gave her a squeeze.

"She's the one who wants to speak to you," he said. "She's the daughter of Elsa Haddish, the fighter."

Osman tilted his head and raised his brows. Lydia wasn't sure if it was because she looked nothing like her mother or because she showed up unannounced.

"Elsa's daughter? Let me say hello to you properly then." He pulled Lydia in for a kiss. "What's your name?"

"Lydia."

"Lydia," he repeated, nodding. "Why don't we all go upstairs to my office so we can talk properly."

They followed him up a narrow staircase to an office with bay windows that faced the street. He motioned for them to sit and closed the door before taking a seat behind his L-shaped desk. Lydia felt like she had been called to the principal's office.

Berekhet, in his delicate, meandering Tigrinya, started things off, explaining that Lydia was just trying to learn more about her family's experience during the war and more specifically about her father. As he spoke, Lydia stared at a small television with a built-in VHS player at the far edge of the shorter side of the L. The screen was paused on a grainy image she recognized of a young boy with gruesome burns on his torso and bandaged limbs.

"Is this for school?" Osman said, responding to Berekhet. "I know it's the summer, but some youngsters like to do research on the war for class projects. I can take you to Freweini, upstairs, who has all sorts of photographs and articles."

Osman turned back to the television, noticing what had captured Lydia's attention. "Do you know what that is?" he asked.

Lydia had seen the footage around Thanksgiving last year. Everyone had gathered at Mama Zewdi's to watch the rebel-made video about the brutal fight to liberate Massawa. She hadn't been able to understand everything that was documented, but she remembered what happened to that child.

"That's from the napalm attack in Massawa," she replied.

"Very good." Osman tapped his pen approvingly on a stack of well-worn legal pads on his desk. "The Derg dropped napalm supplied by the Soviets over civilian neighborhoods. Before the battle, we had been fighting the U.S.-backed Ethiopian Army of Emperor Haile Selassie. That fight was our first against the new Soviet-built forces of the Derg. Did you know that?"

Lydia shook her head that she didn't. Osman had a pleasant

manner of speaking; his style made her feel as if they were having a conversation instead of a one-sided lecture.

"In December 1977, before you were born, we were poised to capture Massawa. The Ethiopian government forces only had control of the naval base and a few strategic port facilities. The base was separated from the mainland by about five hundred yards of shallow salt flats—that's about a quarter mile, not far at all." Osman raised his hands to face each other, demonstrating the short distance. "But we failed to close the gap. Why?" Osman raised his very long index finger in the air. Lydia finally realized that he resembled Arsenio Hall, with those slender digits and elongated face.

"Because the Soviets had arrived. For reasons that we don't need to get into now, the Soviet Union decided to send massive amounts of weapons and technical assistance to Ethiopia. We're talking T-54 tanks, BM-21 rocket launchers, and squadrons of MiG-21 jet fighters. And get this—the Ethiopians were still getting trained on how to use them. In December, we're talking days before Western Christmas, sixty Ethiopian pilots were on some base near the Black Sea trying to figure out where the 'shoot' button was. Back in Massawa, Soviets took their places and were operating the rocket launchers and long-rage artillery themselves. They had South Yemeni pilots flying the jets. Berekhet, did you know that?" He paused and leaned forward for Berekhet's response.

"I did." Berekhet was sitting on the edge of his chair.

"Of course you did. The Soviets were also kind enough to equip the Ethiopians with napalm, and on Christmas Eve, the city was in flames. Hell on Earth. This image you see here"—he gestured over his shoulder at the picture of the badly burned child—"doesn't even capture how bad it was. We failed to liberate Massawa . . . and over the next year, this supercharged Ethiopian Army unleashed itself on us throughout the entire country.

It was as if the war had started all over again. We retreated back up into the Sahel Mountains, giving up all the territory we lost so many brave souls to take. Your mother can tell you all about this."

Lydia considered that timeline. Elsa had told her that she left for Khartoum the following year when Lydia was about three months old, which would have been June. Lydia wondered if her decision had anything to do with this retreat Osman was describing.

"My apologies." Osman gave a sheepish smile that made his hooded eyes crinkle. "Once I start, I have a hard time stopping. I doubt you came for this lecture. Please tell me what it is you're looking for."

"No, not at all," Berekhet assured him. "We are both lovers of knowledge, especially this one." He smiled at Lydia reassuringly.

"I'm not here for a project or anything," Lydia said, scooting closer to the edge of her seat. "I'm here . . . for me. I don't know that much about my father. His name was Efrem Negash. He was a guerrilla fighter and he met my mother in the field . . . they were in the same unit. He was killed, and then my mother left. That's about all I know."

"Did you tell your mother you were coming here today?"

Lydia shook her head. Osman nodded as if he understood.

"Okay. What do you want to know?" he asked.

An obvious question that Lydia realized she didn't have a simple answer for. When she was feeling really dark, like when she watched war footage sent from back home, she wanted to know how her father died, if he knew his death was coming, and if he felt any pain when it happened. Most of the time she just wanted to know what he was like, if he was a bit reserved like her and her mother, or if he was the life of the party like Mama Zewdi. She wanted to know why he decided to leave home and join the war, if that had been a hard decision for him, and if he ever thought about going back to his family. She wanted to know what they shared in common besides their looks. Did he also like to read and watch people from afar?

Lydia reached into her backpack and pulled out the photo.

"That's my father," she said, handing the image over to Osman. "I guess I wanted to know if you recognized him . . . and if you could tell me something about him or how he died."

Osman studied the picture carefully, the corner of his mouth turning up slightly. "I did meet your father, Lydia. We didn't spend much time together, but I definitely recognize him. This photo was probably taken in Zager, where your mother, your father, and the other woman in this photo were stationed. They were in the public administration unit. Do you know what that is?"

Lydia shook her head no.

"That unit worked with civilians in the liberated areas, which were the areas that the rebels freed from Ethiopian rule. They helped to educate the residents and organize them to govern themselves. I went there for just a few days in 1976, but your mother wasn't there. I did meet your father and this other woman, who everyone called 'Twin.' Now I understand why—it was because she looks just like your mother."

"Do you remember what my father was like?" Lydia asked.

"He seemed friendly, well liked," he said, still smiling down at the picture. "You know how some people just put you in a good mood? They don't even have to say anything . . . you just look at them and start smiling. He had that effect on people. And he was great with kids. All the children in the village loved playing with him."

Lydia smiled as she fought back the tears that threatened to fill her eyes. "Do you know how he died?" she asked.

"I don't, I'm sorry. I really wish I could tell you more about him, but we didn't spend that much time together. But I can tell you for certain that the best of us died. There's not a day that goes by when those of us among the living think otherwise." Osman set the picture down and looked at her with his sad, deep-set eyes. "How old are you?"

"Thirteen."

"Hmm, okay." He stretched so far back in his chair that Lydia was afraid he'd topple over. "Imagine that you're sixteen or seventeen years old, or even a little bit older, like Berekhet here, and you're living a normal life. Slowly though, things start to change. You see more of a military presence, people getting arrested and killed, dead bodies in the streets. You aren't allowed to speak your own language in school, you can't ask questions about why this is all happening, and you're not sure who to trust. Over time, your friends leave to join the rebels who are fighting against the oppression and violence. You decide to leave too. But you can't say goodbye to your parents or have a farewell party because that will endanger them . . . you just have to leave everything you know and commit yourself to this cause. The only way to survive is to bury your old self, to forget that you ever had parents, siblings, and a warm house. You become someone else with a new family and new life, but you can't even get too attached to that life because you have to be prepared to die."

Osman looked down at the photo again and handed it back to Lydia.

"It was even harder for your mother," he said gently. "She had to leave both of her families, the one she was born to and the one she made."

Lydia looked down at her feet, trying to feel the sympathy for her mother that she knew Osman was hoping to generate. She looked over at Berekhet, who nodded at her.

"Thank you so much for talking to me. We don't want to take any more of your time," she said, standing up.

"Of course, of course." Osman looked like he wanted to say more but stood up as well and led them back down the stairs and to the front door. As they said goodbye, Lydia thought of something else.

"What about her friend? Do you remember anything about her?"

"I do. She's impossible to forget. A natural leader, very sharp, quiet but in control. People seemed to be in awe of her."

"Where is she now?"

Osman cleared his throat. This was the point where adults lied—Lydia could always sense it.

"I don't know," he said. "She could still be in that unit, she could have been transferred elsewhere, or she could be dead. We won't know until the official reports are released."

"So my mom doesn't know what happened to her?"

Osman nodded. That seemed true.

"What was her name?"

Osman hesitated before answering. "Lydia. Her name was Lydia."

Lydia and Berekhet immediately locked eyes before she turned back to Osman. He looked back at her steadily, giving nothing away. But Lydia felt the knot within her loosen, not by much, but enough to let a little hope in.

"One step forward," Berekhet said as he led her to Seventh Street to the #70 bus that would deliver them to the National Museum of Air and Space. She barely registered Berekhet's lecture about the Parisian design of D.C., how the Capitol in the distance marked north from south, east from west, and about the young Black architect, a son of slaves and protégé of L'Enfant, who surveyed the city.

"I shouldn't have had to do that," she said, finally finding her voice at the entrance to the museum on Independence Avenue.

"Do what?"

"I shouldn't have to go to a stranger's office to find out that my father was a great guy who everyone liked and that I was named after an amazing woman who everyone respected. It's not fair. My mother could just open her mouth and start talking."

"Cut her some slack, Lydia."

"Why?" Lydia was blocking one of the entryways, and Berekhet had to pull her inside the hangar-like hall. "Why should I? I hate her!"

"You don't hate her," Berekhet said.

"*You* can't tell me what to feel. And whose side are you on anyway?"

"Look," Berekhet said with a shrug, "your mom and I might not agree on some things, but I still have a lot of respect for her. My father isn't an easy man, and he never forgave her for running away to join the war . . . you didn't know that?" he said in response to Lydia's look of surprise.

Lydia always knew that Elsa and Dr. Alazar weren't close. Elsa didn't call him or send thick socks and cases of Nivea lotion like Mama Zewdi did to her own relatives. But her mom didn't have much of a relationship with anyone in their family.

"My father had a lot of hopes for her," Berekhet continued. "Apparently, she was an academic superstar, top of the class every year. And he loved that an Eritrean had the number one spot. 'Let them look up at us,' he used to say. Obnoxious, but he was that kind of guy. When she left, he felt that she squandered her opportunity. But I always admired her . . . she was like the bravest person I didn't actually know. We might not understand each other, but I still respect that she had the guts to defy everyone's expectations and put her life on the line."

Lydia shook her head slowly as Berekhet guided her to an unstable-looking contraption with broad white gliders and a formally dressed mannequin lying prone at its center.

"Look, Lidu," Berekhet said with wonder in his eyes. "This is the Wright brothers' 1903 Flyer."

Lydia rolled her eyes and gave her back to it, leaning her arms on the railing.

"No, no, no." Berekhet gently turned her back around. "You don't want to be like one of those people in"—he paused to read the placard—"in Kitty Hawk who told these visionaries that they were crazy and that their so-called plane would never fly, or their wives who told them to stop fooling around and come inside for dinner. You have to admire people like this, Lidu, and not begrudge them if their dreams make their personal lives a little complicated."

"I don't care about this plane," Lydia said softly. "I don't care about the war and politics. I'm talking about my family, Berekhet." She gripped the rail. "Every time I try to talk about this, you all tell me about things that I don't really care about."

"Lydia, you are an American coming of age in the end of the twentieth century. Your life is and will always be a straight line. That's why you can say you don't care about these things. 'War and politics,'" he said with finger quotes, his new favorite gesture, "will never affect the choices you have to make."

"Oh, yeah? You're the son of a doctor. What has politics ever done to you?"

Berekhet led her up to the second floor as he tried to explain. Class was a funny thing in Ethiopia. Dr. Alazar wasn't loaded, but he had stature, indoor plumbing, and electricity, which was all it took to be middle class. Add a fancy car and a medical degree, pasta served a few times a week, and their star shone a bit brighter. The true elites, however, were feudal landowners and the royal family, cliques that Berekhet's father could lay no claim to. Those people summered abroad and sent their children to the best private schools in the city, things far out of Dr. Alazar's reach, even if he hadn't been financially responsible for all the nieces and nephews who showed up at his doorstep. But Berekhet was a smart kid and had won one of the few scholarships to attend the International Community School, Ethiopia's most prestigious school.

"Distance isn't just geographical, Lidu," Berekhet said to the display of Neil Armstrong's Apollo spacesuit. "I went to a different universe just by changing schools. Same city, same home, but I was officially gone."

Lydia eyed her reflection in the glass case, unhappy with what she saw. She immediately straightened her spine and sucked in her stomach. She could see a young couple behind her, probably Berekhet's age. The girl arched her back and leaned over to read a placard, and her boyfriend snaked his arm behind her torso to pull her closer. Lydia tried to arch in the same way, leaning toward Berekhet and studying the case to see how she appeared.

"Look!" Berekhet exclaimed, oblivious. "This is where the astronauts who landed on the moon lived and slept." He dragged her to a hunk of rusted metal that was shaped like an upside-down cupcake liner.

"The International Community School," he went on. "Half of my classmates were the children of diplomats, and the Ethiopian half seemed just as foreign."

A history teacher from Vancouver had taken Berekhet under his wing, introducing him to ideas and books and music that brought the rest of the world much closer. For the first time, Berekhet became curious about leaving Ethiopia. Attending Addis Ababa University was always assumed, as was the expectation that he'd become a doctor like his father, a cloud in the distance that would one day be right over his head. But he took the Test of English as a Foreign Language, an exam required of non-native-speaking applicants by American universities, and started to explore how he might go abroad.

Then came his senior year of high school. In December, just a year and a half ago, his graduating class had finished their coursework and taken the college entrance exam. The spring semester was more relaxed, and in February, Berekhet and his classmates boarded buses for a nine-hour drive north to Bahr Dar on the shores of Lake Tana, where they would shadow students at the Polytechnical Institute and hang out on the lake.

"But 'history,'" he said with the quotes again, "interrupted."

While the EPLF guerrillas were waging war in Eritrea, Ethiopian rebels had also been mobilizing against the brutality of the Derg. From his dorm-room window on the institute's campus where they were being housed, he watched thousands of well-equipped government soldiers retreat as a mass of shabby Ethiopian guerrilla fighters overran the town. The whole thing happened in less time than it took for him and his classmates to get to Bahr Dar, and he didn't hear a single shot. Everything seemed fine after the Ethiopian Army retreated, and so the next day, he was minding his business, sitting outside under a tree.

"Lydia, have you ever just sat under a tree?" Berekhet asked, interrupting his story.

They had exited the museum and were at that moment sitting on a bench under a tree. Lydia tapped his shoulder and pointed upward. "What do you think that is?"

"No, no, that's not what I mean," he said, laughing. "We are sitting on a bench under a tree, but what I'm asking is have you ever sat on the ground under a tree?"

Of course she had, she wanted to say. But she couldn't be sure if her vague memories of doing so were just lifted from the books she'd read and movies she'd seen. Berekhet grabbed her hand and walked her to a fuller tree with low-spreading limbs that was unencumbered by a bench. He lowered himself, rested his back against the trunk, and motioned for Lydia to do the same.

"Imagine you are sitting just like this in the late afternoon. It's cooler than it is now and there's a light breeze. There's a lake . . . you are too far to see it, but you can smell it. You hear a mechanical type of buzzing and you are trying to figure out where it's coming from . . . so you look up." He tapped Lydia's shoulder and pointed up at the cloudless sky. "In the distance, you see the shine of metal. Faster than you can process, the metal becomes planes that are getting closer and louder. And then BOOM!" He clapped his hands. "The planes, the same Soviet fighter jets Osman just told us about, drop bombs not even ten kilometers from where you are. What do you do?" he asked with bugged-out eyes. "You run! You run harder and faster than you ever have in your life."

Lydia looked at the crowds on the Mall, following the movements of a flock of people wearing matching T-shirts that said JACKSON FAMILY REUNION. She tried to imagine fighter jets nearing from the horizon and herself and the Jackson family outrunning them. Then she tried to imagine that she was in Eritrea, and instead of the Jackson family, she and her parents were running under a dangerous sky, her father picking her up and throwing her over his shoulder so that she was looking at her mother, who trailed behind.

Berekhet said that the military troops had regrouped and were firing on the Ethiopian rebel base, and that none of the students got hurt. The rebels stormed onto campus and told all the students to report to the lecture hall. A man in rubber sandals who didn't look much older than them lectured for two hours about revolutionary democracy and the future of Ethiopia. The cycle of violence, poverty, and inequality was finally coming to an end, and he invited them to be a part of this new beginning. They had a day to decide whether they wanted to join the rebels or return home.

The deliberations didn't last long; everyone wanted to go back to Addis. Berekhet felt even more resolute: he wanted to leave Ethiopia altogether; his world had just opened up. The rebels honored their promise. They gave each student 200 birr, told them to buy hats and crackers, and drove them in the buses they'd confiscated to a town that marked a day's trek from the Nile, which divided rebel-held territory from the government side, with militia escorts who would leave them at the banks of the river.

"We're city kids, you know? I mean, we were not from the capital of the United States of America like some people," Berekhet said, twisting his neck. "But all we know is the city. We walk to school, walk to the video shop, walk to church, but we never walked to the next province!"

In the blackest night that Berekhet had ever seen, they walked from midnight to four in the morning, slept for a few hours, and then walked farther until they reached the Nile, where their escorts turned back. They crossed the river, which thankfully was low, and trekked for another six hours in 100-degree heat until they reached the first government military command.

"Were you scared?" Lydia asked, shaking her head in disbelief.

"Nope." He laughed. "We were just really hot and really tired."

He stood and pulled Lydia up to join him. "Let's keep walking. I want to get a picture at the Washington Monument."

Lydia refused to budge. "I really don't want to see Mom right now," she whined. They were a nice, safe distance from Elsa's cart, six blocks down and parallel to Madison. But once they neared Twelfth Street, they'd be on her territory and required to say hello.

Berekhet rolled his eyes. "How long do you think you can avoid her for? Are you not coming home tonight?"

"But I'm having such a great time with my great cousin and his great story," she said, throwing her arm over his shoulder.

He chuckled and shoved her off. "What about my picture?"

"Let me see your map." Lydia unfolded it and tried to figure out how to circumvent her mother.

"Okay, we can go around her. It'll take longer, but we can cross the Mall here to get to Constitution Avenue, walk down to Seventeenth Street, and then approach the monument from the other side." Lydia gently nudged him in the other direction. "Go on. You were saying that you weren't really scared on your trek."

Berekhet followed her lead and confirmed that they weren't. Someone had a boombox—it was a class trip after all—and played Chachi Tadesse for practically the entire trek, until the group threatened to tie the culprit to a tree if he didn't change the cassette. They talked trash and made jokes and catalogued the first things they would do when they finally got to Addis. Lydia found the whole saga hard to imagine, like almost every other story she was told about back home. A surreal and dangerous situation unfolds, but everyone is fine and everything is funny.

Life after their class trip was even stranger. Their university admission test results were withheld, the government announced that high school students would have to join the military before they could enroll, university students themselves were getting mobilized, and Berekhet wanted no part of it. His father used his connections to get him a passport and an appointment at the U.S. embassy, and three months later, he boarded a plane to Washington, D.C.

"So here I am," he said, standing in front of the Washington Monument with his arms open wide like the car dealers he'd seen in commercials. Lydia snapped the picture and put the camera back in her bag.

"No, no, no! We need one of the both of us." He summoned a nearby tourist. "Say cheese!"

Lydia threw her shoulders back, leaned into Berekhet's frame, and smiled directly at the camera.

"Here I am," Berekhet repeated after their picture was taken. "And my story is an easy one, Lidu. I can guarantee that your mother's is not."

25

ZEWDI HAD A PLAN FOR MAKING SURE THAT ASGEDOM AND HER cousin wouldn't meet. At this stage, no one needed to know about their relationship, and Samrawit kept a secret as well as a sieve held water. So Zewdi agreed to meet her cousin at the Beverly Center at three thirty but told Asgedom she had to be there at three. Once they got there, she would "remember" the correct time and force him to leave.

Things started off well. But as Zewdi and Asgedom waited to turn into the mall parking lot, the driver ahead of them started honking and waving in the rearview mirror. In the backseat, two girls, one of whom looked Eritrean, turned their heads curiously.

"That's my cousin!" Zewdi cried out.

When the light changed, Samrawit indicated for them to follow her car halfway around the perimeter of the mall to the cinema, where she pulled over at the entrance to let the girls tumble out. Zewdi watched her careful plan fall apart as Samrawit then walked toward Asgedom's car with her arms outstretched.

"Samri!" Zewdi said, rushing to meet her.

"Zewdi, my sister! It's so good to see you."

Samrawit pulled away from Zewdi's embrace and called out to the girls: "I know this movie ends at five! Do not make Chelsea's mother wait again. Do you hear me, Meron?"

She turned to Zewdi and threw up her hands. "These children have turned us into their chauffeurs. Can you imagine? All we did as kids was run around and play. Where were we going to be dropped off? The next ditch? Am I right?" she asked Asgedom, who had joined them. "Are you family?"

She looked at Zewdi and then back at Asgedom.

"Do you live here?" she tried again. "Zewdi, is he on our side? Let me say hi to you properly."

Samrawit pulled him into a hearty embrace, making a loud kissing sound as she pressed her cheeks to his. Zewdi felt her blouse start to cling to her back. How was she going to introduce him?

"I do live here . . . and we're not family, no," Asgedom said, straightening his shirt. "Zewdi's neighbor's mother, who was visiting D.C. from back home, is my mother's neighbor in Asmara. We met so that she could give me the things that my mother sent with her neighbor."

Look at what Zewdi was making him do. He was a better liar than she expected. She reached for her cousin's arm to steer her back to the car.

"Samrawit, my sister, shall we go? Asgedom needs to be heading off."

"What do you mean? It's St. Michael's Day! Just come to the house! Both of you! We'll have coffee."

"I really should be going." Asgedom stepped back and jingled his car keys. "Zewdi, just call the house when you want me to come back and get you."

Samrawit shrugged Zewdi off and tucked her arm into Asgedom's. "No, please. Join us! Zewdi, get in with me. Asgedom, follow behind. My home is close by."

Zewdi grimaced at Asgedom. He only raised his eyebrows in response. And of course, when they arrived at Samrawit's garden-style apartment complex, she didn't serve coffee. They sat in silence in her living room as she reheated six platters of food. When she saw how little they were eating, she served them herself.

"Where are you staying, Zewdi? You should have stayed here."

Zewdi breathed deeply and began. She had been prepared to lie, but just not in front of Asgedom.

"With the daughter of a good friend of mine from nursing school. She was just a little thing when I left and now she's married . . . expecting her first soon."

Asgedom's face twitched but he kept his focus on his food.

"Lovely." Samrawit got up to put more injera on Asgedom's plate. He was making very little progress. "Where does she live?"

"Baldwin Hills."

"Baldwin Hills! That's a great part of town . . . expensive. What does she do? Is she married to an Eritrean?"

"Something in healthcare, an X-ray tech, I think. And yes, she is."

"Where do you live, Asgedom? And why aren't you eating?"

Asgedom had been discreetly tearing off the chicken from its bone and wiping the sauce on the injera.

"I live in Baldwin Hills as well."

"Really! Good for you! So do you know . . . what did you say her name was, Zewdi?"

"Tsehai."

"Tsehai who?"

"Kiflemariam." The lies kept coming. May God forgive her.

"Do you know this Tsehai Kiflemariam, Asgedom?"

"No, I can't say that I do."

"And what do you do for work?"

Jesus Christ, held captive in a frame directly above Samrawit's head, was holding court over the performance. It wasn't a regular picture, but one of those holographic images that projected him in the same pose, arms extended and expression plaintive, from any position that he could be viewed. Zewdi held his gaze and then futilely tried to evade it, moving her head from side to side.

"Asgedom," Zewdi said, "didn't you say that you had some errands to run? We really should be—"

"Haile's daughter's wedding! Have you seen the video? I'm sure you haven't! He just dropped them off."

Samrawit crouched in front of the television stand and dug through stacks of cassettes and VHS tapes, pulling out two tapes and then a third.

"This was May 31, just a week after independence. Six hundred people attended. Can you believe that? There's videos of the church ceremony, the reception, and the melsi. Beautiful wedding, right in his backyard. I've never seen anything like that. Let's start with the ceremony."

Samrawit put the other two tapes on the table in front of them, each cover emblazoned with CONGRADULATIONS NEBIAT AND TEMESGEN.

"Haile already knows the whole world, but then we won the war. So what could he do but turn the wedding into an Independence Day party. They had to put up another tent for the overflow, rent more tables and chairs. It was incredible. You guys in D.C. celebrated in a hotel, paid for parking by the hour, but we partied all night long like it was back home. Do you know Haile?" she said to Asgedom. "What village are you from?"

"Why don't you play the video, Samrawitay?" Zewdi said.

"It's playing, it's playing. Look at the bride and groom. Don't they look related?"

Samrawit was pointing to the introductory montage of photos set to a Lionel Richie song that Zewdi loved. The sequence shifted into a series of dissolving and reconstituting hearts, each with the bride and groom's smiling faces in the center.

"It's dangerous these days," she said to the screen. "In our time, our parents researched the family and made the arrangements. Now everyone is spread all over the place, not knowing if their girlfriend is actually their cousin. Do you remember Senai, Zewdi? Sophia's brother? He met this girl in D.C., fell in love, and proposed. When he called his parents back home to tell them the good news, they asked for the girl's father's name and her village and figured out that they were cousins five generations apart. Seven is the rule. There's no getting around what it says in the Bible."

Jesus finally showed some mercy, because the intercom chirped.

"That must be Zerai and his family," Samrawit said. She walked out of the apartment toward the outdoor staircase that led to the parking lot, yelling her greetings. Zewdi and Asgedom gave each other a knowing look and hurried to put their plates in the kitchen sink and wash their hands. They rushed to the door as Samrawit was ushering the family of four in.

"Zerai, Netzanet, meet Zewdi and . . ." Samrawit glanced at the purse on Zewdi's shoulder. "Where are you guys going?"

"Samrawit, we really have to go." Zewdi inched closer to the doorway.

"So soon? We haven't even had coffee! And the videos!"

"It was such a pleasure meeting you," Asgedom said as he took Samrawit's hand and then shook the hands of the incoming guests. Zewdi did the same and then kissed Samrawit. "I'll call you!"

In the car, Zewdi took nervous looks at Asgedom, determining how best to break the silence. His expression was placid, but she knew that she should speak first.

"I'm . . . I'm so sorry for dragging you through that."

"It's fine, Zewdi," he said, still looking ahead. "You know how some of our people can be. What could you have done?"

There were options here for how best to respond. Zewdi had to be thoughtful for which one to choose. She could try humor, poke fun at their predicament and hostage situation, maybe joke that they were like kids getting caught. Or she could address it straight-on, try to explain, better this time, how she wasn't quite sure how to manage all of this. But Asgedom beat her to it.

"I know dating isn't easy, Zewdi . . . at our ages, especially. But let's talk honestly with each other. How are you feeling about all of this?"

He looked over at her, but she wasn't ready to look back, focusing instead on his hands on the steering wheel. He had perfectly shaped nail beds and the faintest smattering of hair on his knuckles.

"Well, I can tell you that I'm nervous," he continued. "I've been living on my own and I worry about what it would be like to share my life with someone again. But in marriage you also share the load, you have each other for support, for good times and bad."

This was her cue to agree, to say that she was also nervous about finally having what had long eluded her. Here it was, just a few inches to her left. Asgedom hadn't actually verbalized that he wanted them to be together, but he was close. He was doing a temperature check. All she had to do was assure him that she was close too.

When Zewdi was younger, she used to fantasize about her future family. The children were plentiful and kinetic, a jumble of little people with big eyes who scurried over her like kittens. Sometimes the eldest was a girl, Zewdi in miniature, a deputy who took seriously the domestic education imparted on her and kept the others in line. Other times, the firstborn was a boy, Zewdi's vision stilling into a family photo with Junior clad in a short set and suspenders, standing solemnly at his mother's side. The father (and husband, of course) was always there, but vaguely represented, a pixelated fixture. Zewdi and her childhood friends had talked about boys but never in seriousness. There was no plotting, no personal agency in determining whom they'd be yoked to. It was understood that when the powers that be made those arrangements, the girls would be made aware.

In Saudi, a different, darker preoccupation had revealed itself. Twenty-five-year-old Zewdi was lonely. Her loneliness was a physical occupying force, and at its heart, to her shame, was a hunger, a great and greedy need to be touched. This force predictably activated itself at night, and she would curl up on her side, running her hands over her arms and legs, pretending that it was the touch of another. She grew to dread the night and also to despise her bed, as if it had betrayed her to the enemy. She found refuge instead in the uncomfortable armchair in her sitting room. In the hours made for sleep, she'd watch movies (always romantic, unfortunately, but Egyptian, so much less suggestive); yet the enemy persevered, and she gripped the elbows of her crossed arms.

She deployed her greatest weapon: her faith. Clutching her rosary, she fired off rounds of Our Fathers and Hail Marys until the spaces between the words disappeared. She held out her upturned palms and sang the gospel, doing both the priest's call and the congregation's response. Finally, the heavy artillery, the Holy Book itself, was unleashed. The Book of Mark, Ecclesiastes, page 1, it didn't matter what she chose, but she read, whispered, and then mumbled until precious sleep earned her a temporary truce.

In Zewdi's forties, the war had finally ended. It was a mean peace, since it meant her body was no longer worth fighting for. This was a condition nearly as bad as the one before it. Bitterness, she had found, was nastier than desire. It had also happened that from the moment Asgedom had been introduced into Zewdi's life, another deadly front had appeared: she was now absolutely terrified at the thought of being touched. How could the things that were expected of a wife be expected of her? If the whole point was to reproduce, then what, exactly, were she and Asgedom going to be doing with each other?

In Villa Lucia, the bed, once again, compromised her. With the weariness of a veteran called back to battle, she considered her weapons, either the Bible she brought or the one in the nightstand. She chose her own and then faced her enemy. If God wouldn't give her strength, then at least he could let her sleep.

•

26

LYDIA WAS LEARNING ALL THE DIFFERENT WAYS THAT HER ANGER could take shape. The rage she felt after visiting Osman a few weeks ago had since cooled into an icy indifference. She tried her hardest to avoid Elsa in the apartment, succeeding in spending time with her only when they shared the same bed at night. Sometimes Elsa would try to hold her and ask how her day was, but Lydia would push her off and face the wall in silence. The distance between them was unnerving; Lydia felt that they were becoming strangers to each other, connected by proximity and not much more. She'd look at old pictures of herself as a toddler nuzzling Elsa's neck or peeking from between her legs, unable to recognize the intimacy they once had.

In the middle of the night, Lydia woke up to use the bathroom and heard Berekhet in the kitchen. She followed the light and noise to find him reading a book while absent-mindedly flipping over something in a pan with his other hand.

"I knew you were going to wake up as soon as I started frying these potatoes," he said with a sly look. "I could feel it."

"Yeah, yeah," Lydia said. She reached around to grab a potato and hoisted herself up on the counter.

"Have you been working on your big idea?" Lydia asked. She realized she hadn't been seeing much book writing or new color invention going on.

"You know, it's more about the audacity to think big than it is about the project itself. To have that audacity, I need the right conditions."

Lydia wasn't sure what he was getting at but let it go. Berekhet resumed humming along to a CD playing softly, an aching voice Lydia hadn't heard before. When she asked, Berekhet told her the singer was someone named Robert Plant. He was obviously white, but he sounded unlike any white singer she had heard before, and much better than the other musicians Berekhet had tried to convince her were talented. He practically trembled when lecturing about "Bob Deelan," a faraway, tinny voice that didn't impress her much.

She closed her eyes to hear this Robert guy better. There were no words, just crooning, that voice begging and demanding, turning proud and then pliant. Robert Plant sounded hungry.

"What are you guys doing?" Elsa said from the kitchen entryway. "It's three in the morning."

"Sorry, Elsa," Berekhet said, speaking before Lydia could. "I know it's late. I was up cooking, and Lydia must have heard me. She just got here."

Elsa marched over to the stereo and turned it off.

"Lydia, go back to sleep. And you, too, Berekhet. You have class in the morning."

"I don't have class," he said.

Elsa registered his nerve to respond back with a slow blink.

"Yes, you do. You have composition and chemistry tomorrow," she enunciated with great care.

"I have chem lab, but it's been canceled. And we're having one-on-one editing sessions with our composition professor, so I don't have to go in tomorrow."

"It's still a school night. Go to sleep and wake up early so that you can study. You, too, Lydia. Now."

Berekhet nodded at Lydia, and she slowly pushed herself off the counter and followed her mother into her room. She got into the bed and made a point of facing the wall, aware that Elsa had stopped in the doorway and was watching.

"Lydia," she said, her voice barely above a whisper, trying

to dispel the tension. But Lydia burrowed under the covers and ignored her.

"I'm your mother, and this is my house," Elsa said, the edge back in her voice. "Don't you forget that."

That Saturday, Lydia and Berekhet agreed to have a movie night, which Elsa couldn't spoil. An exhausted Berekhet came home from work at ten p.m. and collapsed on the sofa, promising that he had enough energy to watch Bruce Willis squint for the next ninety minutes. Berekhet usually thought his commentary was essential to the viewing experience, while Lydia's movie-watching philosophy was to let the actors do the talking. This time, he drowsily mumbled through an analysis of how Hollywood reinforced the overly-simplified dichotomy between good and evil that served as the foundation of American foreign policy. By the time the first German died, his head had fallen to the armrest and he was snoring from deep within his chest.

Lydia tried to focus on the movie while also fighting sleep and stealing glances at Berekhet. Once the credits rolled, she scooted closer and leaned over to watch him. He looked better like this, sleeping and not talking, his face relaxed. He barely budged as she curled up beside him and tugged at the blanket tucked under his arms. Her limbs grew heavier and heavier and her eyes started to close. They needed to get up and go to their rooms, but that felt impossible. Lydia soon drifted into sleep, waking up at intervals that could have been minutes or hours. The movie replayed in her dreams, but instead of the LAPD trying to stop the terrorists, it was the EPLF, scaling the sleek Japanese conglomerate tower in their khaki shorts and rubber sandals. Her mother's twin scampered into the elevator shaft as Bruce Willis had, clutching a brick of C-4 and looking up at Lydia, as if to say, *I got this under control, and so do you*. Lydia woke up disoriented, unaware of how much time had passed, and turned over to see if Berekhet was still knocked out. She studied the whites between his partially closed lids and his lightly puckered mouth. The weight of her own head started to feel immense, its mass dragging itself lower and lower, until her face hovered right over his. She held her head there before allowing herself to do the unthinkable: touching her lips to his. Finally, her first kiss.

She pulled back as quickly as she had closed the distance between them, wondering if the kiss had happened at all. Berekhet only fidgeted and exhaled a labored breath in response. Lydia lay beside him for a bit longer before going to her mother's room and getting in the bed, waiting for her eyes to close. The whole thing felt flat, dim compared to her once iron-clad conviction that kisses were much more important.

27

ZEWDI WAS AT WILLIAMS-SONOMA, WHICH MEANT THAT IT WAS officially an emergency. At least once a week, she visited Macy's or Hecht's to inspect their newest cookware offerings, but she only went to Williams-Sonoma when things were bad. Today was one of those days.

To be fair, she'd been in a state since her return from L.A. the week before. She had called Asgedom to let him know she made it back safely, keeping the call short out of fear of him bringing up their next steps, an inevitable topic that she was trying to avoid. She wasn't sure what to make of her anxiety. Was it the fear of upending her life and leaving Elsa and Lydia? Was it the nagging suspicion that she wasn't interested in him enough to commit? Or was it the certainty that another chance for partnership would never come again?

She let all her calls go unanswered and ignored the number on her answering machine that increased every day. Finally, on Saturday, she answered the phone, and it was Asgedom, calling for the big talk. He said that he was enjoying getting to know her and understood why Mama Minia thought so highly of her. He also declared that he wanted to move forward. Until his daughter left for college the next fall, he proposed that they stay in touch and visit each other, and by the next year, she could—if she wanted to, of course—make a home with him in California.

Zewdi's opposition to the idea was so immediate that it shocked her. But her rational mind beat the feeling back, urging her to not be foolish in her response. After steadying her breath, she stammered that she also really liked getting to know him and that it would be good to have a bit of time to think things through. He agreed—it sounded reasonable, after all—although she did detect a hint of disappointment in his voice.

Later that evening, Zewdi had to meet another man who was waiting for her to make a decision. Saturday night at Asmara Restaurant was just as she expected. There wasn't an empty seat in sight, but the orders were skewed more toward beer and liquor than food. People stopped at her table to make small talk, and she kept things light, not letting on as to why she was hanging around.

Ammanuel took her to the back office so she could review the books. They revealed nothing alarming, and if she got people to take the food seriously, which she didn't doubt she could, the calculations looked promising. Since she hadn't run a business this size, she contemplated having an accountant take a look as well before she made a final decision. The office was slightly bigger than her bathroom, with two chairs on either side of the desk and a massive filing cabinet that stopped the door from opening all the way. Zewdi leaned back in the sturdier chair, listening to the commotion in the kitchen through the shared wall: the clatter of plates, metal hitting metal, the tic-tic-tic and whoosh of fire being ignited, someone yelling that the carton of oil was about to fall over, and then the carton falling over.

She left the restaurant, promising Ammanuel that she'd be back; she still had a week to decide, after all. And now, on Sunday morning, after going to church and leaving Lydia to man the injera, she was staring down a display of Le Creuset pots.

"Are you looking for anything in particular today, ma'am?"

Zewdi looked over approvingly at the well-groomed saleswoman who greeted her.

"I'm looking for a few things actually. My daughter is getting married."

As the woman gushed, Zewdi became emboldened by her

little fib. She looked the part after all, donning a regal caftan and nearly $1,000 worth of gold.

"Yes, she's my only daughter. Her brothers are all married, and this is my chance to finally have a say in the wedding." Zewdi laughed.

The woman laughed even louder. "Were you thinking to get started on a registry?"

"Yes, absolutely. I'll bring her soon to finalize, but I'd like to get started now."

Gravy boats, salad sets, and serving bowls. With the feel of each overpriced yet essential item and the affirmative nod of the saleswoman as she added them to the list, Zewdi felt her problems dissipate. She even prepared an explanation for her eventual reunion with the saleswoman to tell her that she would have to cancel the registry. Her daughter's fiancé would be caught with another woman, his colleague, who had come to their home often for dinner and referred to him as her work husband.

This good cheer only lasted for as long as she was in the store. In the car, the dilemma of Asgedom's proposal resettled itself around her neck. It also didn't help that she felt like she was coming down with a summer cold. Instead of being able to go straight home and crawl into bed, she first had to buy garlic and honey because she already knew that no one would offer to get what she needed. As many times as she'd nursed Lydia and Elsa back to health, made pitchers of hot, runny oatmeal to soothe their throats and peppery shiro to open their sinuses, not one of them ever lifted a finger to help her when she fell ill. Zewdi muttered under her breath on the drive to the grocery store, where she decided to also buy a box of Andes chocolate mints that she would keep in her room and not share with anyone else.

Zewdi circled through the Southern Towers parking lot a few times, waving at the residents she knew. She also memorized the license plate of a Toyota Camry parked in a residence spot without a permit. Bud from Big Dog Towing hadn't heard from her in a while and would be eager to come out and do his job. She walked past the faded "Southern Towers" sign and stepped over two wailing Ethiopian children whose mother ignored them while chatting with a neighbor in front of the call box. Zewdi tried and failed to catch the similarly disapproving look of an older white woman with visible comb lines in her hair and real pearls, one of the last of her tribe in the building, as she deftly skirted around the commotion. Like black-light technology over seemingly clean fabric, Zewdi scanned the lobby and revealed dust on the fake lilies and missing fringes on the shiny Oriental rug. Management, as represented by the haunted-looking Somali man sitting behind the desk, was clearly unable to maintain standards.

When she walked into her apartment, Zewdi found Lydia curled up on the sofa watching a movie and Elsa in the kitchen knocking around for leftovers. Why is it you get what you want but not when you want it?

Zewdi called out a hello to them. "I'm just going to go change, be back out." She strode to her room and firmly closed the door, standing momentarily with her back pressed against it. On her nightstand, the blinking number on her phone's answering machine revealed there was a new message since she'd left in the morning. She hoped it wasn't Asgedom.

"Your problem, my daughter," Zewdi could hear her mother say, as if she had left the message instead, "is that you'll never be satisfied."

Her mother had always blamed Zewdi's high expectations on her father, saying that he spoiled her too much. After her parents divorced and her father moved to Ethiopia for his trucking business, he would return to Asmara every year and shower Zewdi with gifts. When Zewdi was in the seventh grade, the same grade that Lydia just completed, he showed up to her classroom with a ribboned box of pastries for her classmates and strode to Zewdi's row with a huge smile on his face. He was a little chubby like his daughter and struggled to get on his knees to present her with a jewelry box that she giddily opened, revealing crescent-shaped gold earrings on a bed of white cotton. He put them in her ears and kissed her cheeks. Of course the teacher gave her permission to leave early with him, but when Zewdi got home, her mother made her take the earrings out, claiming they were too fancy for a young girl to wear every day. That trip was the last time she saw her father. Later that year, he and thirteen Eritrean businessmen were rounded up in Gonder, in northwestern Ethiopia, forced to dig a ditch and wait as the man to their right was shot in the back of the head and fell to his waiting grave. Miraculously, the last man was spared, since the soldiers just happened to run out of bullets. Zewdi's father was the second to last one.

The phone rang. Zewdi nearly jumped out of her skin. She sat gingerly on her bed and took a breath to compose herself before answering.

"Finally!" said an excited voice. "Zewdi, is that you?"

"Sorry, who's this?"

"It's Dahab from Sweden."

Zewdi frowned, trying to connect the dots. "I'm sorry, who?"

"Dahab . . . I'm Efrem's cousin. I'm here!"

In a breathless tone, Dahab explained that she had called so many times and left so many messages, but Zewdi never got back to her, and now she was here in town, as she had told Zewdi about her plans, and not just in town but in Southern Towers on the sixth floor visiting someone else and she wanted to know if she could come by now, yes, right now.

"Of course, come on up," Zewdi said softly to her reflection in the mirror. "We're all here in 1341."

28

Trust Me

1977 WAS SUPPOSED TO BE THE YEAR THE WAR WAS WON. BY THE end of the summer, the rebels had liberated the entire country, except for Asmara and the two ports of Massawa and Asseb. In August, Tedros shared more big news: Twin was being transferred to Keren to lead the civilian governance program. Her promotion meant that a nineteen-year-old woman would be preparing the nation's third biggest city for democratic rule.

Elsa was certain that Twin was the right woman for the job. At her farewell party in the assembly hall she helped build, the older women danced around Twin as if it were her wedding night. Efrem and Tedros lifted her on their shoulders, the flickering light casting shadows on their wild grins. Elsa mostly stood off to the side, refusing the beer that made its rounds, having never tried it and too nervous to start while on the job. Back at the house, Twin curled up next to her in the dark, reeking of hops.

"I saw you pretending not to cry," she said, her breath tickling Elsa's ear.

"Tears of joy, my sister. I'm so happy you're finally leaving."

"Oh, please, I know you're going to follow me to Keren just like you did here."

They choked on their laughter, trying not to wake up Efrem and Tedros on the other side of the wall.

Elsa tilted her face toward Twin, even though she could barely make out her face in the darkness. "I have a letter for my mother I want you to give to her when you get there. Just read it to her. I want her to know that I'm okay."

"Of course," Twin murmured. "I wish you could give it to

her yourself." There was no such thing as requesting leave to visit family once you joined the movement. How could you move forward if you were also looking back?

Elsa let her head rest against Twin's shoulder, feeling it as their breath steadied to the same rhythm. Keren needed Twin—the whole country did. But all Elsa could think about was that by tomorrow night, she would be sleeping alone. She took Twin's hand, kissed it, and rested her palm on her cheek. When she woke up, Twin's hand was still there.

Later that day, Elsa hiked up to the blue church and crouched in a nook below its gates. As she looked out over the hills, she spotted a flash of something dark in the dry gully below. Efrem's head and then the rest of his body came into view. He turned to face the shrouded path from which he had emerged, extending his hand to pull forth another obscured figure that soon revealed herself. He draped his arm over her shoulder. Elsa watched as they wound around the base of a hill, wondering how they'd be saying goodbye.

The next month marked the first deliberations of Zager's new people's assembly that Elsa's unit had been working to reform so that it included women and representatives from all classes, not just the village elites. At dusk, the new assembly leaders proceeded somberly up to the hall, flicking their white cotton shawls over their shoulders and taking their seats on roughhewn logs at the front. The villagers followed behind and crouched on their heels. The sky was clear and Zager quiet, as if the usual noisemakers, both the children and the braying animals, knew that something important was happening.

Elsa, Tedros, and Efrem greeted everyone but sat in the back, not wanting to distract from the proceedings. Once the assembly head called the meeting to order, Elsa was thrilled to see a mother of four young children, who previously wouldn't even make eye contact when she spoke, stand up first.

"Thank you, esteemed council, for this auspicious meeting. I am pleased to share this issue for your consideration."

Elsa and Efrem exchanged a look, tickled at her confidence.

"Several cattle have been trampling on our young crops of peppers and tomatoes. This harvest season, we lost nearly a third of our yield. I believe the cattle belong to Mr. Fissehaye," she said, nodding in his direction.

There was a slight murmur, as the man was one of Zager's wealthiest and had served on the village council before its reform.

"We'd like to ask if the cattle can be better monitored and steered to graze away from our crops."

The assembly head cleared his throat. "Is there anyone else who would like to say anything with regards to this matter?"

An older gentleman with tattered pants stood up. "I can attest to what this woman has said." Another man called out the same.

"Mr. Fissehaye, do you have anything to say in response?"

"I do not," he said, standing up. "I will see to it that this doesn't happen again."

The head conferred with his peers before responding. "Very well. We also require that you reimburse this woman for the damage incurred."

There were a few other items brought up: brothers fighting over their inheritance, two longtime enemies suing each other for bodily injury. At the very end, a teenager who couldn't have been more than sixteen or seventeen years old raised her hand and stood up. She pushed her headscarf back gently, revealing a stunning face with perfectly symmetrical features.

"I am here to petition for a divorce."

The chatter in the crowd silenced.

"I was married off to my husband," she went on, "who is ninety-something years old. Look at him; what am I supposed to do with him?" She gestured at a wizened man whose mouth threatened to collapse over his toothless gums, sitting next to a sheepish younger couple who were likely her parents.

"I cook and clean, but I can do nothing else for him and he can do nothing for me. I want out of this marriage."

The old man struggled to stand and had to be helped up.

"You see the shame that has befallen me . . . the words coming from my own wife's mouth," he said. "I have promised that I will provide her with anything that she requests. I repeat this to you all now, on my word. My age should not be a reason for our divorce. She was given to me, after all."

Several women covered their mouths with their shawls and sucked their teeth in disapproval. "You all should be happy we even let you join these meetings," muttered a man in the back.

"Order," the head said. "We expect order." He whispered among his peers and turned his attention back to the assembly.

"Now, young lady. We can appreciate your concerns. While we hope that your husband lives even more years on this Earth, and in a free Eritrea, God willing, it's safe to assume, respectfully, that he will soon be returned from where he came. Would you not consider staying with him until then, and then your life is yours?"

"With all due respect," the girl said, raising her chin, "I will consider no such thing."

"All right," the head said, stroking his beard. "We'll return with our decision at our next meeting."

Tedros shook his head, as his leg bounced nervously. "I'm going to say something. They can't make this girl stay married."

"You will do no such thing," Elsa hissed, clamping her hand on his thigh. "Let's talk when we get home."

In their cramped living room, Tedros paced as he ranted. "Being forced into that kind of marriage is cruel. Dissolving it is exactly how we ensure more progressive norms. What is there to be confused about?"

Efrem looked over at Elsa. "What do you think?" he asked.

"Of course I agree with you, Tedros," Elsa said calmly. "But we need to let the assembly leaders decide that for themselves. If we intervene so heavy-handedly, they will lack legitimacy. We have been working with them for years. Let's have some faith that they'll make the right call."

Efrem looked Elsa up and down and crossed his arms, barely suppressing a smile. "Tedros, can you believe what we're hearing?" he said, his eyes still fixed on her. "Our resident radical is now the cool-headed advisor."

"Believe it." Elsa held his gaze. "Plus, I already talked to some of the women, and they're going to lobby their husbands."

The next week, the girl was granted her divorce.

Toward the end of the year, Efrem and Elsa were assigned to train less-experienced members of the public administration unit in Semanawi Bahri, the evergreen escarpment northeast of Zager's highlands. After all the time that had gone by, they had finally settled into a less contentious relationship. They still watched the lights twinkle in the middle of the night, and the harmony of those nocturnal meetings had spread to their daily interactions. As much as she didn't want to admit it, Elsa suspected that it was because Twin wasn't there. She felt more relaxed with Efrem when it was just the two of them, less inclined to pick fights and prove herself.

They managed to get a ride to the base in Semanawi Bahri, but after the training, they had to walk the nearly fifty-mile ascent back to Zager, the terrain gradually rising from 1,500 to nearly 5,000 miles above sea level. After they trekked through the lush vegetation of Filfil and Solomuna and reached the dry foothills that marked their proximity to Zager, it began to drizzle, and eventually, the rain turned into a heavy pour, lashing the earth in sheets. They ducked into a cave to wait it out, and by the time it stopped, it was too dark to proceed. Elsa suggested they sleep there and resume their journey in the morning.

Efrem spread his scarf on the uneven ground and lay on his back with his hands clasped behind his head. Elsa placed her scarf on top of both of them and gave him her back. She listened as he breathed deeply and slowed her breath to match his. She had shared more intimate spaces with him and Tedros than she had with her own siblings. They were fighters, comrades united for a cause that superseded any baser impulse.

But she turned over, and her hand touched his or maybe it was the other way around. Neither of them moved away. That was all it took.

Elsa did allow herself to enjoy it, the weight of his body on hers, his mouth on her neck, and the sweetest of silences. They took their time, and when they were finished, Efrem was the first to speak. As he held her in the darkness, he told her about his childhood, how his grandfather used to call him "the pisser," since they had shared a bed since Efrem was three, how his mother begged him to not join the war as his three older brothers had, to let her have at least one child at her side. Elsa felt bold enough to run her hands over his chest. She tried not to think about whether he had lain with Twin the same way, playing with her hair as he reminisced about his family.

He asked Elsa to share something about herself, to prove that she was actually human and not a walking, talking avatar of the Little Red Book.

"How about we start with your name? You know mine."

"My name is Elsa."

"Elsa," he murmured in her ear. "Who are you the daughter of?"

"The revolution."

"Very funny. But I'm being serious."

"Haddish. Who are you the son of?"

"Negash. Tell me something else about you."

Elsa resisted, burying her face in his neck, wanting to enjoy the moment for as long as she could. He kissed her and gently pushed her on her back, waiting with a hopeful, almost childlike look. So she started from the beginning, telling him the story of a new mother who felt a sharp pain in her thigh.

Elsa felt that she talked more than she had in her whole life. When she was done, Efrem took her into his arms and held her the way a mother would hold her child. Elsa felt a lightness, and strangely, she thought of Dr. Alazar. As she described him to Efrem, she saw him more clearly: a young man, who, at the start of his own career, had been charged with taking responsibility for his dead brother's kids and a slew of other relations who appeared on his doorstep. All those people had to be fed, clothed, and educated—there was no time for anyone's grand ideas—and along came Elsa with her theatrics. She chuckled softly and nestled closer to Efrem, wondering how she would have fared with a similar responsibility.

In that dark cave, with its earthy mustiness, Elsa had never slept so deeply. She woke before Efrem, sensing the sun's rise, and watched him sleep. When he finally opened his eyes, he pulled her closer and said right in her ear, "Good morning, Twin."

Why couldn't he have said her name instead? She pulled out of his embrace and sat up, declaring that they should resume their trek back to Zager. He was startled and reached out for her arm, but whatever had opened up inside Elsa was closing shut. Efrem was talking, but Elsa couldn't hear a word he was saying. She got dressed and told him there was nothing to say.

"What is wrong with you?" He gripped her arm firmly. "Something just happened here . . . this was real."

"Just for now though, right?" Elsa yanked her arm back and bolted out of the cave. Efrem caught up with her, and they continued their trek in silence. Every now and then, he would make an unhappy sound. Elsa would respond by walking faster. As they were cutting through a dry ravine, Efrem grabbed her hand and told her to stop.

Elsa shoved him off and pushed ahead.

"Elsa, I'm serious. Look!"

In the valley that lay before them, a large swath of grass on both sides of the riverbed was charred and covered with slate-colored ash. A rebel demining unit must have burned the area in an attempt to trigger the landmines that the Ethiopian military had planted.

Efrem lowered his stance and kept his limbs loose, as if he could launch himself to safety. But the panicked look in his eyes betrayed how he really felt.

Elsa looked down at the earth below her feet, praying that her quickening breath wouldn't somehow trigger a mine. The charred earth extended all the way to the sharp slope of the mountain range on either side. Only the ablest of goats would have been able to find purchase on the range's craggy surface. Farther down, after about half a mile, the riverbed curved eastward and there seemed to be a break in the range. The only way out was to make it to that break.

Elsa turned around to face Efrem, her expression matching his fear.

"Think our guys have a hundred-percent success rate with clearing mines?" she asked.

"We're about to find out," he said, his voice so low she could barely hear him.

Elsa closed her eyes until she managed to steady her breath. Then she went first, walking gingerly on large stones and following any foot- and hoofprints. She and Efrem kept a healthy distance between them, and after every ten steps, Elsa would stop and look back at him. His hands were trembling and he didn't make eye contact, keeping his gaze glued to the ground.

When they finally reached the curve in the riverbed, an explosion roared just around the bend. They scrambled as fast as they could onto a deep ledge near the base of the range just before the break. In the middle of the riverbed was a cow, grunting and writhing, its hind legs blown up. A fine cloud of dust and stone and bone fragments settled on them.

A young herder appeared across the embankment and rushed toward his cow.

"Don't move!" they both yelled.

The herder stopped and squatted, gripping his own head as his cow's lolled futilely on the ground.

Efrem also sat on his haunches, rubbing the grit out of his eyes. "We need to get back to the base and get the deminers to sweep the area again."

"I don't think we should leave this site unmanned though." Elsa felt her teeth chatter as she spoke. "Suppose someone else comes here and gets blown up. One of us should wait here to keep watch."

"You want us to separate? No way. That goes against protocol. Let's just tell this kid to keep watch."

Efrem waved at the herder. "Hey, are you okay? Can you wait here while we get help?"

The herder shook his head and said something back in Tigre.

"Don't you speak Tigre?" Efrem said to Elsa. "You grew up in Keren, right?"

"I left when I was really young." Elsa wrung her hands. "I don't remember anything that can help us right now."

"I'll make him understand." Efrem stood up carefully and pantomimed that he and Elsa were leaving and for him to stay put. But the kid just squinted with a bewildered expression.

"Efrem," she said sharply, "I'm leaving. Stay here."

"You don't listen." He tapped at his temple. "Just listen to what I'm saying. We shouldn't split up."

But Elsa had already scampered down the ledge. "Trust me, Efrem. I'll be back."

"Be careful," he said in a low voice, sounding defeated.

Elsa carefully reversed the steps they'd taken into the valley, turning back only once to see Efrem still squatting, watching her with his hand shielding his eyes from the sun. The longer she journeyed to the base they had just come from, the more she doubted the wisdom of her decision. Efrem was right: fighters were never supposed to separate. As the sun continued to rise, the heat intensifying her anxiety, she prayed for a sign, something to reassure her that she hadn't put Efrem at risk.

A few hours later, as the descent sharpened and vegetation turned more lush, her prayers were answered. She spotted a rebel-manned Land Rover maneuvering toward her over the rocky path. The driver, a medic coming back from Massawa, delivered her to Semanawi Bahri, where she rounded up the deminers and drove with them as far as they were certain the land was safe. Once they got out of the truck and began walking the same path that she and Efrem had traversed, the scent of sulfur assaulted her, its odor too fresh to be from the landmine that the cow had triggered.

When the riverbed was in sight, Elsa heard a piercing wail from around the bend, and broke into a sprint, ignoring the desperate shouts of the deminers. When she reached the curve, she saw the herder hysterically gesturing at a newly blown-out crater of land.

The entire scene became refracted in Elsa's vision: a far-flung leg, bits of fabric and flesh strewn about, Efrem's head facedown, all the elements moving in an ever-changing tableau, yet one that never made him whole. She lurched toward the bombed-out crater. Two of the deminers chased after her as the third shouted from the ledge for them to return to safety. They tackled Elsa and carried her back to the ledge, one of them practically sitting on her as she screamed Efrem's name. The deminers radioed in another unit, and the two who had subdued Elsa drove her back to Zager, a one-hour ride in which no one said anything at all.

Once they dropped her off on the main road, Elsa lurched down the path into the village. She approached the acacia tree Efrem was lounging under the first time she had seen him two years ago. Her knees buckled as she imagined him throwing his hands behind his head and Twin laughing at something silly he said. Could she reverse time? If she had never shown up to Zager, would Efrem still be alive?

Elsa swayed under the still tree. She reached out and plucked a long, thick thorn from a branch. Holding it like a pen in her right hand, she traced the thorn from the inside of her left wrist to her elbow, hard enough to draw blood. That wasn't enough. She pressed her face into a thick group of branches as if it were the blooming vine of bougainvillea that reached across the facade of her mother's home. The thorns pierced into her cheeks, and Elsa felt relief for something that hurt more than the thoughts in her head.

Elsa tried to compose herself by the time she reached her unit's home—fighters weren't supposed to be carrying on the way she was. Tedros was stoic, the grief visible on his face, but he kept on with his work. The villagers knew not to say anything, respectful of the rebels' code. If anyone else inquired about Efrem, whether a comrade or civilian, they would be told he had been stationed elsewhere. After some time, as the story changed but maintained its vagueness, they'd come to understand. That's how it was.

August 1991

29

ELSA BLEW OVER THE STEAMING BOWL OF LENTIL SOUP SHE SET ON the dining table. "You sure you aren't hungry?" she said to the only parts of Lydia's body that weren't tucked into the armchair. "There's some pasta too."

Lydia grunted that she wasn't and pulled back her right leg, which had been swinging from the armrest. Elsa nodded at the back of the chair, wondering if her daughter's brattiness was going to be a permanent condition. As she was pondering whether to respond, Zewdi reemerged from her bedroom, still clad in a lavender caftan with gold trim.

"I thought you were going to change?" Elsa asked, tearing off a piece of toasted pita and dipping it into the soup.

Zewdi didn't respond. Instead, she strode past her into the kitchen, leaving Elsa in the wake of her sandalwood fragrance.

"Everyone's ignoring me today? Fine." Elsa watched Zewdi set out her good tea set next to the stove. With precise, economical movements, as if she were being evaluated by five-star hotel management, she arranged raspberry jam cookies and baklava on the two-tiered crystal dessert stand she used only for special occasions. Breezing past Elsa again, she straightened the coffee-table runner before moving on to the entertainment stand and inadvertently blocking the view of the television.

Lydia adjusted in her seat but didn't say a word. Elsa assumed that she could sense that doing so would be at her own risk.

"Please turn the television off," Zewdi said to the screen. A group of Girl Scouts were traipsing in the woods with their golden-haired troop leader.

"But I like this movie," Lydia said with a softer voice than she had just used to address Elsa.

Zewdi's back rose with a deep inhale. She turned around to face Lydia. "We're about to have company."

"So?"

"Lydia," Elsa said sharply.

Lydia huffed and sat up, pointing the remote at the television. "You have to move out of the way . . . you're blocking the thingy."

"Just turn it off," Zewdi said.

Elsa pushed her dining chair back and stood at Lydia's side. "Turn it off."

Lydia jumped to her feet and jabbed the remote in Zewdi's direction. "If you could pleeease move out of the way, then I can—"

Zewdi stepped to the side, and the television went quiet.

"—turn it off," Lydia said.

In the abrupt silence, they all stilled, eyeing one another in anticipation. Elsa looked cautiously at Zewdi, waiting for her to finally reveal whatever was in her hand.

"Who's coming over?" Elsa asked.

Zewdi smoothed her neckline and finally made eye contact with her. "I tracked down a cousin of Lydia's father."

Elsa's body froze. Her brain chose the other extreme, hurling her thoughts into a spinning vortex that she was failing to control.

Zewdi kept speaking, and formally, as if she still worked for the princess and needed to report on an unexpected inconvenience that she was sure she could resolve.

"This cousin, Dahab is her name, lives in Sweden. It turns out that she's here . . . in this building. She just called to say that she's coming up."

Elsa gasped. She turned to her daughter, who was looking wide-eyed at her.

"Isn't . . . why isn't that a good thing?" Lydia asked.

Elsa palmed her forehead. All of a sudden, there was a faint smell of something burning.

"Is the stove still on? Zewdi, did you leave something on it?" she asked.

Zewdi shook her head slowly. "I don't smell anything."

Lydia sniffed. "I don't either."

Elsa rushed to the kitchen to check. The range was off, but she was sure that she could still smell gas. Elsa hovered her face over each burner, and the smell soon dissipated.

Someone cleared their throat. Elsa turned around to see Zewdi in the kitchen entrance with her hands pressed against her abdomen.

"Everything okay?"

"Yeah, yes. I thought . . . it was nothing." Elsa splashed her face with water and wiped it roughly with a kitchen towel. She brushed past Zewdi and found Lydia sitting primly on the edge of the loveseat. Zewdi followed behind and stood next to her, resting a protective hand on the girl's shoulder.

"This *is* a good thing, Liduye," Elsa said, facing them both. "Of course it is. I never meant to . . . I always wanted to find them." Elsa searched desperately for any truth she could offer with this lie, which was that whenever she thought of Efrem, she saw him crouched in the rocky ledge, watching her as she left him, despite his pleas that they stay together. She could never tell her daughter what happened that day, or the other reason, beyond her guilt, that she'd kept Lydia from her father's family.

"How do I know that?" Lydia's jaw clenched. "I feel like you want to act as if my father never existed."

"No, you don't understand. It's just that . . ." Elsa set her eyes on Zewdi. "It's just that I didn't know about this. So maybe Zewdi can tell us just what she's done. What did you do?"

"Where should I start, Elsa?" Zewdi's eyes flashed as she

put one hand on her cocked hip. "What about all those years I asked you about Efrem's family . . . all those years that Lydia, poor Lydia, has been asking to know more about her father? What did *I do*, you have the nerve to ask? Something. I actually did something."

Elsa shook her head, unable to process what she was hearing.

"And you know what?" Zewdi continued. "It didn't take much. We're not from China, for God's sake. There aren't a billion of us. I just kept asking around until I finally got a hold of this woman who was . . . how can I even say it . . . positively overjoyed to find out that Efrem had a child, that he still lives on through *this child*." She pointed at Lydia.

Elsa moved closer to Lydia, who had a wounded look on her face. Her breath felt short. She stopped in an awkward position between the edge of the armchair and the coffee table, willing herself to not collapse.

"Zewdi," Elsa said with an edge to her voice.

"I did not tell this woman to come," Zewdi said. "A while back, she told me she was going to be traveling this way, and I thought she'd give me more of a heads-up . . . and that I could . . . you know . . ." Zewdi fluttered her hands. "But she's here now, so we'll have to talk to her and see what's what."

"If you had more of a heads-up, you were going to do what exactly? Let me know what plans you had for me and my daughter? You know she's *my* daughter, right?"

Elsa spit the words out, knowing it would cost her.

Zewdi laughed dryly, as if the jab landed exactly where she had expected. "I know whose daughter she is."

"I didn't—"

Zewdi raised her hand. "I know my place very well."

"That's not what I meant."

"I know exactly what you meant. There's a lot you could be saying right now, Elsa, but that's what you chose."

As Zewdi spoke, Lydia kept her eyes fixed on Elsa, her expression like when she tried to work out math problems in her head.

"You could have said thank you." Zewdi's voice cracked. "Because even though you keep secrets about everything and never stop to ask about what *I* might be going through, I still love you enough to care about you and *your daughter.* Or you know what else you could say?" She pointed at Lydia. "You could say, 'Lydia, I'm going to stop being selfish and tell you whatever you want to know so that you can feel a little better about not having your father around.' But." Zewdi clapped, punctuating each word with a slap of her hands: "You. Didn't. Say. That!"

Elsa felt each clap like a strike across her face.

"Who do you think you are?" Elsa said. "No, really . . . who do you think you are?" Her voice trembled as it rose. "Do you think you're so perfect? Do you think you would have handled things differently? You have no idea what you would have done in my shoes because you weren't in them!"

There was a knock at the door. They all turned to look at it. Elsa wasn't ready. She took one last look at Lydia, who had her arms wrapped around herself. She tried to communicate with a pleading look that she was sorry, but Lydia kept her attention on the door. Elsa should have been trying to comfort her instead of defending herself, but it was too late now. Zewdi took a quick glance at herself in the foyer mirror and opened the door, bringing four people into view.

A woman who had to be Dahab pushed past her, eyes fixed on Lydia.

"Is that our daughter?" she said in a high-pitched tone. "Come here, my child, come here!"

The diminutive woman pressed Lydia into her chest and rocked her from side to side.

"Where is your mother?" she called out, whipping her head around.

Elsa hesitated before presenting herself. Dahab didn't resemble Efrem; she had a slight bearing and narrow gashes for her eyes and mouth. But Elsa surrendered to her embrace, somehow feeling Efrem's presence. She pulled back quickly as Zewdi ushered Dahab's entourage to sit down. Dahab forced Lydia next to her on the loveseat and clasped her hands between hers.

"I'm your auntie Dahab," she said, her voice trembling with emotion. "I see Efrem in you, I do. You're tall, you have his coloring. But it's all in the eyes. Do you speak Tigrinya?" she asked Lydia, who was studying the woman carefully, as if she were also looking for some sign of her father.

"I'm sorry, but my English is a no," Dahab continued with a cutting motion of her hand.

"Does this child speak Tigrinya?" she repeated, turning to Zewdi and Elsa.

"Dahab," Elsa said slowly, "It's good to finally meet you."

"Yes, it has taken much too long for us to meet. Sit here, sit next to me." She stood up and pulled Elsa down to the other side of her. Lydia adjusted so that all three of them could fit.

Elsa stiffened, wanting Zewdi to take charge; she was so much better at these things. But once Zewdi got everyone settled, she went into the kitchen, where Elsa could hear her putting the kettle on.

Elsa faced the audience that had accompanied Dahab, hoping to cue an introduction. They had variations of the same face: beaked noses and wide-set eyes, quivering chins that indicated mixed messages of either mirth or distress.

"My husband, Kifle." Dahab pointed to the first in line. "And his sisters, Fana and Nigisty."

They nodded in unison. Dahab removed one of her hands from Lydia's to grip Elsa's, linking the three of them.

"We didn't know Efrem had a child. Can you believe that? All this time, we didn't know! Can this child understand me? Lydia, are you following?"

"Yeah, I am," Lydia said in English. Elsa widened her eyes to indicate that she should at least try. "I can understand you," Lydia said in halting Tigrinya.

"Oh my goodness. You're perfect." Dahab grabbed Lydia by the cheeks and kissed her before linking hands with her and Elsa again. "Your father and my father were first cousins, but they grew up like brothers. My father always had a feeling that Efrem was going to run off and join the war. He told Efrem's mother, your grandmother, Haregeweini, God rest her soul, that 'these children are not yours, you can't try and keep them for yourself . . . they belong to the nation.'"

Dahab's gaze traveled across the room before resettling on Lydia. "I was about eight or nine when Efrem left. I was very attached to him . . . everyone used to call me his shadow because I was always by his side. He loved that. He wasn't one of those teenagers who didn't want a little girl trailing behind him like a lost puppy. He liked teaching me things, watching me grow." She looked back at Lydia with a wistful smile. "When he disappeared, I was so angry. I refused to eat, I tore my clothes. I was hurt! But as a child, that's how I expressed it. The family came up with all sorts of stories, that he went to Asmara for school and that he'd be back, but I'd been paying attention. I knew where all the youth were running to. And I had this feeling I'd never see him again."

Lydia put her other hand over Dahab's. She was staring desperately at her, as if she wanted to crawl into the memories Dahab was reliving and see them for herself.

"Later, I found out that my father tried to track him down," Dahab said. "But when I was just a little older than you are now, he was jailed and killed. But my God, if he knew that Efrem had a child . . ."

She got choked up and began howling as if the grief of Efrem's death were new. Her sisters-in-law also started shrieking and weeping, covering their faces with their sheer scarves. Elsa couldn't take it. She looked over at Lydia, whose eyes were darting all over the room. In all these years, she never let her sit with Eritreans as they mourned, not wanting her to be traumatized by the wailing and dramatic fits of grief. Elsa certainly wasn't going to have her start with this. She got up to comfort Lydia, and Zewdi appeared with a box of Kleenex and gently, yet firmly, told the women to stop.

"You're right." Dahab patted her face. "We should focus on the good news, on why we're here." She smiled up at Zewdi, who returned with the tea and set it on the coffee table. "This woman, this angel, called me and told me about this blessed child. Please, Elsa," Dahab said, fighting back another sob, "tell us what we've missed for all these years."

Everyone's head swiveled to Elsa, who released her hand from Dahab's and pinched the skin between her thumb and index finger, avoiding eye contact.

"Well," she said carefully, "I was stationed in Zager in October of '75 to work with the public administration unit, and that's how we met. Efrem was really adored by everyone, his comrades, the children, the villagers. We were these guerrillas who just showed up and set up shop . . . We could only do our work if the people trusted us, if they could relate to us. Efrem had that gift; he just knew how to put others at ease. And Zager became home for us, at least for a few years. But then he was martyred in '77 . . . before either of us knew that Lydia was coming."

Elsa finally glanced up at her audience. Dahab was listening intently and still looked like she was trying to keep from crying. Her in-laws were listening politely with their cooling tea. She could barely see Lydia, who had leaned back on the sofa and was obscured by Dahab. Only Zewdi sat with her head lowered, as if she was in prayer.

Dahab's husband, clad in a sports jacket several sizes too big, cleared his throat delicately. "Was he . . . how did he . . ." He fiddled with the label still on the cuff of his sleeve.

Dahab whispered something in Swedish, tilting her head toward Lydia. Elsa was grateful that she intervened.

"And you left after he was martyred?" Dahab asked. "Once Lydia was born? When was that? Why did you leave?"

"She left so that Lydia could have a better life," Zewdi answered in a low voice. "And at least one parent."

Elsa found Zewdi's eyes and nodded at her.

"Of course," Dahab said gently. "You've sacrificed so much . . . and here we are, finally reunited and finally free, thanks be to God."

The room fell quiet. They all seemed to be taking in the tower of untouched sweets on the table. Dahab turned to Lydia and patted her cheek.

"We don't have any relatives on your father's side in the States. But you can always visit us in Stockholm, and we're going to Asmara next summer. Are you all?"

"Maybe," Elsa responded, even though she had never once mentioned it. "We're thinking about it." Lydia didn't even try to hide her surprise.

"Forget maybe! Lydia should see the village her father is from, the house he grew up in. And I'm sure you'll want to see your comrades. The only reason we knew Efrem had died was because my uncle harassed a fighter who eventually confirmed it. He also told him where Efrem had been stationed and the names of some of the people in his unit, Petros or Tedros or something, and a woman . . . what was her name?"

"Her name was Lydia," Lydia said pointedly.

Elsa jerked her head toward her daughter. How did she know that?

"Lydia! Yes, that's it!" Dahab clapped her hands. "Oh, is that why you . . ." She turned to Elsa in excitement. "Is that why you chose the name?"

"Yeah, Mom. Tell us all. Is that why you chose my name?" Lydia asked in English. Elsa could see a hint of challenge in her eyes.

Dahab looked between the two of them. "Is she okay?" she asked Elsa, unable to understand what Lydia said.

"There's no point in asking her," Lydia said in Tigrinya to Dahab. "She either won't tell you or she'll lie."

"What are you saying?" Elsa hissed in English.

Lydia addressed everyone. "My mother never told me who I was named after. I had to figure that out myself. Elsa doesn't want anyone to know anything. She didn't even want you to be here. She was mad at Zewdi for calling you."

Elsa felt her face burn. She reached over Dahab to grab at Lydia, as if she were still a toddler she could subdue. But Lydia just shrugged her off and jumped to her feet. She faced everyone with her hands clenched into fists at her sides.

"She never tried to find you. I don't believe anything she says, and you shouldn't either."

Lydia's Tigrinya started off strong but was unraveling the longer she spoke. The tenses flew from past to future and the genders switched indiscriminately. But Elsa could make out what she was saying, and the Swedes seemed to be following along as well.

"That's enough." Zewdi took assured strides toward Lydia and tried to sit her back down. "This has been emotional for all of us, but don't talk about your mother like that."

"My mother? Who, her?" she pointed at Elsa.

Was that the cruelest thing your child could say? Elsa looked down at her hands, helpless in her lap, wondering who she was if she wasn't Lydia's mother.

"She's not my mom. Lydia is my mother. That's why she named me after her . . . and that's why she never tried to find you all . . . because she'd have to admit the truth."

Dahab and her entourage were silent, shifting uncomfortably in their seats. Her husband and his sisters, with their birdlike features, looked as if they wished to fly away. But Elsa could tell they were somewhat skeptical, thinking that Lydia's emotions had gotten the best of her. Zewdi, on the other hand, was locked in on Elsa, as if Lydia's declaration was the first thing she had heard in a long time that made sense.

Elsa stood up, feeling her body tremble with each movement. "Lydia," she croaked, "I am your mother."

"No, you're not." Lydia's eyes welled with tears. "My parents are dead!"

Lydia pushed Zewdi out of her way and ran out of the apartment, letting the door slam behind her. As soon as it closed, Elsa collapsed back on the loveseat, weeping the way she had when she saw Efrem laid out in front of her on that dry riverbed.

Zewdi rushed to her side, and Dahab took her in her arms.

"She doesn't mean any of that," Dahab said. "She's young and overwhelmed and taking it out on you. You heard how I reacted when Efrem left . . . I practically threatened to kill myself."

"Elsiye, please." Zewdi stroked her arm. "You know your daughter loves you. You've given her everything."

Elsa quieted and extricated herself from their embrace. She could feel her temples start to throb. One of the in-laws murmured to Dahab, who wiped her eyes and nodded.

"Unfortunately, we have to go. We're driving to Harrisburg tonight to see another family member and then flying back to Stockholm from Baltimore in two days. But promise to stay in touch," Dahab said, her voice still husky. "We don't want to lose you and Lydia, now that we've found you."

Elsa promised, and as she said goodbye, she thought of

something she had to ask. "Did your relative hear anything about Lydia?"

Dahab looked surprised at the question and shook her head. "He only told us about Efrem. I'm sorry, Elsa."

Zewdi led them out and then threw herself down on the sofa. Elsa collapsed next to her, and they sat with each other in a rare silence.

30

LYDIA SHOVED OPEN THE STAIRWELL DOOR AND DRAGGED HERSELF down the two flights of stairs back to her apartment. After entering, she stood for a few moments with her back to the door. Nothing had changed. This was still her home. That was still the room she shared with Elsa. It didn't matter how many of her father's cousins magically appeared—he was still dead.

Mama Zewdi was right. It couldn't have been that hard to track down her father's family. In fact, Elsa had to try *not* to find them. Watching Dahab, a perfect stranger, completely unravel when she met Lydia confirmed that her feelings had been valid, that the relief and joy of being connected was the right response, the human response. Why was that so hard for Elsa?

Lydia's epiphany that Elsa wasn't her real mother had only crystallized when she uttered it. She was suspicious when she had discovered the elder Lydia's name, but it wasn't until she saw Elsa stonewall Dahab, who had only asked for basic details, that she realized how much Elsa was hiding.

It felt good to shout at Elsa, to make her feel small in front of all those people. To put it in Eritrean terms, she had achieved a decisive victory that left the enemy vanquished. But now that she was alone, she doubted her revelation. Elsa felt like her mother, and more important, the thought of her secretly raising another couple's child, even if they were all friends, just didn't seem likely. What kind of person would keep that child from her mother's own flesh and blood?

Lydia walked toward her room, hoping to find Berekhet, just

as his alarm clock began to howl, the bell clanging at louder and louder decibels.

Something was off. Wind was coming from somewhere, and his door shuddered and then slammed toward her, as if it were being shut from the other side.

"Berekhet?" she called out with her hand on the knob. There was no response. She hesitated and then stepped into the room.

The bed was made, sloppily though, the comforter laid out the wrong way and sheets bunched up underneath, but still the most effort he'd ever applied. All his books were gone—only hers remained on the bookshelf—the floor was bare, and the closet was empty. She opened every dresser drawer, only to find an orphaned sock and some Peoples Drug receipts.

Lydia sat on the bed, facing the open window as the curtains whipped toward her. Then she lay down, listening to the clanging of the alarm become discrete units of sound, thinking of her last interactions with Berekhet. Berekhet had been scarce the week after their movie night. Lydia was terrified he knew what she had done and was trying to avoid her. That next weekend, she had heard him enter the apartment in the middle of the night. As she watched the hallway light under her door, she thought about getting out of bed and asking him to make her something to eat. She could act like nothing had happened and watch him fuss in the kitchen. Nothing really did happen, after all. She was also certain that Berekhet had slept through it, as he did through everything else. But then the light in the hallway went out, and Lydia started to doubt herself.

The next afternoon, Lydia had sat in the hallway reading with her back to his door. Eventually, she heard the bed creak and his feet pad the carpet. He opened the door and looked down at her, as if he had been expecting to see her there.

"Hey, stranger."

"Hey," Lydia said self-consciously. "Haven't seen you much this week. Been busy?"

"Yeah, I have," Berekhet said, scratching the stubble on his face.

"Doing what?" Lydia looked past him into his room. Something seemed different. There was less stuff strewn about, and the edge of a big cardboard box peeked out of the closet.

"Trying to survive. It's like a jungle sometimes; it makes me wonder how I keep from going under . . . as I heard our rapping brothers say."

Lydia cracked up, trying her best to make it seem like she was laughing with him and not at him.

"Oh, come on. I know I said that right."

She laughed even harder and then immediately burst into tears.

"What happened?" Berekhet said, dropping to his knees to comfort her. "Was it that bad?"

Lydia didn't know what had come over her. Berekhet put his arm around her and leaned back so that she could rest her head on his shoulder.

"I think this isn't about the song."

Lydia shook her head, too afraid to say anything else. They sat quietly for a while. Then Berekhet got up, only saying that he had to get to work.

Now the room still smelled like the cologne he'd begun wearing, something crisp and masculine in a pretty blue bottle he chose because it evoked the Caribbean. He'd borrowed an elaborate coffee-table book about the Caribbean islands and become obsessed, declaring that one day he'd experience those turquoise waters for himself.

The wailing alarm clock quickly brought her back to reality. Berekhet was gone. A lump swelled in her throat, but she was not going to cry. Crying got you nowhere. She sat up, slammed her hand on the clock, and rushed outside of the apartment to the elevator. As soon as the doors opened, she ran through the lobby and down the sidewalk shouldering the complex's driveway toward the exit.

"Lydia!"

She stopped and turned around. Dahab was running toward her, away from her husband and sisters-in-law, who were standing in front of a waiting taxi with identical looks of concern.

"Wait!" Dahab was clutching her purse across her chest with one hand and waving frantically at Lydia with the other.

Lydia turned back around and kept running. Right when she reached Seminary, she barely caught sight of a cyclist barreling down the sidewalk before jumping out of the way and into the street, twisting her head to see Dahab, whose mouth was open in a silent scream. Lydia felt the car's impact almost as soon as she saw it and then she saw nothing at all.

31

ELSA PACED IN THE WAITING ROOM, BARGAINING WITH GOD. A young couple sat huddled in the corner, the woman sniffing into a Kleenex and the man bouncing his knee up and down. Zewdi entered the room, cradling crackers and little tubs of juice.

"For the love of God, sit down," she said. "You're making me more anxious."

"Any luck with Berekhet?" Elsa asked. Zewdi had called the house three times since they'd arrived at Alexandria Hospital.

"Still no answer. And I tried the 7-Eleven."

Zewdi offered the couple the snacks she'd managed to secure from someone on the nursing team. They shook their heads politely.

Elsa checked her watch. An hour had passed since Lydia was admitted into the emergency room. Not long after Lydia had stormed out of Zewdi's apartment, Dahab burst back in with tears streaming down her face, struggling to explain that Lydia had been hit by a car. Elsa felt everything go quiet, Zewdi's screams and Dahab's cries sounding muffled, as if they were all underwater. They raced downstairs. Elsa outpaced them down the sidewalk, feeling her breath catch as she could see Lydia's body slumped on the ground. She didn't hear anything again until the ambulance appeared.

A weary-looking doctor with smudged glasses nearly falling off his nose appeared at the doorway.

"I'm looking for the family of Lydia Negash?"

"That's us." Elsa darted toward him. Zewdi quickly rose to her feet and stood at Elsa's side.

“Are you her mother?” he asked.

“Yes.”

“Your daughter is going to be okay,” he said, gently nodding.

“Oh, thank God!” Zewdi exclaimed, clutching Elsa’s arm.

“She has three broken ribs and laceration of the spleen, which has caused active internal bleeding. Her vitals are stable, but we need to stop the bleeding. We suggest a non-operative procedure to target the bleeding vessels and stop their flow.”

“Okay, whatever you say. When can we see her?”

He looked down at his watch and nearly lost his glasses in the process. “With any luck, in about two and a half hours. We’ll update you as soon as we can.”

When they were finally able to see Lydia in her room, Elsa went straight to her side, waiting for her to regain consciousness from the sedation. She checked her arms and legs and smoothed her hair back, fussing over Lydia the way she used to when she was a baby. She missed those years when she could touch and take in her child as much as she wanted.

Zewdi went to the other side of the bed and kissed Lydia’s hand. “Oh, thank you, Mary, mother of God. She looks okay, doesn’t she?”

Elsa murmured her agreement, pulling a chair up close enough to the bed that she could stroke Lydia’s hand. There weren’t any bruises or broken skin on Lydia’s face. She looked peaceful, like nothing traumatic had just happened to her.

“How are you always so happy?” Elsa remembered asking Efrem that night in the cave.

“Because I don’t try to be,” he had said with a laugh. “I don’t try to be anything. I don’t try to be brave or strong or memorize the Little Red Book like some people. There’s only one thing that I do. Every day, I try to imagine that I’ve lost something precious to me. I imagine that I’ll never see my mother again, that I’ll lose a limb, or that Eritrea will never be free. I hold that thought in my mind because if I scare myself now, I won't be scared later."

Elsa clasped her hands over Lydia's and brought them to her face, trying to hide the tears that fell from her eyes.

In March 1978, a few months after Efrem's death, Elsa was helping a Zager resident repair a broken fence in her chicken coop when she spotted a familiar figure in the distance. The woman was heavily pregnant, her hips swinging from side to side. Despite her labored gait, she bounced ever so slightly on the balls of her feet.

Elsa walked slowly toward the approaching figure, wondering if she was imagining its presence, until the woman, with a face just like hers, stopped right before her.

"Is this the greeting I get?" Twin asked with her hands outstretched.

Elsa tried and failed to speak. She knew she would see Twin again but never prepared for what she would say.

"Don't worry, it's not contagious." Twin laughed as she tapped her midsection, then threw her arms around Elsa.

Elsa slowly put her arms over her shoulders, and as soon as she felt Twin's firm belly press into hers, she found her words. "I missed you," she whispered in their embrace. "I'm so happy you're back."

Elsa steered her to the house they once shared. Villagers came out and greeted Twin warmly, if offering slightly tepid congratulations on her pregnancy for reasons she would soon understand. Elsa could tell that Twin was looking out for Efrem to appear, even though she never mentioned his name. That night, once she and Elsa were finally alone in the room they used to share, lying by each other's side, she asked Elsa about his whereabouts. She had come to surprise him with her pregnancy and deliver their baby in the makeshift maternity ward hidden in the hills on the outskirts of the village.

Elsa closed her eyes, grateful for the dark. This was the moment she had been dreading. She opened her mouth, trying to find the words but bursting into wretched sobs instead.

Twin sat up, resting on her elbows.

"What happened?" she asked.

Elsa couldn't speak. She kept crying for it all, her guilt surrounding Efrem's death, what had transpired during her last night with him, and that he would never know his child. She couldn't verbalize any of that, so she said nothing. But Twin understood the one thing Elsa's tears had to mean. Instead of dissolving into grief, she turned over and held herself tight.

They didn't mention Efrem again. Twin went up into the maternity ward, along with other expecting rebels from nearby posts. Someone sent word when Twin's water broke, and Elsa was at her side when her daughter was born, holding her hand as she squatted and cried out for mercy. As soon as the child was in her arms, Elsa could see the light return to her friend. As if she could hear Elsa's thoughts, Twin looked up and nodded with tears in her eyes. Elsa sat behind her and held them both, feeling Efrem's presence in the room.

Twin's return also meant that she brought news of Elsa's mother. When Elsa asked how she had received her letter, Twin shook her head, and it was Elsa's turn to interpret the silence. There would be no exuberant postmortem, no one to make sense of the end. Elsa just hoped that it was peaceful.

For as long as Twin was in the ward, that baby was either in her or Elsa's arms. They both clung to her for dear life, marveling at every wiggle of finger and toe and predicting the little quips Efrem would have made. In a rare bout of indecision, Lydia couldn't commit to a name and called the peaceful baby a litany of nicknames until she could finally settle on one that was just right.

They had a happy little life for three months until Twin had to go back to her post in Keren. Mothers usually left their babies with the ward's caregivers until they were old enough for the Zero School, the underground school and dormitory farther north in Nakfa.

"I wonder what she'll be like," Lydia said as she cradled the baby in her arms, her index finger stuck in the newborn's grip. She smiled softly and looked at Elsa, yet her expression was intense, posing a request she didn't need to utter. Elsa held her gaze, nodding ever so slightly, indicating that only death would keep her from fulfilling her promise. Twin kissed her child on the forehead and stood up before handing her over to Elsa.

Mao Zedong's theory of protracted war wasn't linear. He accounted for a strategic retreat, in which the liberation movement, under existential threat, would draw back in order to rebuild its capacity and fight again. Right when victory was close, the war took an unexpected turn. The Soviet Union fully intervened in support of Ethiopia, enabling the Derg to launch airstrikes across the country and weaken the rebels' hold. In November 1978, the Ethiopian military recaptured Keren, which had become the de facto capital of the liberated areas, and Elsa was desperate for news of the damage they wreaked. The answer she got was averted eyes and vague responses. She assumed the worst—Twin must have been killed.

Faced with Chairman Mao's prediction, the EPLF forces made the impossible decision to give up all their hard-won territory and withdraw north into the mountains, taking along civilians who were willing to follow. Elsa retreated as well, but going east to Khartoum, where she named their child Lydia.

There was a knock at the door. Osman entered the hospital room.

Elsa was surprised to see him but not irritated, which surprised her even more.

"Osman." She rose to greet him. "What are you doing here?"

He presented her with a small vase of flowers before enveloping her in a gentle embrace. "I heard and just wanted to see how your daughter was doing."

Elsa looked over at Zewdi, who fixed her face in a picture of innocence. Elsa was sure that she had called him but decided to let her play dumb.

Zewdi rose from the cushioned nook built under a portion of the window. "It's so kind of you to come. Please, have a seat. I'll let Elsa catch you up while I go try Berekhet again."

Osman sat gingerly in the nook. Elsa set the vase on the window ledge and turned her chair to better face him.

"How is she?" he asked.

"She's going to be okay, that's what the doctor says. I wasn't so sure when . . ." She stopped, feeling her eyes start to well. "But now that we've talked to the doctor and can see her, I feel better."

They settled into a comfortable silence, with Elsa's foot flexing to the beeping of the EKG. She told him what happened, but selectively, leaving out Dahab's arrival and her fight with Lydia.

"She's a tough kid, smart as well. I'm looking forward to talking to her again," he said carefully.

"Again?" Elsa set her foot on the floor, grounding herself. "When did you talk to her?"

Osman interlocked his fingers and let out a deep breath. "She showed up at my office wanting to see if I could help her learn more about her father. She had this picture of you, her father, and Lydia Tekeste . . . the woman you're looking for."

Elsa glanced at Lydia for an explanation, as if she could have given one.

"Did she just show up at your office by herself? How did she even know how to reach you?"

"I don't know, but she came with her cousin, Berekhet. I told her that I had met her father, but, unfortunately, I didn't know him well . . . I could tell she was disappointed."

"Was that it?"

Osman hesitated before continuing. "She asked who Lydia was. She wanted to know if you knew what had happened to her, and I said that you didn't."

Elsa leaned back. So that was how Lydia started to put things together. Her poor child running across town, trying to figure out the truth. Elsa pressed her fingers to her temples. The truth was a convoluted thing. How could she even begin to explain it to her daughter? How could she describe what it felt like to go back into the hills and hold that orphaned baby in the big and violent world they had found themselves in? To realize that all she had left was that child, and all that child had left was her. In that moment, there was no choice, as if every other path before her went dark. Just as she knew in Dr. Alazar's car that her life in Addis had come to an end, and that a new one had begun when she first laid eyes on Twin's face, she was certain, clutching that child in her arms, that she had to do whatever she must to keep her safe.

"Am I a bad mother?" she asked out loud.

"What? No, of course not!" Osman said, knowing only half of the story. "Elsa, look . . . as someone who doesn't have kids, I have no idea what this is like . . . but your daughter needs to know more about you. She needs to know more about her father. The more you keep from her, the more she'll resent you and the more she'll turn to others. You don't want that."

Elsa closed her eyes and nodded.

"Did you find out what happened to Lydia?" she asked quietly.

"You never gave me the letter."

"I didn't. But what I asked is if you found out what happened to her?"

Osman looked down at his feet.

"Tell me."

"Elsa."

"She's dead, right?"

Osman's silence was all the confirmation she needed.

"When?"

"In '78, when Keren was recaptured."

"What happened?"

"I don't know that, Elsa. All I heard was that she didn't make it."

"Look at where we are." Elsa gestured at Lydia, the tubes running out of her arms, the machines beeping at her side. "Look at me. I thought I lost my child today. Whatever it is you know, I can handle it. Just tell me."

Osman sighed deeply and clasped his hands again. "An Eritrean spy for the Ethiopians spotted Lydia and someone else in her unit sneaking back into Keren, likely aiming to destroy the Ethiopian military weapons depot. This is according to a trustworthy resident who was secretly working with Lydia and watched this all happen himself. Soldiers approached, and Lydia told her partner to escape while she gave him cover. He ran off as the soldiers started to fire. They hit Lydia in both legs, and she collapsed. She threw a grenade behind her, missed her target, and then clutched her last grenade to her midsection, detonating it when the soldiers neared. She didn't die immediately. It seemed like she said something to them . . . and then they shot her several times."

Elsa pressed down on her knees to brace herself and then stood at Lydia's side. The steady beeping of the machine confirmed what she could see with her own eyes, her daughter's chest rising and falling with steady breath. Elsa closed her eyes and focused on her own breath, submitting, with each internal release and return, to the fact that she was still among the living. What would she do, the rhythm asked her, with that unwieldy gift?

32

LYDIA WAS A LUCKY GIRL, SHE WAS TOLD. THE PROCEDURE WENT well, and her fractured ribs would heal on their own. It still hurt to breathe, so she was given pain medication and careful instructions to breathe big, deep breaths. Elsa repeated the guidance in front of the doctor, breathing deeply with her hands on her chest.

"I'm sure you're excited to be going home!" said one of the nurses and the happiest person Lydia had ever met.

Lydia said she was, the positive response more for the nurse's sake than for her mother's. When Lydia had come back to her senses, she still had a nagging suspicion that her hunch about Elsa not being her mother wasn't true. She didn't know why she felt that way. Maybe it was seeing Elsa hover over her, the familiar smell of her hand cream, the tiny moles beneath her eyes. That face was the first face she had ever known. Lydia had to respect Berekhet's Rule Number 3: she could be wrong. But she was still upset and unsure about how to hold both things at the same time.

Lydia also wondered if she had made up Berekhet's disappearance; maybe the drugs had messed with her memory. Maybe he was at home right now, making a stack of chocolate-chip pancakes to welcome her back. But then how could she explain the emptied-out bedroom? He had cleared it out only because he realized the great burden he had been placing on her and wanted to return the use of the room to its rightful owner. In a gesture of good manners, he was going to offer to sleep on the sofa instead. Lydia would refuse—he was their guest, after all—and demand that he put his belongings back.

At her discharge, she was wheeled out and handed over to Elsa, who immediately began fussing over her in the passenger seat.

"Where's Mama Zewdi?" she asked.

"She's at home getting lunch ready. She made a special lasagna for you."

Elsa got into the driver's seat and closed the door, trapping them together in silence.

"Are you in any pain?" Elsa asked when she pulled out of the parking lot and turned onto Seminary.

"No, Mo—" Lydia stopped herself. She wasn't ready to let her off the hook.

"Well, breathe deeply . . . like this."

Elsa tried to rest her hand on Lydia's chest, but Lydia pushed it away.

"Is Berekhet home?" she asked.

Elsa waited a beat before answering while she fiddled with the rearview mirror. "No, he's not."

Lydia turned toward the window.

"It was so irresponsible for him to just pick up and leave like that," Elsa said. "What a waste."

"You didn't help!" Lydia said with as much force as her ribs would allow. "You just judged everything he did and pushed him away. It's your fault he left!" She started to cry, but it hurt and she clutched at her chest.

"Lydia, please," Elsa whispered. "I'm hurt that he left too . . . that's not what I wanted to happen."

Lydia calmed herself down and steadied her breath.

"But," Elsa said softly, "we need to talk about what you said to Dahab."

The red light at the intersection with Pickett turned green, but Elsa didn't move until the car behind her started to honk.

"I know you're my mom," Lydia said.

"What?" Elsa clutched the wheel harder.

"I was just so mad at you . . . I'm still mad. You don't tell me anything, basic things that I deserve to know. But I know you're my mother . . . and I didn't mean to do all of that in front of Dahab."

Now Elsa looked like she was the one with the difficulty breathing.

"Did you not want me?" Lydia asked. "Did I ruin your life?"

"Ruin my life? You are the most important thing in my life."

"That's not what I asked."

"Do you remember when I told you about my aunt Kidan who used to live in Mogadishu?" Elsa asked. "The one who opened up a bar and had a huge villa and Fiat 34? Every Easter, she used to send us money for new clothes, and when I was around your age, we were told that she was finally coming to Addis. We were expecting this glamorous woman with hired help and heaps of jewelry, but this hunched old lady with messy hair showed up. All she had with her was this beat-up trunk, and when we looked inside, there were only dirty linens. Can you imagine, Lidu? She would tell us to go fetch her gold bracelets or some fancy dress, but there was nothing there, nothing of value."

They approached their complex, and Lydia looked away from the spot where she got hit.

"What, exactly, am I supposed to get out of that story?"

"Lydia, the woman was filthy rich but she never had a family, never had kids, not one person to protect her. She got old and a little"—Elsa tapped her forehead as she pulled into a parking space—"and her house help or maybe the people who worked for her took everything from under her nose and sent her home with nothing but dirty underwear! That would have *never* happened if she had kids. You are lost without a family, Lidu, lost! How can you ask me if I didn't want you? You are the most important thing I have. What else do I have to show for myself if not you? Who am I if I'm not your mother?"

"You don't get it," Lydia said. She felt so tired. Her mother made her feel tired. Her whole life made her feel tired. The thought of walking into their home and seeing her empty room made her feel tired.

"You're telling me that you're happy you had me so that I can take care of you when you're old and make sure that no one steals your stuff. Do you think that's why I'm mad? Do you think that's what I want to know?"

"Lydia . . ."

"MOM! Just tell me what you've been keeping from me!"

Elsa dropped her shoulders and leaned back into the seat. "Okay," she said softly. She told Lydia about how her father died, about life in Addis with Dr. Alazar and how she'd tried to kill herself. More cars appeared in the parking lot. It was just a regular day for everyone coming back home, everyone but Lydia, who was trying to imagine Elsa as a young girl laid out on a bathroom floor. As Elsa went on, Lydia tried, for the first time, to see Elsa not as her mother but as a teenager running away from home to join the war and becoming best friends with someone who believed in what she did. She saw the girl hiding her feelings for a boy that her best friend liked, and that boy dying gruesomely. She saw the girl's best friend get pregnant and die soon after giving birth to a baby she loved very much. She saw the girl raising that child as best she could, while never forgiving herself.

The sky darkened. Kids were still playing outside. Lydia steadied her breath. Then she and her mother went home.

33

ZEWDI COULDN'T REMEMBER A TIME IN HER LIFE WHEN SHE HAD prayed harder. Even after the doctor said that Lydia would be fine, she lit every candle and prayed her special rosary from Jerusalem until Elsa brought her home.

Zewdi wanted to give mother and daughter some privacy when Lydia was discharged. She left the hospital early to prepare all of Lydia's favorite dishes: lasagna, beef zigni with potatoes, and Betty Crocker spice cake with cream-cheese frosting. The good china was out on the table, and her *Best of Motown* cassette was playing from the stereo.

Zewdi heard the door open and rushed out from the kitchen. "Welcome home!" she called. But only Elsa was there.

"Where's my baby?"

"She was so tired, Zewdiye. All she wanted to do was sleep. I didn't have the heart to force her to come up," Elsa said as she walked past her and dropped to the sofa.

"I can bring the food downstairs. She has to eat!"

"As soon as I got her showered and she got into bed, she was out like a light. I'm too tired to eat anything myself."

Zewdi felt herself deflate. "Well, at least let me make us some tea."

She returned to the kitchen and waited for the water to boil, looking at all the food crowding the countertop.

"I called Dahab," Elsa said from the other room, fighting through a yawn. "I told her that Lydia was doing fine, and that we'd keep in touch."

"Oh?" Zewdi said carefully. "That's good."

"I meant it too. I want Lydia to know her family."

Zewdi poured the tea and brought it to the living room, along with a few slices of cake. Elsa sat up slowly and curled her legs under her. In the two days that Lydia had been hospitalized, Zewdi could see the toll it took on Elsa's face. This family of hers was falling apart, and for once, she didn't know what to say.

"Thank you, Zewdi." Elsa raised her bloodshot eyes to hers and smiled.

Zewdi shook her head. "Please don't say that. If I didn't go behind your back and call Efrem's family, Lydia wouldn't have gotten so upset and run into the street." Zewdi set down her tea and stifled a cry.

"No," Elsa said forcefully. "That's not on you, that's on me. And Lydia needed to meet Efrem's family . . . I did too. If it wasn't for you, it wouldn't have happened."

"You don't need to. . . ."

Elsa raised her hand and continued. "And I'm sorry for making you feel like you didn't have a right to get involved when you're just as much Lydia's mother as I am."

Zewdi bent her head, just realizing how much she needed to hear that said. She cradled her cup, steeling herself to ask what she had been wondering about since the accident.

"Is what Lydia said true?"

Elsa's face broke wide open, revealing the pain of every choice she had made and those she hadn't. Zewdi gripped her hands and then kissed them. Enough. For both of them, it was enough. There would be time to explain later, but everything that really mattered Zewdi already knew.

Zewdi sat next to Elsa and wrapped her in her arms.

"It doesn't matter, Elsi. None of it. All that matters is that you have given everything you have to protect that child and give her a loving home. She feels loved and safe. You hear me?"

Elsa nodded into her shoulder, trying to quiet her cries. Zewdi reached for her tissues and wiped Elsa's face, slowly nudging her upright.

"That's enough. After today, we start over, okay?"

"Okay." Elsa nodded.

"Good, that's what I want to hear. Now, go and get some rest. When Lydia wakes up, tell her I'll make pancakes and sausage for breakfast."

Zewdi walked Elsa to the door and hugged her goodbye. She put all the food away, wiped the counter down, and scanned the kitchen for another distraction from what she knew she had to do. She decided to clean the floor under her fridge. She pulled the fridge out, prepped a bucket of Lysol diluted with water, and got on her knees with a rag in hand.

"What are you doing?" she said out loud to herself.

"Zewdi Naizghi, what are you doing?" she repeated.

It was still early in L.A. She picked up the phone and dialed Asgedom's number. When he didn't answer, she hung up and called again. He answered the second time but with a hint of irritation in his voice.

"Hi, Asgedom, it's Zewdi."

"Oh, hello, Zewdi. I hope you're doing well. It's quite late there, no? Would you mind if I called you back? We have a no-phone policy during dinner . . . well, the kids aren't here, but I still like to maintain the policy. If it's too late for you when I'm done, I can call you tomorrow. That might be—"

"Asgedom, this won't take long. It's best if we just chat now."

"Well, all right, let me just—"

"I prayed for someone like you. I prayed for a companion who was kind, family-oriented, and God-fearing. I have to admit that I gave up hope, but meeting you renewed my sense of what is still possible in my life."

Zewdi paused. There was silence on the other end, but she could somehow sense that he was adjusting himself.

"But I can't accept your proposal. It kills me because the more I've gotten to know you, the more I can see how good of a man you are and how lucky any woman would be to have you. But God is telling me that he hasn't willed this for me. As much as I want what you're offering, it's not mine to accept."

Asgedom took a deep breath. "Well . . ."

Zewdi smiled. Thank God they weren't speaking face-to-face, because he would have misinterpreted her cheer. It was just that she already knew him so well and was prepared for his Asgedomness. He was measured and long-winded as he expressed his disappointment. But ultimately, he said that he understood and was appreciative because an unhappy marriage was such a painful thing to bear.

As he spoke, Zewdi activated her mental Rolodex to identify who he might be better suited for. They said their goodbyes, and when she hung up, she collapsed on a dining chair and burst into laughter.

What would her mother think if she could see her now? That made her even more hysterical. She got up, took out a Baccarat crystal goblet from the top shelf of her china cabinet and a bottle of areki from the bottom drawer, and served herself a healthy pour.

"Saluti!" she cheered before knocking it back.

The celebration was missing something. She went to her room to grab those Andes mints she had tucked away and poured herself another shot. She had one more call to make.

34

EVEN GOD HAS A ROUTINE. DR. ALAZAR USED TO SAY THAT TO ELSA all the time. For all his education and status, he was adamant that work was just work. The painter cleaned his brushes, the farmer watered his crops, and the surgeon made neat cuts. A week after Lydia's return from the hospital, Elsa, the hot dog vendor, went back to work. She prepped her cart, lined up the chips and soda, and waited for business. When she didn't have customers, she stepped out of the cart and did a vague approximation of stretching, keeping track of the nearing sun.

"Look who's back."

Elsa jumped at the sound of Ricky's voice behind her. She never understood how someone who walked with a cane could creep up with such stealth.

"Ricky," she said with her arms outstretched.

"Don't 'Ricky' me. And I don't want your iced tea either. You win the lottery or something?"

Elsa shook her head sheepishly.

"Okay, so you still need this job. And clearly none of your limbs are broken." He patted his face down. "Where have you been?"

Elsa didn't even know where to begin. "That's a long story, my friend."

Ricky laughed and nodded. "Yeah, I get it. I got some of those myself."

"Peace offering?" Elsa held out a bottle of Lipton's.

Ricky looked at Elsa solemnly. "Only if you promise to tell me that story one day."

"I promise."

They shook hands and grinned like kids with a secret. Elsa looked out over the tourists hustling up and down the space between Constitution and Independence Avenues and had another thought.

"Ricky, I need to take care of something quickly. Can you handle the cart for me for a bit?"

"Sure thing, boss lady."

What a strange thing it was to just walk again! Throughout her entire childhood, if she wasn't sleeping or studying, she was walking. Throughout the war, all she really did was walk up and down mountains. But since she moved to this country, she couldn't think of the last time she just set one foot in front of the other and *walked*. It felt good. She swung her arms vigorously forward and backward and across her torso like she used to do in training. She picked up the pace and launched into a light jog, laughing at how stiff she felt. A real runner with a headband and all the gear nodded at Elsa as she passed. Elsa nodded back seriously, wiping at her brow. The sun was upon them, and Elsa could feel her shirt start to stick.

As Elsa approached Aster's cart, Aster was looking at her as if she had taken her shirt off and tied it around her head.

"What's wrong with you? Are you okay?"

"I'm fine," Elsa said, jogging in place. "I just wanted to move my legs a bit."

"Who's watching your cart?"

"Ricky."

"Do you need to go to the hospital?"

"What? No, Aster. I just wanted to walk a bit."

Aster crossed her arms. "But you're running."

"Yeah, I know . . . I was walking at first and then I started jogging. I'll be back to my cart soon."

Elsa resumed her jog toward the Washington Monument but quickly tapered off into a brisk walk, finding it hard to continue jogging with Aster's eyes boring into her back.

The line at the monument was surprisingly short. Elsa decided to join it, listening to families chatting in different languages, embarrassed at how far people had come to see something that she had never bothered to. She tried to remember the last time she and Lydia went on any kind of outing together. Lydia had done all the tourist stuff on school trips or with Zewdi, but maybe this year they could all take a trip somewhere together.

Her vision of that trip included Berekhet, and it pained her to remember that he was gone. She knew what she had done was wrong—come down entirely too hard instead of letting him find his way. If anyone should have known that it was the wrong approach, it was her. She certainly didn't appreciate when she was on the receiving end of it; and she had to explain the failure of that approach to the man who had perfected it. Elsa's call to Dr. Alazar had filled her with a dread she hadn't felt since he used to summon her to go over her grades. He responded to her news with a stony silence, to which Elsa thought to share that she had faith in Berekhet and believed that he'd make something of himself, on his own terms. Dr. Alazar's silence turned arctic. But Elsa realized those words were also for herself, and most important, that she believed them.

After the elevator ride up to the observation deck, Elsa peered out of the south-facing window. Just beyond the grand sweep of the Tidal Basin and Thomas Jefferson Memorial, past National Airport and the Pentagon, she could see Zager again, superimposed over the wide expanse of trees and mere glint of Southern Towers. The villagers were cheerful, the women empowered, and the children happy and healthy. Efrem and Lydia were still there, full of life and confidence for the future they were working toward. They waved at her, motioning for her to join. Elsa waved back, laughing at jokes she couldn't hear, promising that she'd be there soon.

35

LYDIA SHOWED UP TO THE FIRST DAY OF THE EIGHTH GRADE FEELing different. It wasn't that she looked much different, even though she finally got some things right. Her hair was straightened and miraculously not frizzing up. She was also sporting new espadrilles and a pretty blouse that Mama Zewdi had splurged on. But it was more that she felt less preoccupied with her classmates, and maybe because of her indifference, they were being nicer to her, at least in their own ways. Joel and Matthew greeted her without any jokes at her expense, and Lindsay asked if she wanted to sit with her at lunch.

At home, Lydia had finally put her things back in their place. Setting up the room for Berekhet seemed like it had happened much longer ago than in May, and it had been strange to return things to how they used to be, as if he had never been there at all.

Her mother had tried to make it a happy occasion. After selling the car she had bought for Berekhet to a neighbor down the hall, she surprised Lydia with a trip to Marlo to buy a new bed. Lydia chose a sturdy white frame with a bookshelf built into the headboard. Elsa also gifted her a framed version of her picture with Efrem and the elder Lydia, which she positioned on her nightstand.

Lydia had rummaged through her books, deciding what to showcase in her new shelves and what to leave in the older one against the wall. As she debated between all of her *Baby-Sitters Club* books, she could imagine Berekhet tossing them aside and rolling his eyes. He wasn't even there and he was still judging her. Wasn't that nice?

Lydia threw her favorite one, *Claudia and the Sad Goodbye*, toward the bed, where it bounced off and landed on the floor, releasing a single lined sheet of paper. Lydia picked up the paper and recognized the handwriting as soon as she unfolded it.

Dear Lydia: You found it. I knew you would. Your room is yours again. Thank you for giving it up. I'm sorry I didn't say goodbye. You, little sister, deserved that. But in the words of André Gide, who you should really be reading instead of this stuff, "One doesn't discover new lands without consenting to lose sight, for a very long time, of the shore." Have you rolled your eyes yet? I'll wait while you do . . . . (this is me waiting). Lidu, we will see each other again. And when we do, I hope that I'll have something to show for my travels. Your mother loves you, never forget that. And be kind to her, as she knows that you'll lose sight of the shore too. Your brother forever, Berekhet.. P.S. Keep reading.

Epilogue

WHEN IS GOD MORE GENEROUS THAN ON A PERFECT SUNDAY afternoon? Zewdi stood at the end of the bar, her elbow resting on its edge, as she had posed in *The Washington Post* article chronicling what she had birthed. The front windows facing U Street revealed her vision come true: patrons huddled over bistro tables on the outdoor patio, bushels of purple azaleas beaming under the September sun, beckoning pedestrians to smile at the warmth and ease on display and consider experiencing it for themselves.

Zewdi straightened her chef's coat and greeted a family she recognized from church, guiding them to the last open table inside the restaurant. A toddler fussed at the next table over, and Zewdi glided back to the bar, returning with a coloring book and crayons and promising to send over mimosas to the grateful parents.

Near the entrance, a golden beam of light illuminated Elsa and Lydia, sitting next to each other on carved wood stools, manning a single burner and a clay jebena resting on its woven perch, steam rising from its narrow spout in a hopeful curl. Now, as a fourteen-year-old, Lydia was learning how to conduct the coffee ceremony. In the third and final round, Elsa guided her to pour the brewed coffee in an uninterrupted stream into the rows of handleless cups that they would serve to the restaurant guests.

The beam of sunshine was wide, and Zewdi stepped into it. There, in the light, God reveals who you are, answering the questions that wreck you in the dark. Right out front, emblazoned on the new awning that she had commissioned, was the answer: Zewdi.

Acknowledgments

While this book is a work of fiction, I researched the real lives of people who experienced the years of war and upheaval that are the novel's context, including female guerrilla fighters in the war for Eritrea's independence. I am indebted to everyone who shared their personal stories. They include Asmeret Abraha (Guande), Eritros Abraham, Teklai Afwerki, Tsige Alem, Alem Araya, Abrehet Arefaine (Gual Fano), Solomon Asmelash, Professor Senait Bahta, Dr. Tade Belachu, Gebray Beyan, Mikael Debass, Ambassador Araya Desta, Dr. Laynesh Gebrehiwot, Mihret Ghebremeskel, Andemichael Ghebreselassie, Weini Hailu (Gual Encheyti), Her Excellency Fawzia Hashim, Yordanos Kifle, Shemainesh Kiros (Trinidad), Samrawit Michael, Tsion Michael, Dashim Misgina, Haile Misginna, Abrihet Ogbatsion, Ambassador Hanna Simon, Semaynesh Tekue, Tsehaynesh Tesfaghaber, Alemseged Tesfai, Haregu Tesfamariam, Azeb Tewolde, Rahel Tewolde, Berhane Woldu, and Dr. Kaleab Zeru. I also extend heartfelt thanks to my family for sharing their memories. My deepest appreciation to Nigisty Ghebremichael, Netzanet Ghezai, Haileselassie Giorgis, Mulugeta Giorgis, Azieb Habtemariam, Dr. Elsabet Tekle, and Selam Zerabruk.

My research was made possible thanks to the generous funding of Cambridge University's Harper-Wood Creative Writing & Travel Award. Alemseged Tesfai was a tremendous source of personal support and inspiration, and his book, *Two Weeks in the Trenches,* served as a helpful reference. Zemhret Yohannes, the director of the Research and Documentation Center of Eritrea, generously offered his insights, suggestions of interview subjects, and the help of his staff. Danait Fisseha provided critical research support and an encouraging spirit.

Dan Connell's *Against All Odds: A Chronicle of the Eritrean Revolution* was an invaluable account of the reality of the war on the ground and the global geopolitical forces at play. I especially drew from his reporting on the efforts of the EPLF's public administration unit in Zager. The books *Inside Eritrea's War for Independence: Journey from Nakfa to Nakfa: Back to Square One* and *The Tenacity and Resilience of Eritrea 1979–1983* by Dr. Tekeste Fekadu, and the *Massacre at Wekidiba: The Tragic Story of a Village in Eritrea* by Habtu Ghebre-ab provided essential historical background.

This novel does not present the comprehensive history of Eritrea's struggle for independence, which was started by the Eritrean Liberation Front. I would like to acknowledge everyone who sacrificed greatly in the war. I would also like to acknowledge the incomparable generosity of the Sudanese people for sharing their cities and homes with Eritreans seeking refuge.

Thank you, Toyin Adeyimi, for your kind introduction to the writing life and encouragement to apply to the Callaloo Creative Writing Workshop. At Callaloo, I benefitted greatly from the community of fellow writers and instruction from Ravi Howard and Maaza Mengiste. Maaza, thank you for your continued mentorship.

This novel was born during my creative writing education at New York University. I am immensely grateful to the administration and my faculty and classmates. Thank you especially to Nathan Englander, Zadie Smith, and Darin Strauss. All my gratitude to Dionne Ford, Enkay Iguh, Coco Mellors, and Jessica Ramirez for your support and encouragement since our time at the Lillian Vernon Creative Writers House.

Raj Pipella, words can't express my gratitude for your generosity of spirit and time in the hallowed halls of WeWork. Selam Daniel, thank you for being a tireless cheerleader and thoughtful reader. Lula Hagos, I am grateful for your proofreading expertise. Yelena Zeru, my partner in reminiscing on the good old days, thank you for your stellar memory and input.

I am indebted to everyone who offered encouragement, sanity checks, and room and board on this long journey. Thank you to Kobina Aidoo, Keondra Bills Freemyn, Nikki Duncan, Hana Elkhazeen, Azza Elsheikh, Eden Ghebreselassie, Salah Goss, Meron Hagos, Michael Hagos, Tarig Hilal, Fatima Khambaty, Eden Kidane, Natasha Logan, Menelik Major, Chelsea McKinney, Milena Mikael-Debass, Natali Sosnizkij, Ryan Spence, Laurie Thomas, Selma Woldemichael, and J Wortham.

To my agent, Ayesha Pande, I am most grateful for your wise counsel and steady hand as we got this book to the finish line. Thank you for believing in me.

Glory Edim, I am thrilled to have brought this book to the world with you. Thank you for your light. And thank you for connecting me to the wonderful team at Liveright, including Fanta Diallo, Kadiatou Keita, and Nick Curley. Gina Iaquinta and Maria Connors, I am so grateful for your astute editing and care for Zewdi, Elsa, and Lydia.

Thank you to my entire family for your support and for honoring my request to stop asking about the book's progress. For brevity's sake, I'd like to especially thank Weldemariam Mezghebe, Mebrahtom Mezghebe, and Tesfu Mezghebe.

To my parents, Tsehai Habtemariam and Haile Mezghebe, thank you for your unconditional love and support. I couldn't have been born to better, more loving parents. Thank you for the incredible gift of raising me in the beautiful and complex universe that is the Eritrean community.

And to my little one, I wonder what stories you will tell.

"**Well-Read Black Girl Books** is a collection of magnetic debut fiction that invites readers to explore powerful narratives rooted in diverse cultural experiences. These stories offer readers an opportunity to step into new worlds, expand their horizons, and experience the transformative power of fiction. Just as the Well-Read Black Girl community celebrates literature that resonates deeply, these books are crafted to not only be read but cherished, shared, and revisited for years to come—characters that stay with you long after the final page."

—**Glory Edim**, founder of Well-Read Black Girl